S – A JOURNEY INTO SERVITUDE

Stopping in front of him she knelt, feeling small and vulnerable as he towered over her. She laid the two thick birches at his feet.

'Please, Master,' she said, her voice trembling with emotion. 'This woman begs you to accept her as your own.'

As he stooped to pick up the first of the whips, she turned and draped herself over the bars of the wooden frame, her hands gripping tensely, her legs wide and her buttocks offered high.

By the same author:

THE AWAKENING OF LYDIA
LYDIA IN THE BORDELLO
LYDIA IN THE HAREM
MADAM LYDIA
'S' – A STORY OF SUBMISSION

'S' – A JOURNEY INTO SERVITUDE

Philippa Masters

This book is a work of fiction.
In real life, make sure you practise safe sex.

First published in 1998 by
Nexus
Thames Wharf Studios
Rainville Road
London W6 9HT

Copyright © Philippa Masters 1998

The right of Philippa Masters to be identified as the
Author of this Work has been asserted by her in
accordance with the Copyright, Designs and Patents Act
1988.

Typeset by TW Typesetting, Plymouth, Devon

Printed and bound by
Cox & Wyman Ltd, Reading, Berks

ISBN 0 352 33286 7

*All characters in this publication are fictitious and any
resemblance to real persons, living or dead, is purely
coincidental.*

This book is sold subject to the condition that it shall not,
by way of trade or otherwise, be lent, resold, hired out or
otherwise circulated without the publisher's prior written
consent in any form of binding or cover other than that in
which it is published and without a similar condition
including this condition being imposed on the subsequent
purchaser.

One

The departure was emotional. S cried along with Carla as they hugged with mingled joy for S's future and their sorrow at parting. They had become very close in the weeks since S had answered that strange, fateful advertisement, the advertisement that had changed her life.

'Freedom through submission?' it had said. Hating her dull, dull life as a solicitor's secretary, she had answered it and been allowed into the extraordinary, exciting world of Seigneur and Carla, a world of sensuality and submission which had drawn out her true inner nature. And now, as the voluntary slave to her beloved Kano, Prince Adenkano N'Kwandwe, she was leaving Seigneur to fly off with her Prince to a whole new life.

Seigneur kissed S for the first time ever, on the cheek like a benevolent uncle. Even Katherine and Erika, who had taught her so much about love and love-making, were there. If S felt any trepidation at the prospect of her new life far away it did not show in her radiant yet tear-brimmed eyes.

'You are looking beautiful,' Erika murmured as she kissed S goodbye, the full, searching kiss of a lover. 'Especially with your new decorations.'

S blushed with pleasure and looked down at herself. Three large diamonds hung suspended from each of her gold nipple rings, and a whole fringe of them were hanging almost like a little triangular apron from the ring on her pubis. Her hands and feet had been decorated with delicate, elaborate patterns of henna dye, and on her head was a cap of silver filigree encrusted with yet more diamonds, hundreds of them.

Apart from that she was entirely naked, and gloried in the fact. It was what her Master wished, and thus was perfect. She sensed rather than heard him coming down the stairs, and straightened to attention, her head bowed as he required. He shook hands with Seigneur and Erika, and kissed Carla and Katherine before walking out of the front door towards his limousine. S hurried to pick up the two heavy suitcases and followed him, wincing a little at the soreness in her bottom. He had beaten her very thoroughly last night before spreading her and fucking her until she nearly fainted.

If the chauffeur of the limousine was surprised to see a tall, elegantly dressed man approaching his vehicle followed by a small naked woman struggling under the weight of two large suitcases, he gave no sign of it. Nor did he so much as raise an eyebrow when S heaved the cases into the capacious boot and then climbed in beside them, curling herself into a ball and settling down on the carpeted floor of the car boot like a contented cat. He was, however, considerably surprised at the happy smile on her face and at the clear marks of a recent beating on her backside as he closed the boot lid on her.

Unlike the chauffeur, the men working on the large private jet aircraft registered amazed delight when a naked girl was lifted out of the Prince's car boot along with his suitcases. The mechanic checking the

2

undercarriage banged his head as he straightened up with shock. The men loading the mass of luggage that had already arrived rushed across to the limousine, ogling S while pretending to be concerned with the cases.

S stood perfectly still on the tarmac at the rear of the car, her hands behind her back as her Master required. Prince Adenkano climbed out of the limousine as soon as the chauffeur opened the door for him and, without even glancing at S, strolled towards the steps leading up to the body of his aircraft. Halfway there he clicked his fingers and S hurried to fall in behind him like an obedient puppy. She was acutely conscious of the stares of the ground crew, and did not know whether to be embarrassed or proud.

The cabin of the jet was plush and opulent, more like a lounge than an aircraft. Along one side was a thickly upholstered couch facing a long, low table. On the other side there were three pairs of seats, facing forward and equipped with seatbelts. A stewardess dressed in a brilliantly coloured, flowing costume directed S to the rearmost seat, while the Prince went to the foremost. Two large, hard-looking men wearing dark suits took the middle pair of seats, and the stewardess buckled herself in beside S.

Nobody spoke. In minutes the engines had been fired up and with a high-pitched, whistling scream the plane was taxiing out towards take-off. S stared out of the window as the ground rushed past and then rapidly fell away as the aircraft climbed. Her heart was racing faster than the jet.

Less than two months ago she had been secretary to a dull provincial solicitor, living a dull provincial life, and hating every lonely minute of it. Then she had answered that mysterious,

3

enigmatic advertisement, and Seigneur and Kano – she still thought of her Master as Kano – had come into her life.

Her period of training had been hard but oh, how happy she was that she had managed it. Nothing in her life was dull now! Her Master had chosen her. Without even knowing who he was, she had submitted, offering herself to an unknowable future life as the willing slave of an unknown Master. She could still feel the thrill of joy when that Master had turned out to be Kano, Prince Adenkano N'Kwandwe, the man she had come to adore even when she thought he was no more than Seigneur's servant.

And now she was being flown off to his homeland as his voluntary, eager slave. The shiver of happy excitement that ran through her was such that the stewardess sitting beside her glanced round, first in alarm, then with amusement.

The flight was a long one. The stewardess served coffee. S slept after a while. She was awakened by the stewardess gently shaking her arm. The two hard-looking men, bodyguards by the look of them, were sitting on the couch playing cards. The Prince, her Master, was nowhere to be seen but S had no time to wonder about his absence as the stewardess hurried her out of her seat and towards a door at the rear of the cabin.

To her astonishment, S found herself in a perfectly appointed bathroom, although with sloping walls and a low ceiling. Silently, the stewardess motioned her to stand still in the centre of the compartment, then carefully removed the filigree cap that had adorned her head and unclipped the strings of diamonds from her nipple rings and the little triangle of diamonds from her pubic ring.

S obeyed as, still silent, the stewardess gestured her into a small shower cubicle with aluminium walls and a perspex door. The stinging jets of hot water began without warning and S bumped her elbows several times as she span round under their pressure, gasping as the shower beat on her body. The spray stopped as suddenly as it had begun and the door of the cubicle slid open. The stewardess was holding a huge, thick towel, smiling, now as naked as S herself.

'My name is Ankinda,' she said, her dark eyes smiling. 'I get you ready for the landing.'

S did not reply because she had not been given permission to speak, but she gazed at the girl as Ankinda gently towelled her dry. She had a triangular, kittenish face, with large eyes and full, sensuous lips beneath a pert nose. Her hair was cropped into a cap of thick black curls which gave her a boyish look that was belied by the feminine curves of her torso and limbs.

Like S, she had been ringed on her nipples and pubis. Perhaps it was a badge of Kano's ownership, S thought. Her breasts seemed almost too large for the slender delicacy of her ribcage, and stood full and high, the gold rings trembling on her dark, prominent nipples. Her chestnut skin gleamed tautly and her legs were long and shapely, their graceful curves drawing the eye to the round prominence of her buttocks and the soft plumpness of her hairless pubis. There, what Carla had laughingly called a 'clitty ring' bobbed and bounced against the tight slit of her sex. S found herself wondering whether Ankinda found the presence and constant stimulation of the ring as deliciously distracting as she did herself.

Once S was dried Ankinda oiled her all over, from her neck down. For S it was a disturbing process. The oil gave off a delicate aroma of spices mixed with

5

something like vanilla and a hint of coconut. S found herself becoming almost as aroused by the scents as she was becoming by the movements of Ankinda's hands as they slid softly, insidiously over her body.

Her breath quickened when the smiling girl oiled her breasts, paying special attention to her nipples. She blushed when Ankinda smiled at the way her nipples hardened beneath the cunning fingers. She tried to think of something else as Ankinda's hands slipped and smoothed along her parted thighs, circling slowly higher, nearing the cleft that was becoming disturbingly warm and moist.

S knew that Ankinda was trying to work her up. She fought it, but lost the struggle when the oiled fingers reached the crux of her thighs, smoothing first over the swells of her buttocks and teasing the length of their cleft, then moving to her mons and vulva, softly, lingeringly. The caresses around her clitty ring and along her swelling labia set off the inevitable spasms in her belly as S swooped into a come which had her thigh muscles spasming and her belly undulating towards the insidious fingers – fingers which teasingly withdrew as soon as her orgasm erupted.

Shamefaced, for she had not been given permission to come, S sat down on the stool Ankinda gestured her towards. The girl brushed her hair back and fixed it with a band before slowly and carefully applying make-up. There was no mirror so S could not see what was being done, but she guessed the effect must be exotic because Ankinda paid a lot of attention to her eyes, using kohl and mascara and two different eyeshadows. The lipstick was of a very dark red and Ankinda applied it to her nipples as well as to her mouth.

Her work with the cosmetics finished, the African

girl inspected S critically, nodded her satisfaction, and proceeded to brush her hair slowly and luxuriously. S loved having her hair brushed and relaxed into a mindless reverie as Ankinda worked on her. She snapped out of it the instant Ankinda spoke, and obediently followed the girl back into the main cabin.

As they did so, S stopped in her tracks and gasped. Kano had returned to the cabin while the girls had been in the bathroom. He had changed out of his European clothes and now looked magnificent in robes of white, with patterns of black and red and gold rioting over the flowing folds. A cap of leopard skin crowned his proud head; a dozen heavy gold chains hung down on his deep chest; gold bracelets and rings decorated his wrists and fingers. Oh, he was beautiful and S choked with pride that she was his slave!

Her near-trance was broken when Ankinda gave her a little slap on her bottom and positioned her at the side of the aisle behind the last of the pairs of seats. Apparently oblivious of her nudity and the appraising glances of the two hard-looking men – surely bodyguards? – Ankinda went to Kano, bobbed him a deep curtsy, and spoke rapidly in what seemed to be their native language. The Prince glanced towards S and nodded, and Ankinda returned.

From beneath one of the seats she pulled a small metal case which she placed on the seat itself. S's eyes grew huge when Ankinda opened the case, for it was absolutely crammed with diamond jewellery. She had never imagined, let alone seen, such riches. Carla had not been exaggerating when she said that S's new Master was wealthy. There must have been enough for a dozen kings' ransoms in that case.

Ankinda rummaged almost casually among the

treasure before drawing out a wide, heavily encrusted choker. She fixed it around S's neck so that the delta of strung diamonds hung neatly down almost to S's collar-bone. Next came an equally encrusted head-dress which fitted over her crown like a cap, and from which long strings of diamonds hung to her shoulders at the sides and back, entirely concealing her hair.

A thick gold chain fringed with strings of diamonds was hung between her nipple rings and then, most amazing of all, a skirt made entirely of strings of glistening jewels suspended from an equally heavy gold chain was hung around her hips. It must have weighed several pounds, and S did not even try to guess at its value. The fringe of diamonds hung down all around except for a six-inch gap at the front. They followed the curves of her hips and buttocks, falling to just below the tops of her thighs, but left her pubis entirely exposed. When Ankinda clipped a long leather leash to her pussy ring, S began to have an idea why. Whatever happened when they landed, she was going to be led along like some exotic pet as a demonstration of her Master's ownership. She felt a strange surge of pride. That was why he'd had her decorated so beautifully and pricelessly – because she was his.

Ankinda took the end of the leash and led S to where Kano sat. He inspected her calmly, nodded his approval, and gave a gesture with which she was now very familiar. Ignoring the two bodyguards and the naked Ankinda, S instantly dropped to her knees. Lifting the hem of her Master's robes she burrowed her head underneath. It quickly came up as a lump beneath the richly decorated cotton cloth between his knees. The lump moved in slow bobbings as her hands and mouth worked to please him. The cabin was silent except for the low noise of the jet's engines and the quiet slurping and suckling noises from beneath the robe.

After perhaps ten minutes the Prince's body tensed and his face tightened into a rictus of pleasure as his hips jerked. Slowly, S emerged from beneath his robe, her face pink and glistening with pleasure, her throat working as she continued to swallow. Ankinda helped her to her feet, and repaired her lipstick before strapping her into her seat for the landing.

The final preparation before S was led from the plane was to have her wrists cuffed behind her back. With seeming inevitability, the manacles were of gold encrusted with diamonds, but none the less secure for that. Ankinda led her out of the aircraft and down the steps, holding the leash attached to her pussy ring loosely. As she stepped through the low cabin door and straightened up on the top step S quailed. The crowd, albeit a hundred yards away at least, seemed vast and the noise tremendous. They were cheering and ululating at the return of their Prince, and cheered anew when they caught sight of S.

Ankinda, once again wearing her colourful costume, led S slowly down the steps from the jet and across to where a cortège of limousines waited, their engines purring. Prince Adenkano was settling into the third of the five black stretch limousines, his one open to the skies. The first two and the last two were filled with mean-looking men with walkie-talkies and bulges beneath the left sides of their jackets, all scanning the crowd through their mirrored sun-glasses. An escort of a dozen motorcycle police flanked the cortège.

The sunlight glinted in a million sparks from S's exotic decorations as Ankinda conducted her to a position behind the Prince's open-topped Rolls

Royce. S watched in fascination as the stewardess uncoiled the leash clipped to her pubic ring, at least ten feet of it, and attached it to the rear bumper of the car. To cheers from the watching crowd the group moved off slowly, but still fast enough to cause S to stumble and trot hurriedly to ease the shock of the sudden tug on her pussy ring.

The cortège kept up a fast walking pace and the crowd that lined the route cheered and waved flags and banners of welcome as their Prince returned to his palace. S struggled to keep up, no semblance of dignity left to her as the leash pulled at her pubis to make her keep pace, her lungs soon heaving and sweat running from her body to match the tears of humiliation caused by the laughter and catcalls of the crowd.

Yes, she was beautifully and richly costumed. Yes, she belonged to her Master, his voluntary slave. But did he have to debase her so far? Did he need to show her off as a public slave hauled along behind his car by a ring in her pubis? It was too much! S felt as though he was displaying her to the whole world, and the whole world was laughing.

By the time they reached Prince Adenkano's palace S was in a semi-trance of conflicting emotions. The crowd that lined the route became no more than a blur and their calls and laughter was only a rumble of indistinguishable noises. Indeed, the chinking of the hundreds of diamonds with which she was bedecked seemed louder to her ears.

Far more important to her swirling senses was the persistent tugging of the leash on her sex, more or less gentle according to how well she kept up with the car. It had its inevitable effect, and long before they finished the half-mile journey she was panting more from arousal than from the effort of walking.

She was so far gone that she hardly registered the high, white walls surrounding the palace grounds, nor the wide wrought-iron gates through which they passed, except to feel grateful for the absence of the crowds. The column of five vehicles followed a long asphalted drive which curved through an avenue of tall shady trees until it swung round in a wide half-circle, to halt in front of an imposing white portico.

Even before the cars came to a halt a dozen girls scampered out of the main door and formed a line on either side of the wide steps. All of them were beautiful and dressed alike, in loose, colourful turbans with long matching skirts. They were bare breasted and, S noticed, wore a variety of nipple decorations.

They were followed out of the palace by an imposing figure dressed like an English butler, in pin-striped trousers and a black cut-away coat. He moved with tremendous dignity to the Prince's car and, bowing low, opened the door. All the girls at once dropped to their knees and touched their foreheads to the stone of the steps. They maintained their humble obeisance until the Prince, apparently ignoring them, entered the opulent building, whereupon they rose as one and followed him in.

The butler unhitched the leash from the back of the car and led S slowly up the steps and through the wide, heavily varnished door. There was no sign of her Master, nor his entourage of glowingly-clad, bare-breasted girls. S gazed around her in wonder as the butler, tugging gently on the leash attached to her pussy ring, led her across a sumptuous, marble-floored foyer that must have been at least forty feet square. Huge mirrors in gilt frames hung on every wall. Deep sofas upholstered in dark red velvet with

11

gold piping stood against those same walls, with low, marble-topped coffee tables in front of them. The chill of the marble floor to her feet was eased by several thick Chinese silk carpets that were dotted about seemingly at random.

The silent butler led S through an inconspicuous side door and along a narrow, far less richly decorated corridor, then down some steps. He ushered her into a Spartan, white-painted room. The contrast between this room and the magnificent foyer could not have been more stark. No more than ten feet by eight, it contained only a metal-framed bed with a thin mattress, a wash basin with a little shelf and a mirror above it, and a toilet. Several white towels hung from a metal rail; a hairbrush lay on the shelf above the wash basin; there was nothing else.

S found the butler's silence oppressive and rather frightening. It was almost as though she was a thing rather than a person. He unclipped the leash from her ring, unlocked her diamond-studded handcuffs and spoke for the first time, his voice cold and very English.

'Remove the jewellery, please, and place it on the bed.'

S unhooked the chinking, sparkling skirt from around her hips and laid it gently on the plain mattress. The headdress quickly followed, then the choker and the nipple jewels, and S stood naked. She blushed as the butler's dispassionate gaze swept over her. He picked up each of the fabulous pieces of jewellery in turn and dropped them into a plastic bag as though they were mere trinkets.

'Lie down, on your back. Raise your hands to the bed-head, please.' The word 'please' was ironic, for he was clearly issuing orders.

S obeyed without hesitation. The butler shackled

12

her wrists to the vertical bars of the bed-head, fixing them with rings S had not noticed before. His glance swept over her one last time and, picking up the plastic bag containing the fabulous jewellery, he left the room without another word.

S heard a key turning in the lock. She settled herself to wait. She had wanted a new life, a new world. She belonged to her adored Kano now, she thought with wonder as she drifted into a contented sleep.

Two

S awoke from dreams that had swirled with Kano's eyes, and his kisses, and the wonderful fire of his beatings, and his rearing manhood, then changed to rain and the sound of waterfalls and running taps. She started up with wide eyes, her legs clamped together. She needed to use the toilet. Needed it badly!

She tried to get up, but her wrists were still manacled to the bed-head and the loo was five feet away. As if by a miracle the door burst open and a young woman entered. Without a word she unlocked S's restraints, and grinned as S rushed across to the toilet. No finer method could have been designed to confirm to S how low her status was as her waters gushed from her and the woman gave a rich, deep laugh.

'My name is Gladys,' she said when S had finished and dabbed herself dry. 'I am to be your watcher.'

The name Gladys seemed incongruous for such a statuesque and exotic woman. She was fully six feet tall. The high-boned, handsome face beneath the huge turban was marked with three horizontal tribal scars on each cheek, which had the weird effect of increasing her beauty. Her breasts were full and pendulous, with dark areolae and long, thick nipples. Beneath the long, wraparound skirt her hips were full and wide and the feet which peeped out beneath, bare of footwear, were large and strong-looking.

Even then, in those first minutes, S found herself fascinated by the grace and delicacy with which the impressive woman moved, with the strength of her gestures, with the soft sway of her heavy breasts.

Gladys gestured S to sit on the bed and went out through the door, leaving it wide open as though inviting S to venture outside. She did not move. After a minute or so Gladys returned carrying a tray, which she handed to S.

'Eat,' she said.

The tray bore a small bowl of porridge-like stew with flakes of meat and vegetables in it, some pieces of fruit, already peeled and sliced, a jug of iced water, and a beaker to drink it from. There was no spoon or other cutlery. S glanced up at the woman towering over her.

'Eat,' Gladys repeated.

It was many hours since S had eaten or drunk and she fell to at once, glugging at the delicious water so eagerly that some of it splashed over her chin and down onto her breasts, scooping up the stew with her fingers and cramming it into her mouth, hardly even bothering to chew she was so hungry. She cleared the bowl completely, wiping the last traces up and licking her fingers. The fruit, mangoes and something resembling segments of orange which S did not recognise, was savoured more slowly, the fresh flavours made even more delicious by their contrast. At last, everything eaten and all the water drunk, S looked up at Gladys, who was smiling broadly.

'Good! Good appetite. I like that,' she said, with a low, rich chuckle. 'Now, wash yourself, and we get on.'

'Getting on' meant S standing with her back to the

16

wall and her hands behind her head while Gladys worked on her nipples. She dipped her fingertips into a pot of some kind of cream then, with a slight frown of concentration, teased and tugged and rolled S's nipples for all of fifteen minutes. 'Hmm,' she murmured, more to herself than to S. 'Master like them big.'

As if the action of Gladys's fingers was not distracting enough, the effect of the unknown cream was to make S's nipples almost hyper-sensitive. In moments they were standing hard. In minutes they were straining until S felt they must surely burst. She was soon panting and moaning softly as the statuesque woman rolled and tugged, rolled and tugged, and star-bursts of sensation set off a deep throbbing in her vagina.

She felt the threat of an orgasm welling in her loins and fought it, just as Mary and Miss Erika and Seigneur had trained her to do. Gladys had not given her permission to come. After ten minutes her nipples were straining so much that she was far beyond any thought of orgasm. All she wanted was that this exquisite torment should stop.

It did at last, just when S felt she must collapse in tears, the effort of keeping still while Gladys worked on her almost impossible to sustain. She felt a little wave of gratitude when Gladys told her she was a good girl, but was conscious of little save the throbbing in her breasts and the soft fluidity in her loins. When Gladys had her turn and bend over so that she could inspect the darkened stripes that decorated her backside, S was blushingly aware of how obvious her state of arousal must be.

Gladys ran a gentle hand over the curves of S's proffered behind. 'Hmm . . . Master must like you a lot. You mark up nice!' S struggled to keep still as the

17

hand began to explore the cleft between her soft buttocks, then moved insidiously down to trace the shape of her labia. S parted her knees a bit further to allow access, and Gladys's hand slipped between her legs to cup and stroke her mons.

'A little bit of stubble down here!' Gladys's voice was throaty as she pronounced what could only be an excuse for caressing S the way she was. S was surprised that Gladys thought she needed an excuse.

S stifled the little pang of disappointment when Gladys removed her hand, but obeyed instantly when she was ordered to lie sideways across the bed, with her hips over the edge and her knees wide. She waited while Gladys disappeared for a couple of minutes. She reached down with one hand. There was indeed a hint of re-growing hair, but hardly more than a hint. She had shaved only two days ago. She snatched her hand away when Gladys re-entered the cell.

The tall woman knelt between her knees and poured some kind of lotion into the cupped palm of her right hand.

'This will sting a bit.'

Gladys's words were an understatement. S managed to keep still while Gladys smoothed the lotion all over her mons and labia and down over her perineum, but was soon squirming and biting her lip in an effort not to yelp out loud as a burning sensation consumed her splayed loins. She sobbed with relief when Gladys began to wash her off with mercifully cool water.

'This better than shaving.' Gladys's voice was still throaty. 'Take off all hair and make sure it slow to grow again. My, but you have such a pretty cunt!' And without warning the towel which had been dabbing S dry was replaced by softly demanding lips, and then spreading fingertips and a seeking tongue.

18

It was so sudden and unexpected, and so voluptuous that S, already worked up, was instantly on the edge. Her hands flew to her face as she fought it. Her head rolled and her torso rippled, pushing her hips up to get more of the wonderful sensations at the same time as she tried to deny them.

'Please may I come!' Her plea was half-scream, half-sob.

Gladys chuckled. 'If you don't come, child, I'm gonna whip your arse raw for you!' and her mouth returned to its wicked work. She pressed her hands onto S's hip-bones, holding her down as S bucked into violent orgasm, her cries echoing from the bare walls of the cell. At last, Gladys knelt back, her eyes shining and her mouth and chin glistening.

'You'll do, girl. You'll do,' she said as she rose and moved to wash her face at the basin.

S did not see her Master for what felt like days and days. She could not be sure just how long it was because the lights in the basement area where her cell was located were never turned off. She saw no one except Gladys and apart from her visits remained manacled to the bed.

Gladys allowed S to do nothing for herself except feed and use the toilet. She bathed S in the palatial bathroom next door to the cell. She dried her, brushed her hair, polished her body rings. At every third or fourth visit she stood S against the wall, hands behind her head, and worked on her increasingly sensitive nipples for a quarter of an hour at a time, crooning throatily as S moaned and wriggled as the strange cream took effect.

Once a day, or what seemed like once a day in this disorientating world, Gladys laid S crosswise on the bed and checked the smoothness of her splayed vulva by rubbing it with soft hands. It was not really necessary, for the hair was indeed slow to grow again, but it became a sort of ritual which they both looked forward to.

S would lie down on the bed and spread her knees. Gladys would kneel between them and smooth her hands over the love petals so prettily offered to her. Then that knowing, insidious, overwhelming mouth would descend and S would buck and shudder into helpless, wonderful orgasms. She was a good girl, though; she always asked permission first.

After a while, S began to worry. Why had her Master not sent for her? Was what Gladys did permissible? Would she be in trouble for letting it happen? Why did Gladys not require her – allow her – to be more . . . well, active? Back in England, during her training, Miss Erika had been very demanding in that respect. The image of Gladys's voluptuous breasts flashed into S's head as she lay manacled to the bed-head, and she felt a familiar lurch in her lower belly. She pressed her thighs together and flexed the muscles of her pelvis; it helped a little.

Things changed when the butler accompanied Gladys on her latest visit. Gladys unlocked S from the bed and allowed her to use the toilet before making her stand against the wall in the now familiar position. This time, though, she did not use the cream on her nipples but simply tweaked and rolled them a little until they stood out full. Then the silent butler stepped forward. Using a pair of callipers similar to the ones Mary had used a lifetime ago, when S had been sent to Miss Erika's for 'training up', he carefully measured each engorged nub.

'Excellent!' he murmured. 'Excellent! Right side exactly one centimetre, left side slightly more. Well done, Gladys. Get her ready,' he added as he turned towards the door. He had not spoken to S, nor even looked her in the eyes.

'What's happening, Gladys?' S asked tentatively as the statuesque woman led her along a wide, brightly lit corridor, the leash tugging gently at the ring in her pubis.

'Hush, child. All in good time.' The reply was quiet, but held just a hint of excitement.

The room they eventually entered was like a strange combination of bathroom, dressing room and doctor's examining room. To one side was a wide, open-fronted shower cubicle. At the far end, side by side, stood a toilet, a bidet and a wash basin. On the side opposite to the shower unit was a wide, deep shelf on which stood a thick pile of towels and a vast clutter of cosmetic jars, perfume flasks, lipsticks, and brushes and combs.

But what dominated the room completely, and caused S to glance at Gladys nervously, was a high, black-covered, padded table eight feet long and four feet wide. Near one end two thick steel rods stood vertically, one on each side. From their tops hung chains from which dangled wide leather straps with heavy steel buckles. More straps, much longer, hung from various places along each side of the table, and at each corner of the head end lay yet another strap, smaller and narrower, and clearly designed to capture somebody's wrists. S shivered, certain that her own wrists would soon be captured there.

Gladys turned on the shower and tested its temperature, then gestured S forward. The first shock of the stinging spray took her breath away, and it was a moment or two before she realised that Gladys had discarded her skirt and turban and joined her in the steamy cubicle. As S submitted to being soaped and sponged and rinsed and turned this way and that, every millimetre of her skin receiving gentle and scrupulous attention, she became entranced by the woman washing her.

Naked, the water from the shower setting her chestnut-coloured skin gleaming, Gladys was even more magnificent than before. Her legs were long and muscular and shapely, and her full buttocks were high and firm, with not a trace of fat. Her navel made a deep, shadowed indentation in the voluptuous curve of her belly, and there was a distinct curved ridge delineating the soft vee of her mons. Like S, she was bare, the plump rolls of her labia closing softly on a long slit that positively screamed to be touched. The ring piercing her just above her hidden clitoris was of gold and much larger and heavier than the one S wore.

Gladys towelled S dry more vigorously than usual, seemingly oblivious of their joint nudity, then she sat her on the little stool near the dressing shelf. She brushed S's hair even more vigorously than she had towelled her body, and soon it was almost floating with static electricity.

It became obvious to S that she was being prepared for something special. 'Am I – I mean have I been sent for by my Master?' she whispered tentatively, hope surging. Gladys did not answer, and S knew better than to ask again.

She followed the statuesque black woman across to the wall with the toilet and bidet, and obediently knelt on all fours. She got nervous when she felt Gladys applying some kind of grease to the pucker of her anus, but did not dare ask what was happening. She tried to co-operate when she felt the insertion of the cold metal of the clyster, but her sphincter instinctively contracted against it despite her best

22

intentions. Gladys spanked her bottom just once, and S consciously relaxed. The nozzle seemed to go in an awfully long way.

Despite her determination to be a good girl, S could not prevent a 'whoof!' of shock and discomfort when the liquid began to gush into her. She managed a tearful smile of gratitude when Gladys stroked her cheek and told her she was a good girl.

She managed to remain still and unprotesting as Gladys douched her. Obviously she was being thoroughly cleaned, inside and out. It *must* be because Kano, her beloved Master, had sent for her. Her heart gave a little leap of excitement and she even gave Gladys a roguish little grin as she dried her after the bidet.

When Gladys gestured her towards the examining table, S went serenely. She did not know what was going to be done to her, but if her Master wished it then so be it. Gladys was very gentle as she fastened S's wrists with the straps at the head of the table, and then fixed her ankles to the stirrups high on the steel rods. A single strap was fastened across S at waist level and then Gladys went and sat down on the little stool, out of S's line of sight.

Partly because of her excitement at the thought of going to Kano and partly because of her very exposed and vulnerable position, the short wait that followed was not easy. S gave an audible gasp of relief when the door swung open and a tall man in a white coat entered, followed by two pretty Asian-looking girls carrying boxes.

S craned her neck nervously as the man stepped to the end of the table and leaned forward. From his pocket he produced a stainless-steel speculum. Parting her labia with the fingers of one hand, he inserted the instrument deep into S's vagina, spread

23

her almost painfully wide and inspected her channel by the light from a pencil torch. It took only a couple of minutes, but S was sure she did not breathe at all the whole while.

When he had extracted the cold instrument, the man turned his attention to her pubic ring. He pulled on it sharply enough to make S gasp aloud as he stretched her sensitive skin. He turned it to check how easily it slid through the hole of the piercing. After a minute he moved to the side of the table and turned his attention to her nipple rings. He pulled each of them hard enough to make S bite her lip and to stretch her breasts until they were almost conical. Staring up at him through tear-brimmed eyes, S realised that he was in fact carefully examining the holes through which the rings passed.

After turning each of the rings through its piercing he grunted as though satisfied and, without turning, clicked his fingers loudly. One of the Asian girls stepped forward at once, opening the lid of the box she carried and offering it to the white-coated man, who had still not spoken a single word.

The hand that reached into the box emerged clutching what looked like a large pair of wire-cutters. S froze as he moved them towards her left nipple, then sagged with relief when it was only the ring he cut.

Her neck and shoulders were aching badly with the effort of holding her head up, but she dared not look away from what the man was doing. She gave a swift glance of gratitude to Gladys when, as if she could read her mind, the tall woman slipped a thickly folded towel behind her head as a pillow, but instantly looked back to what the man was now doing.

He opened the slender ring and removed it, then replaced it with a rod two and a half inches long. It

24

came in two parts and was thicker than the ring had been, so insertion was a delicate business. Fortunately, the piercings were well healed by now and the process was more awkward than painful. The man lubricated the first, longer part of the rod with antiseptic cream and, gripping the nipple, manipulated it through the piercing. The other part of the rod was connected by a snap-on device, and a small cross-piece on each side of the nipple ensured that the rod could not be removed.

S stared down at it while the man worked on her other breast. It was a much more obvious and outrageous decoration than the little rings had been. S realised that she would never again be able to wear a bra and that the presence of the rods would be glaringly obvious beneath any upper garment she might wear.

When the second rod was in position, the man moved to the foot of the table again and began to work on her pubic ring. To S's relief it was not a rod this time but another ring, thicker and heavier than before, about the same size as the one Gladys wore. As soon as the man left the room, still without having uttered a single word, the two Asian girls moved in and began a different form of decoration.

The henna with which S's hands and feet had been decorated for the plane journey out here had long since faded off. The girls released S's wrists and, taking a hand each, began the delicate task of painting the backs of her hands and her wrists with complicated patterns. That done, they repeated the process on her feet and ankles. Then they worked on her breasts, decorating their whole surface with filigree whorls and lines until they looked strange and exotic, almost, S thought, as though they belonged to somebody else.

Next came her navel and the sweep of her hips and pubis, which they painted with thin, curving lines designed to draw the eye towards the new, gleaming ring that nestled on her pudenda and the soft, hairless slit below it. Finally, helping S carefully off the table and keeping her standing, for the henna needed time to dry and take its full effect, they decorated her buttocks with more swirls and eddies, all drawing attention towards her tight cleft and the pucker that lay within.

They kept her standing still for an hour so that the decorations could 'cure', as Gladys called it, then she was given a second shower and the Asian girls set about doing her hair and making up her face. All the while, S's excitement was mounting. Surely all this careful preparation meant that her Master had sent for her. Oh, how she wished there was a mirror so she could see herself! She prayed she looked beautiful for him.

Three

S processed into the vast hall exactly six feet behind her Master. She was holding a large fan made of ostrich feathers on a long pole, wafting it gently above Kano's head. A circlet of solid gold rested on her brow, from which a large tear-drop-faceted diamond was suspended between her eyebrows. A heavy gold chain was fixed between her nipple rods, pulling her breasts inwards. From it dangled a gold-handled whip, its single, tapering thong wrapped in silk and reaching almost to her knees. The same skirtlet of diamonds she had worn on the parade from the airport was fixed around her hips. A thick, braided-leather leash was attached to her new pussy ring and was draped up over her shoulder and around her neck.

The multiple symbolism of all this did not escape her as S followed the Prince into the hall. His wealth was being amply demonstrated, as was the submissiveness of this, his voluntary slave, and his exalted status as the owner of such a creature as well as his physical command, symbolised by the whip that hung from between her breasts.

Without having glimpsed a mirror, S knew she looked beautiful. She had seen it in Kano's eyes when Gladys had presented her to him. He looked wonderful, tall and imperious in his brilliant robes, his appearance wildly different from that of the Kano she had first met a few months ago, but his eyes were the same – warm, soft, and deep enough to swim in.

Throughout the banquet which constituted the formal part of the occasion S had nothing to do except stand behind her Master's chair and waft her fan above his head. It was a redundant performance because the hall was air-conditioned. She knew, though, that she was really there for no more than display, and was acutely conscious of the many eyes that examined the Prince's new acquisition. When the ceremonial meal was finished and it became drinking and mingling time, S put down her heavy fan and followed close behind Kano as he circulated.

She was very much a centre of attention. She did not understand the language in which the crowds of people spoke. She did, though, understand the proud, dismissive gestures with which Kano gave permission for people to examine her decorations and touch her body. She seemed to be the only European in the hall, and people were very curious.

Fingers tugged at her nipple bars, and traced the henna patterns on her breasts and backside. Hands cupped her vulva. Fingers intruded. She became lost in an exotic fantasy, naked among all these people, the object of their curiosity and blatant exploration. Kano seemed pleased at the flush of helpless arousal which reddened her chest, and at the way she soon began to pant in her efforts at self-control. Then someone thrust several fingers into her oozing vagina and she lost it without warning and shuddered into orgasm.

It was as though her unwilling climax was a pre-arranged signal. At once the crowd fanned back into a circle. From nowhere Gladys appeared. She unhooked the whip from between S's breasts and whispered instructions. S dropped to her knees and held herself on all fours, the jewels with which her naked body was decorated clinking and jangling. She prayed that the whip would not hurt too much, but prayed more that she would not let her Master down by appearing undignified.

She was aware of Gladys curtsying and handing the whip to Kano. She was aware too of the many faces watching agog. Then she lost awareness of everything except the line of fire which striped across her backside when her Master brought the whip down.

It was just the one stroke. S waited tensely for the second but it did not arrive. Slowly, nervously, she raised her head and looked up. Kano had handed the whip to Gladys and was walking away from her. Since she had not been given permission to move, S remained where she was, on all fours, her knees spread, while the party continued around her.

S remained thus for a long time, aware of the abject image she presented but secretly thrilled at the attention she was attracting, and at the soft smile on Kano's face as he strolled back to his throne-like chair at the head of the hall. He was pleased with her, she was sure, and the thought made her soft with happiness. Perhaps later he would take her to his bed.

That thought, too, affected her. Suddenly everything about her situation seemed to fuse into a single overwhelming reaction, both emotional and physical. She imagined herself crawling to her Master's bed. She felt the new, heavier gold ring moving on her sex – the sex which her kneeling, spread pose blatantly offered for the inspection of anybody who cared to look. Unconsciously, her back arched a little more to present a better view. Her breasts felt swollen and heavy. Her thighs were liquid, her breathing ragged. The whole universe seemed to be centred in the love-lips she could feel swelling and unfolding and glistening with her juices.

Slowly, against her will, S was overwhelmed by a series of gentle, rolling orgasms which rippled through her from her toes to her scalp. No one touched her, except with their eyes. There were many eyes, all focused between her legs as S's torso and hips undulated and her juices flowed. Her eyes were clamped shut, her mouth was slack, visions of Kano's beautiful penis pulsed in her head. She did not know that the hall had become almost silent as the guests watched her with mingled awe and amusement. She did not know that silent tears were seeping from between her clamped eyelids and dripping onto the parquet floor.

'You made an exhibition of yourself.'

The words had been spoken calmly and were all the more ominous because of it.

'Yes, Master. I'm sorry. I didn't mean –'

'Be silent!'

Now this was her punishment, and it was far more cruel than the beating she had expected – even hoped for, because he always made love to her so wonderfully after he had spanked her.

She stood by the head of his palatial bed, still wearing the exotic jewellery she had worn at the banquet. Her arms were raised above her head and fixed by thick, soft ropes to a hook high on the wall. A spreader-bar had been placed between her knees so that she could not bring them together for even minimal relief. A soft light illuminated the bed, on which her Master's gleaming body flexed and tensed under the attentions of two luscious and very active girls, one of whom looked local while the other was clearly Asian.

S tried to take her punishment stoically. She knew she fully deserved it for publicly disgracing her Master with her wanton display in the banqueting hall. Somehow, all the training in self-control she'd had in the last few months had gone out of the window. Her orgasms had been without permission and very public.

As she watched the two girls, envy cut into her like a knife of fire. It should be her there on that bed! She would have done anything and everything to please him, to make up for her lapse – and done it with more passion and adoration than these two naked hussies. Yet at the same time, she knew that to be allowed to lie with Kano, to be permitted to coil against his hard body, to touch and taste and excite him, would have been a reward she did not deserve.

Tears of envy and sorrow rolled over her heavily mascara'd eyelashes as the Asian girl formed her mouth into a perfect oval and began to kiss and lick Kano's penis before engulfing it with her soft lips. The other girl was kissing his chest while her hand gently cupped and squeezed his testicles. S cried silent tears of jealousy as the two girls worked to please her Master. If her hands had been free she would have torn their hair out.

The two girls left the bedroom with the dawn, and Kano slept. He had not spoken a word to S, nor paid her the slightest attention all night. She stood like some bizarre sentry, her nakedness decked out with priceless jewels, her knees trapped by the spreader-bar, her arms numb from being raised above her head so long, and she gazed down at his slumbering form with luminous eyes.

His face looked so peaceful in sleep, so gentle. S knew he could be gentle as well as demanding, and she knew it was this combination of gentleness and discipline which bound her so helplessly to him. Her eyes moved down from his face to the firm curves and planes of his hard torso, every inch of which she longed to cover again and again with soft kisses. They took in his long, muscular thighs and then, inevitably, centred on the manhood lolling soft and sweet on the mat of thick curls at their join. She knew it could rear to magnificence, had been magnificent most of that long night – but for the benefit of the other two girls rather than her.

Her Master was still asleep when Gladys and the butler crept into the bedroom to release S from the wall. She whimpered as the blood began to rush back into her lowered arms, and Gladys placed a warning finger against her lips. Her legs, too, were cramped from the spreader-bar, and she was virtually hobbling as she followed the butler out of the room, followed in her turn by Gladys. The steaming bath to which Gladys then took her was a wonderful relief, and afterwards S fell almost instantly into an exhausted, dreamless sleep.

When Gladys eventually woke her, the atmosphere felt different. Gladys was different. She was still gentle but there now seemed to be a distance in her manner. She supervised S's toilet and shower, but this time waited while S towelled herself dry rather than turning the process into a prelude to more personal attentions. She waited while S brushed her own hair, and offered her no make-up or jewellery.

S plucked up the courage to ask a question. 'Is Master still angry with me?'

Gladys sighed. 'Not just you, child,' she replied quietly. 'I am your watcher, remember. It is my fault if you don't behave. Look.'

She turned, bent forward and pulled off her long, wraparound skirt. S stared at the lush rump that was presented to her and gave a little cry of shock and sympathy. The ripe, chestnut-hued curves of Gladys's backside were criss-crossed with darker stripes. Without thinking, S reached out and touched the stripes, feeling the little raised weals with trembling fingers.

'Oh, I'm sorry! I'm so sorry!' she blurted. Then a wild thought struck her. 'Did he – you know, afterwards, did he –'

'Oh, no. It was not him,' Gladys replied, straightening up and rewrapping her skirt. 'I am not so lucky any more. It was Mr Patrice, the butler. Master gave me to him a couple of years ago. I'm lucky really. It could have been one of the drivers, or even the guardroom. Now, come.'

Stunned by the thought of such a magnificent woman as Gladys being given away to a butler and her head whirling with the concept of such a casually dismissive world as Gladys's words had evoked, S followed her watcher out of the cell and along a bewildering series of corridors and flights of steps.

They came at last to a vast, high-ceilinged kitchen bustling with people. Girls and women ranging from nubile teenagers to plump matrons worked at preparing vegetables, or washing dishes and pans. Men in white coats and chefs' hats stood at ultra-modern ranges stirring huge pots with wooden spoons the size of canoe paddles. At the far end of the room Mr Patrice sat at a table talking to a man who looked almost entirely round and wore the biggest chef's hat of them all.

S was suddenly desperately conscious of her nakedness as Gladys led her across the room between the benches and sinks and cooking ranges. Everybody in the kitchen except her was wearing clothes, the men white ducks and jackets as well as their hats, the females aprons and skirts and white turbans. S wore nothing except her three gold body ornaments and the fading patterns of her henna decorations.

Even so, and even though she was the only European present, she seemed to attract little attention until she reached the table at which Mr Patrice sat. It was an almost dreamlike progression. The noises of the busy kitchen seemed to become louder and sharper. The figure of Gladys walking in front of her, and that of Mr Patrice the butler, seemed to become oddly over-focused.

It seemed to S that they arrived in front of the table in slow motion. Gladys whispered to the butler and S felt as though the words came through her skin. The crash as Mr Patrice banged his fist on the table-top felt like a thunderclap and the instant silence which fell over the kitchen was almost painful. Without turning around S knew that every eye in the room was fixed upon her.

Gladys turned to her and held out her hand. Although nothing was said S knew exactly what was about to happen. Gladys, her watcher, had been spanked by the butler on behalf of Kano for S's misbehaviour. Now, on behalf of the butler, she was about to pass on the spanking to S, and publicly.

Gladys took S by the hand and led her to the edge of the table. S bent over, knowing it was right that her lack of discipline should be thus humiliatingly chastised in front of the kitchen staff. Had she not been servant to the servants back at Miss Erika's mansion?

S spread herself on the cold table-top, pressing her breasts and stomach down against its hardness. She stretched her arms high and spread her feet wide, keeping her legs straight and pushing up her bottom so as to present herself properly for her punishment.

Gladys employed a large wooden spoon for the spanking. She had a strong arm and despite her determination to be a good girl and keep still and quiet, S screamed and leapt up as the first blow landed centrally on her left buttock. She danced and rubbed her bottom frantically, staring at Gladys with shocked, tearful eyes, but the other woman only looked irritated and gestured with the spoon.

Biting her lip and praying for self-control, S spread herself once again across the table. The second blow mirrored the first, this time on her right buttock, and was just as hard. S managed to keep more or less still, but could not suppress a loud wail at the fire of it.

Gladys was an expert with a large wooden spoon, and soon S was sobbing and grunting helplessly as her watcher spread the conflagration over the curves of her backside, picking a different, untouched spot with each stroke, and beating each writhing cheek in turn. To S it became almost a dream, as though the fire in her backside was separated from her brain by a mental wall. She felt the pain and heard the noise, but they had become separate sensations. It seemed to go on for ages, although it was actually only a few minutes, and S swore in her heart of hearts that she would never, never let Gladys down again.

When it was over Gladys had to lift her swooning victim from the table, and half-carried S back to her cell. Once there, her eyes now soft and solicitous, Gladys bathed S's burning rump with icy water and smoothed it over with cold cream, before dotting it with tiny, tender kisses.

Then she allowed S to make love to her, murmuring little sweetnesses and stroking S's hair as she worked her tongue between Gladys's long, muscular thighs. S was once again tearful, but now they were tears of gratitude and love. Gladys's orgasm was slow and voluptuous, her scent and savour driving S into a small orgasm of her own.

'Thank you, Gladys,' S whispered as she snuggled against the warm, enveloping body of her watcher/lover.

'Hush, child,' Gladys murmured, her voice soft and satisfied and comforting. 'You got a long way to go yet.'

S knew that to be all too true. She had let down her Master; had made an exhibition of herself and got poor Gladys punished for it. As she drifted into sleep, her face nestled against Gladys's warm breasts, she determined that she would face anything to make up for it, to Gladys as well as Master.

S groaned aloud next morning as she tried to get off the bed. Her backside felt so stiff and sore even the slightest movement made her wince. Her groan woke Gladys, who was instantly contrite and concerned. She smoothed her hands over the curves of S's bottom, easing off when S hissed in reaction. She ordered S to keep still and hurried out of the room, clucking like a mother hen.

She returned after a moment clutching a large towel and several small, dark brown bottles. With extreme gentleness she eased the towel under S's loins and spread it so that S was lying on it from knees to breasts. S heard the chink of a bottle being opened and smelled a sharp, spicy aroma.

'This will hurt a bit at first,' said Gladys. 'But it make you better quickly.'

S felt Gladys smoothing some kind of oil over her bottom with the flats of very gentle hands, covering her from waist to thighs and from cleft to hips. It felt lovely and relaxing, and even the aroma seemed to be having an easing effect. Gladys wiped her oily hands on a corner of the towel and opened a second bottle. This one gave off a different, deeper perfume, rich with exotic herbs and flowers.

'Ah! Ah!' This time it did hurt as Gladys had warned, for she was now kneading the flesh of S's buttocks with strong, skilful fingers. S gasped and clutched at the bed with clawlike fingers as she forced herself to keep still under this new torment. It was worth it, because after only five minutes or so S began to feel a deep easing of her muscles and a swelling of most luxurious relaxation.

Gladys worked on her increasingly languid charge for perhaps fifteen minutes, massaging her from her waist to halfway down her slack thighs, but concentrating on the swells of her bottom cheeks and the deep cleft between them. Then she stopped and wiped her hands again before wrapping the edges of the towel up and wiping the oil from S's body.

'Keep still,' she said. 'This next bit most important.'

She reached down and pulled S's legs wide apart. S heard the snick of yet a third bottle being opened, and then the soft slurping of oil being rubbed onto hands. The touches became different now, a very different kind of massage.

S began to pant as Gladys's hands moved over the sensitive skin of her inner thighs and the curves of her cleft. Instinctively, she opened herself a little more and lifted her hips slightly to give greater access.

Gladys's fingers were now at her centre, exploring the moist slit of her vulva, moving down through her cleft to tease the pucker of her anus and to press and scratch lightly on her perineum. She was taking her time, easing S's labia apart and smoothing her fingertips back and forth along the throbbing inner lips. S gave a helpless little sob of surrender as two things happened at once – one fingertip began to circle her clitoris as a second pressed rhythmically against her anus.

Her tight little rose-hole automatically clenched. Nobody had ever touched her like this. But Gladys now slipped a couple of fingers into her vagina and the reaction caused S to relax enough for the fingertip to ease into her bottom. The oil on the finger made full entrance easy. The double penetration was unbelievable! The fingers moved in her, gently, commandingly, and S began to roll her head and buck her hips.

'Good. You come now!' She heard Gladys's voice through a red mist. 'Lots of comes help a lot when your arse beaten.'

Gladys gave S lots of comes, keeping her gasping, changing her touches, bringing S to the peak and letting her down a little before taking her over the top again, until S was begging for it to stop, her body wracked and spasming. Only then did Gladys have mercy on her, easing her down until only occasional ripples coursed through her body and S lapsed into an exhausted dream.

The dream was interrupted when, what seemed like an age later, Gladys rolled S onto her back then lifted her in her arms as though she was no more than a child. Gladys carried her through to the bathroom and lowered her gently into a steaming hot tub, leaving her there for a while, breathing in the heady scent of bath oils and feeling the heat of the water reach right down to her core.

The combined effect of the massage and the orgasms and the hot bath was amazing. S found that she could now move easily and although, when she checked in the mirror, her bum was very red from the beating, it did not actually hurt any more. She turned to Gladys with moist eyes. Her lack of discipline had got this beautiful woman beaten; she had, rightly, beaten S in her turn; then she had taken all the pain away with her wonderful hands. With a sob, S threw herself into the other woman's arms and kissed her wildly on her mouth and cheeks and eyes and brow, clinging to her, only regaining her self-control when Gladys levered her off.

Her face was a mask of severity but her eyes had a glow of warmth as though she was returning, in some small part, S's outburst of emotion.

'Hold it, child,' she said. 'You got a lot to learn and a lot to do before you got anything to celebrate. Now, get into your room and make yourself pretty while I go and get dressed. Then we'll get some breakfast and I'll start showing you around the palace and telling you some of your duties.'

S scampered happily off to her room and surveyed the wide range of cosmetics on the shelf beneath the mirror. Some were familiar brands while others were new to her, with labels in foreign languages, some even printed in what looked like Arabic script.

Then she faced a quandary. Would her Master want her in English-style make-up, light and subtle, or would he prefer her to wear something more dramatic, with lots of kohl and eyeshadow and heavy blusher and lipstick? S opted for the latter. If she got it wrong Gladys would tell her, and she could clean it off and change it.

She opened lots of jars and pots, feeling like a child in a sweet factory. She would make herself *so* beautiful for him. After smoothing on a light foundation she began working on her eyes. Two different shades of eyeshadow, a light chocolate and a dark gold, blended together and extended out beyond the outer edges of her eyelids. Thick kohl for her eyebrows, extending them as well. Black mascara for her eyelashes, and narrow lines of kohl around the edges of her eyelids, taking the lines outward and curving them up until she looked quite catlike.

She chose a deep claret lipstick and edged her lips with a deeper, almost purple liner. The blusher she chose echoed the lipstick, and she brushed it on carefully, shaping her cheeks and underlining her cheek-bones, making her face triangular and even more feline. A final, faint dusting of powder and she sat back to survey her work.

S stared at her reflection in wonder. In putting the make-up on she had concentrated on one tiny part of her face at a time. Now she saw the whole effect she gasped. It was magical! She was a different woman, exotic, alluring. With hardly a thought, she reached for the lipstick again and began to smear it on her nipples. They were already engorged and the action felt pleasant. The thought that her new appearance might please Kano was even more pleasant. She felt a gush of heat between her legs at the thought that he might find it arousing, and take her to his bed or at least allow her to take him into her welcoming mouth.

Four

'You look magnificent,' Gladys said when she returned from getting dressed. 'At both ends!' she added, patting S on the bottom which glowed red as if it too had been treated with blusher.

S thought Gladys was really the magnificent one. She wore a long wraparound skirt of green silk covered with a pattern of rioting gold swirls. Her loose turban was of the same material, and in between she was naked save for a wide gold choker and her nipple rings. Her chestnut-coloured skin gleamed with the scented oil she had put on after her shower. Her full, firm breasts caught the light as they swayed and trembled with her movements. S would have hugged her had she dared.

Gladys placed a long steel chain and what looked like a pair of handcuffs on the shelf among the array of cosmetics. She beckoned S closer and turned her around. They were not handcuffs, but elbow cuffs. Gladys fixed the first ring to S's left arm just above her elbow and the second, the one with the chain attached, to her right. She pulled S's arms tight back and fixed the adjustable chain, imprisoning her in a position which was just short of discomfort and which forced her breasts into prominence.

The other chain turned out to be no more nor less than a leash, with a spring clip at one end and a loop at the other. Gladys lifted S's heavy pussy ring, clipped the leash to it and, holding the loop, led her off to begin their tour of the palace. S felt very self-conscious as she followed Gladys, but somehow being trussed up like this felt very right.

The tour began with what Gladys called the public rooms – the marble-floored foyer through which S had first entered this new world; the banqueting hall where she had disgraced herself by coming in public and without permission; a ballroom; a 'receiving room' where the Prince, her Master, met delegations of his subjects, diplomats and groups of businessmen; and a Council Chamber where he legislated for his Principality.

What astonished S even more than the sheer opulence of everything she saw was the number of people milling around. Men in business suits, others in flowing, brilliantly patterned robes, even a few wearing the Arab *keffiya*. The men were outnumbered by women and girls, some standing in attendance by groups of men, most hurrying about with messages or carrying trays of drinks and sweetmeats. All wore skirts and turbans in glorious colours and all were bare breasted.

Since S was the only European and the only woman who was completely naked, she attracted a great deal of attention from the men, and even from some of the women. At first it was deeply embarrassing to feel all those eyes crawling over her, to see the heads turn and men nudging one another, to feel waves of lust washing towards her.

Then it changed; she suddenly understood. Their reaction to her was not simply surprise at seeing a naked woman being led by a leash attached to her pubis, nor simply carnality – though that was certainly there. Had she not been beautiful they would not be reacting the way they were. She was beautiful. Their reactions to her were based on the fact that she was beautiful, and they wanted her, wanted her body, wanted sex with her.

Her embarrassment became pride. She raised her head and pulled her shoulders back even further, pushing her breasts forward proudly. She gave an added sway to her hips, feeling the heat and wetness building between her legs. By the time they got to the Council Chamber S was trembling with arousal and anticipation. He would see her now; Prince Adenkano N'Kwandwe, her wonderful Master, would see her now and find her beautiful, and would send her to his bed and slake his lust on her. As she was led through the door S felt her nipples harden even more and a surge of liquid fire coursed through her vagina.

He was not there. The chamber was empty of people. Curved desks with microphones on them faced a tall, elaborately carved throne, but the throne was empty. S almost sobbed with disappointment. She had built herself up to this moment. She had been *so* certain he would be there, would see how much she loved him, would find her desirable and would fuck her, maybe even there and then, on the hard wooden floor. Oh, how much she wanted him to fuck her again.

Her shoulders rounded now with disappointment and a sense of loss, S obeyed the sharp tug Gladys gave on her pussy ring and followed her on to the next part of their tour.

This part took in the servants' quarters, where S might eventually live, storage rooms for clothes, furniture and all kinds of foodstuffs imaginable, a butcher's shop where the Prince's meat was prepared, a huge garage which housed his fleet of limousines, and the guard room in which the Prince's bodyguard was centred.

Her entry into this particular room caused something of a sensation among the soldiers present. There were perhaps twenty of them, all reacting in the most obvious way to the sudden appearance of a bound and naked European woman amongst them, but S hardly noticed. She looked around dull-eyed, took in the presence of the grinning soldiers and the two-tiered cots around the walls and the guns everywhere, but was still so drained with disappointment at her Master's absence that she registered little.

Their last call was to the kitchens, where only yesterday Gladys had beaten her with that awful wooden spoon. S registered the hum and clatter of activity, saw the table across which she had spread herself to be spanked, noticed the sidelong comments some of the male chefs made to one another. She became aware that Gladys was telling her she would spend much of her working life here in this kitchen. It did not signify except to add to her disappointment. This was not the sort of place Kano would visit often, if at all. How, oh how, was she going to get herself back into his good graces if she was hidden away in the kitchens where he would not see her . . .

'Now, child, you do as you are told here.' Gladys's voice was stern. It was next morning, and S was being presented for duty in the kitchen. 'Remember who gets the first taste if you go wrong.'

S was very conscious that it was Gladys who would 'get the first taste', and she the second, and worked feverishly hard at the menial tasks she was given. It was, she knew, yet another test. She scoured cauldrons so big and heavy she could hardly manipulate them. She scrubbed floors. She humped big sacks of vegetables and meal. Everybody, or at least it felt like everybody, assumed the right to order her about. Get this, get that, move this there, bring that here. And everybody seemed to have the right to cuff the back of her head or take a swipe at her bare bottom if she did not move fast enough.

By the time the Prince's lunch was ready – a huge meal for he always seemed to have a multitude of guests – S was almost delirious with exhaustion. Every muscle ached. Her backside stung from where it had been slapped by hard hands or spanked with various kitchen implements when she was not quick enough or was clumsy with an unfamiliar task. Her breasts were sore from the many times chefs had taken a crafty feel. When Gladys came for her at last she could have cried with relief.

She complained to Gladys as soon as her watcher had clipped on the leash and led her out of the kitchen. Instead of comforting her, Gladys gave a loud sigh and immediately turned around and went back into the kitchen, pulling hard on S's pussy ring.

'I told you you had a lot to learn, child,' she said, sitting down on a stool and dragging S close. 'And you can start by learning your place.'

Gladys grabbed S by her wrist and suddenly jerked her forward, upending her across her lap. The kitchen fell silent as everybody turned to watch what was about to happen. Gladys held S down with her left hand and spanked her upraised bottom with her right. She ignored S's squealing and wriggling, and the tears which soon began to flow. The spanking was over in a couple of minutes, but when she stood up S's bottom had taken on a fresh new glow and she could not help rubbing at the stinging with both hands.

She looked at Gladys with contrite, tear-brimmed eyes. 'I'm sorry, Gladys,' she whispered.

'Thank me!'

S stared at Gladys in amazement. Not only had she just been spanked in front of all these kitchen workers but she was required to be grateful. She swallowed and took a deep breath. But of course Gladys was right; she did need to know her place.

'Thank you, Gladys,' she said, her voice clear if a little tremulous. 'Thank you for spanking me and teaching me my place.'

S was at last in the presence of her Master, but in very different circumstances from those she had wished for. He was at lunch, holding court with perhaps a dozen guests, and looking magnificent. Girls, one for each guest as well as for the Prince, carried dishes to the table and poured drinks. Another girl stood behind Kano wafting a large ostrich-feather fan. S, though, was confined to standing by the huge serving table and assisting the busy serving girls, fully twenty feet away from her Master. She was not sure he had even bothered to glance in her direction, and her spirits were low.

They were not helped by the fact that every single one of the serving girls was delectably beautiful; far more beautiful, S thought, than she was herself. They moved with a proud grace that she could only envy. Their hips swayed, their backs were straight, their naked breasts bobbed and swayed as they moved. They smiled coquettishly whenever the man they were serving fondled their breasts or stroked their bottoms, which seemed to be happening a lot.

They were, S realised, far more comfortable with their sexuality, and that of the men they were serving, than she was herself, and she envied them. She thought back to her time at Seigneur's place when she was being trained. Her own sexuality had been challenged then, or rather her recognition of it. She

46

remembered being presented to two delivery men as their 'tip', and fucked wildly on a pile of potato sacks in the back of their lorry. She remembered asking Arthur, the commis chef, whether he would please fuck her because Mary had told her she should. She remembered long nights delving and nuzzling between Miss Erika's thighs; days and nights of being naked and available. Yet still she could not be as comfortable with her nudity, her femaleness, as every one of these girls appeared to be with theirs.

S was brought back to the present by a sudden burst of laughter at the table, and one of the serving girls grabbing her wrist and leading her over. All the men's faces were turned towards her except Prince Adenkano's. He was whispering into the ear of the man next to him and apparently ignoring her, though she hoped in her heart that it could not be so.

The serving girl brought S close up to the guest she had been waiting on. He was a large man, rather sweaty above a shirt collar that seemed too stiff and too tight. He proceeded to inspect S with bloodshot eyes and pudgy fingers. She kept absolutely still as he inspected her breasts, bouncing them and tugging at the gold rods that pierced her nipples. He felt the weight of her pussy ring, and then rubbed his hand down over her vulva. He said something to her Master Kano, who merely waved a hand dismissively. Then he thrust two fingers into her.

S fought for self-control. Her instinct was to scream and run away from this awful humiliation, yet her Master seemed to have permitted it, to wish it, and therefore it must be right. She looked beyond the man, beyond the table, at one of the paintings on the wall, distancing herself. She parted her knees a little to allow the man better access.

He now had four fingers in her, stretching her

cruelly, working them in and out until the squelching from her over-stimulated vagina became audible. She fought it, using all the training Mary had put her through, all the timed sessions when she had to avoid orgasm no matter what the stimulation.

It seemed to go on for a lifetime, her body palpitating, the man's hand working in her sheath, all eyes boring into her. Then her beloved Master Kano caught her eye. He smiled and nodded. It was permission, and she came volcanically, shoving her vulva down on to the intruding hand, gasping and pumping, her juices a flood. Her sudden convulsions after such long resistance surprised the man fingering her and he almost snatched his hand away, but she grabbed his wrist and held him there so that she could finish herself off.

She was aware of the increased volume of the table conversation and of the laughter among the assembled men as she walked weak-kneed back to her post by the serving table. Their laughter did not matter. It was the laughter of excitement rather than ridicule. Kano had willed it, had allowed one of his guests to touch her, had shown his power. S could see from the brief glimpse she was allowed of his eyes that he was pleased with her, and she was happy. What did it matter that a fat stranger had made a public display of her and that her juices were trickling down her thighs for all to see? Kano had permitted it and approved it, and that was all that mattered.

But oh, how much she wished it had been him and not the fat stranger.

As the days and weeks drew on, S's life took on a pattern. She was in Kano's presence for most of each day, but at a distance from him. After working in the kitchen as a skivvy in the mornings she would attend his luncheons as assistant to his serving girls, but was never allowed to serve him herself. The same pattern prevailed at dinners in the evenings, even State Dinners.

S, always the only girl kept entirely naked except for elaborate jewellery, was never permitted to do more than assist the other girls. Occasionally she was brought forward so that one of Kano's guests could inspect her, especially when she had been recently spanked for some mistake or other. She never got used to approaching some beckoning stranger and bending over so that he could admire the red marks on her bottom, but she did it dutifully because it was what her Master wanted.

Being in Kano's presence during his public meals but never being acknowledged by him, or even allowed to go near him, was a form of exquisite torture, but the nights were far, far worse. Then, beautifully made-up and decked out with gold and diamonds, she had to attend in her Master's bedroom. What made it so awful was that she was never, ever the girl he took into his bed.

Two girls, never less but sometimes more, would assist Kano to undress and bathe, while all S was allowed to do was to accept his discarded clothes from their hands and put them away. Then she was obliged to stand there while they washed and dried his glorious body, taking the used towels from their lucky hands and putting them into the laundry basket.

After that came the worst torment of all. Kano would stroll naked and magnificent to his bed. The girls who had undressed and bathed him would then strip off their skirts and turbans, hand them to S, and join their Master. Standing there holding the girls' clothes while they worked to pleasure her Master sent S nearly mad with jealousy.

Watching the girls privileged to take his penis into their mouths filled her with rage. She could have done it so much better. She could have given him so much more with the gentle adoration of her lips and tongue and fingers. She would have been so much more grateful to receive the gift of his orgasm into her throat.

When he fucked them she was torn between the wild desire to tear the girls' eyes out for being so lucky and the almost irresistible urge to throw herself on the writhing couple and pour kisses on Kano's back and buttocks and thighs, to lick and bite and taste him. And when at the end, after the sex S had been denied, one of the girls would bring towels and a bowl of scented water and reverently rinse Kano's genitals before he settled down to sleep, S always had to fight back tears of frustration.

She could not understand why her Master was treating her this way. Back in England, after she had given herself to him as his voluntary slave, it had been wonderful. He had allowed her to bathe him. It had been she who experienced the joy of sucking his glorious cock. It had been she he had fucked to delirium time after time. And now she was only allowed to watch – no, *made* to watch!

Any number of times Gladys found S crying herself to sleep back in her own room, and the hugs and the gentle love-making that followed were a kind of compensation, but not enough. The repeated orgasms Gladys gave her sated S's physical needs and even gave her a sense of being loved, but did nothing to ease her mental and emotional torment.

Her self-discipline deserted her and she broke down during the fourth week. Her Master had taken two of the most sensuously beautiful girls into his bed. She had suffered watching them vie to kiss and lick and suck his rampant manhood. She had watched him fuck them turn and turn about, his torso glistening as he bucked on them, their gasps and wails of ecstasy assailing her ears. At last, after they had rinsed him and put their skirts and turbans back on, she broke. Tears streaming, she rounded on him, near to hysteria.

'Why not me? Why are you being so cruel! Why don't you fuck *me*? I'm better than those sluts. I love you!'

Her sobs cut off any possibility of further words. She felt herself being grabbed and pulled out of the room. Only when she was back in her own room, still sniffling unhappily, did she begin to appreciate the enormity of what she had done. That aspect of her behaviour was brought fully home when Gladys came in a couple of hours later.

She was moving stiffly, yet there was a soft smile on her face. S knew the system – she had transgressed and Gladys had been punished for it, and now Gladys would punish her. And rightly so. But what did that strange smile signify? The answer came immediately.

'He beat me,' Gladys said, almost contentedly. 'He beat me himself, using a stick. Look.'

She whipped off her skirt and showed S a bottom ridged and striped from a severe thrashing. S gasped and made to reach out for her, but Gladys cut her off.

'And then he fucked me! The Prince fucked me . . . First time in two years!' Her eyes were dancing. 'He did me really hard. It was great!'

She grabbed S in a bear-hug and gave her a big kiss of joy. S felt mixed emotions. She was happy at her friend's happiness but she could not help also feeling stabs of jealousy at her good fortune. When Gladys released her S went silently to the big shelf beneath the mirror. She picked up the largest of the hairbrushes, the one made of glossy, dark hardwood with the long cylindrical handle, and offered it to Gladys without a word.

'I'm sorry I have to do this,' Gladys said as S draped herself across her knees.

The spanking was not a hard one by Gladys's standards, but was still sharp enough to make S squirm and hiss. Soon both cheeks of her bottom were stinging and glowing brightly and tears were dripping onto the floor.

Gladys did not let S up when the spanking was over. With one hand still pressing down on the small of her back she eased S's legs apart with the other. Knowing fingers began to touch and tease and despite the pain in her bottom – or perhaps because of it – S was soon responding. Through a mist of declining pain and increasing arousal she heard Gladys speak, so quietly it was almost as though she was talking to herself.

'This not as good as Master,' she said. 'But it's nearly as big.'

S felt something thick and hard begin to press lightly and rhythmically against the entrance to her vagina. She relaxed her muscles without even thinking, and it began to slide in. It was big and smooth and hard, and felt so good. It slid in easily on her wetness, stretching her and reaching to her depths. S had not been had by a man in weeks, and soon the muscles of her vagina were rippling and clenching in welcome. Even when she realised, just before the end, that what Gladys was using must be the handle of the hairbrush it made no difference. Her orgasm was too close, and she writhed and jerked against the object as wave upon wave of unstoppable sensation coursed through her.

Afterwards, S was rather ashamed of herself. She

had heard of things like dildos and vibrators, of course, and had wondered what possible pleasure such devices could give a woman. Now Gladys had fucked her with the wooden handle of a hairbrush and she had come uncontrollably! Blushing, she stood up and took the brush from Gladys. She rinsed the handle clean of her juices, replaced it on the shelf, and stood facing Gladys, awaiting her next order.

She knew that her outburst to her Master Kano had been a really, really bad mistake and that she was in serious trouble. She waited for Gladys to tell her what her fate was, and was kept waiting for a long while. She knew it must be something truly awful when at last Gladys looked up and she saw there were tears brimming her eyelashes.

'We are being sent away for a while. To one of Master's estates.' Gladys's voice was cracking slightly. 'Master is going abroad for a time, and he says we must use that time to learn proper obedience.'

Gladys was saying 'we', which meant that she too would be sharing S's punishment, which made everything all the more awful.

'We leave in two or three days,' Gladys continued, her tone flat now. 'In the meantime you are to be taken to the guard room. You will stay there and you will be obedient. I am to go there three times a day, when they change duty shifts, and receive a report on you. If the report is less than perfectly satisfactory, I am to cane you.'

By the time she finished her little speech Gladys's tone was miserable. But not as miserable as S now felt. To be banished was bad enough, even though it was only for a while, but to be locked up in a guard-room cell sounded truly awful. She had visions of herself pacing a small barred cell with stone walls, and living off bread and water. The reality was wildly different.

Five

First the butler, Mr Patrice, came in. Gladys held S's arms tight behind her as he cut off the beautiful gold rods piercing her nipples using a special tool, and replaced them with dull steel rings. He did the same with the heavy gold ring between her legs, inserting instead a short, thick stud intended to do no more than keep her piercing open. Then he buckled a wide leather collar around S's neck and a pair of leather bracelets around her wrists. There were rings on the bracelets and at the front of the collar, and using a short length of steel chain he fixed her wrists to her collar. The chain was a foot or so long, so that S could move her hands a little, but she was nevertheless very effectively manacled.

Still without having uttered a single word the butler clipped a dog lead to S's collar and led her away to her fate. The fact that Gladys was crying silent tears in the corner did nothing to ease S's fears.

As soon as they reached the guard room S realised that her vision of being locked into a clammy cell had been very, very wrong. There were no cells. There was nothing save this one large room, with all its bunks around the walls and its long table down the middle, and its complement of soldiers. Big men, fit from military training. The Prince's elite guard.

Mr Patrice led S into the middle of the room. He

unclipped her leash, said something in the local language, and left. Several of the lounging soldiers stood and approached, grinning, their eyes telling their thoughts. S cowered as they ran their hands over her. With her hands manacled as they were she could do nothing to protect herself.

She tried clamping her knees together but their hands got between her legs anyway. She tried cramping her elbows in close to shield her breasts, but it made no difference. Then she suddenly remembered what Gladys had said about being obedient, and about collecting a report on her and caning her if it was less than satisfactory. She also remembered that if she earned punishment, Gladys got punished as well, and knew she could not do that to a friend.

S straightened her spine, pulled back her elbows, and parted her knees. It was what she was here for. She had given herself to Kano as his voluntary slave, to do with as he wished. He had sent her here, for the pleasure of his soldiers, and since her Master wished it that is what she would provide.

Surprisingly, they were not rough, though they squeezed her breasts very thoroughly, tugged at her nipple and pussy rings, and thrust hard fingers into her. She bore it, inexplicably aroused by what they were doing. By the time they led her across to one of the cots and she lay down on her back, she was going with them.

They did not pounce on her as she expected. In fact they seemed almost casual about what they were going to do to her. And no wonder, S thought ruefully; they probably had a lot of girls in here.

The first to approach her, encouraged by his companions, looked to be the youngest of the group. He was surprisingly gentle but overeager, or possibly inexperienced, for he came on only his third or fourth thrust. He had not removed his clothes but simply opened his fly, and S felt his zipper scratching her inner thighs as he bucked on her.

He pulled out quickly and was replaced almost at once by a second soldier. This one was older, bigger, and much more self-controlled. He took his time, gripping S with his hands cupped under her shoulders and moving slowly and powerfully. His orgasm when it came had S groaning and pushing on to him.

'Please, sir,' she managed to gasp. 'Please may I come!'

Whether or not he gave permission was irrelevant as the swelling cramps of orgasm undulated through her body in time to the gouts of heat he was spurting into her. She was still on the crest when he withdrew from her and the third man took his place, and she came continuously as he fucked her. The waves were smaller now, sea-swells rather than breakers crashing against rocks, but powerful enough to send her into a red-misted dream.

She did not know how many of them fucked her, or how many times. She did not ask permission to come, for she felt she was drowning in one long orgasm. She was vaguely aware of the several times penises were thrust into her mouth, but she sucked them automatically, swallowing like a robot when they finished.

S was still in this near-trance when it came to change of guard, and at first she was not aware that Gladys had come for her. She climbed wearily off the bunk. Her hip-joints felt stiff, her vulva felt swollen and bruised, the mattress on which she had lain was a sticky mess with all the sperm that had leaked out of her.

Cooing like a mother hen, Gladys took S off for a hot bath, pampering her, smoothing her loins with a lotion which eased her and made her feel less swollen, telling her she had done well. Then she led her back into the guard room, where the next watch had taken over.

Then it became almost surreal. As the new squad of guards looked on, Gladys gestured. S bent herself across the table as Gladys picked up a thick rattan cane.

'Only three,' she heard through a mist of fright. 'Because she is a good girl. Now just you guys go easy, understand?'

The three strokes of the cane were awful, but S managed to keep still for them and to stifle her screams. Then Gladys was gone and she was left to the pleasure of the soldiers.

The new squad did go easy on her. After all, they had a full eight hours. S was rather puzzled when the first thing they did was to take off their boots, tie them together by the laces, and pile them in a corner. When the one with the stripes on his arm ordered her, in a mixture of gestures and pidgin English, to polish the boots she was astonished, but also relieved. At least it meant that they were not going to fuck her. Not yet anyway.

After polishing their boots S brewed up a huge pot of strong coffee. It was while she was serving it up in big enamelled mugs that they began touching her. Like the others, they were not rough. It seemed to S that the hands on her breasts and backside and between her legs were more to do with establishing status than with titillation. Here she was, a naked woman among half a dozen soldiers, sent by her Master to obey and give pleasure, almost swamped by the sense of their maleness and the certainty of what would soon follow.

The situation set off such a lurch of arousal in her

belly that when the sergeant gestured her to her knees the fingers that went to his zip were fumbling and eager. His cock was already hard, and bounced out of his trousers so suddenly it almost slapped against her face. Her hands went to him gently, cupping his balls and circling the base of his thick shaft. She licked his length, breathing in the scent of his masculinity, then opened her mouth and circled his satiny glans with an eager tongue before sinking her mouth onto him. Somewhere in the back of her mind S realised that she was doing this as much for her own pleasure as his and, strangely, was not shocked with herself.

A couple of girls carrying trays of food came in while S was sucking off the sergeant, but she was too engrossed in what she was doing to be distracted by their giggles. She felt his balls tighten in her hand and knew he was about to come. She crammed her mouth down on him, taking him almost to her throat and gulping and slurping as he flooded her mouth. She kept him in her mouth even after he had finished and had begun to soften, swallowing everything and licking him clean. When she at last released him and knelt back, red-faced from her efforts, he patted her head and smiled his satisfaction and S felt an odd little surge of gratitude.

After the sergeant, most of the squad wanted to use her mouth. S was fucked a couple of times but she was still a bit sore from the last squad and it did little for her. Sucking them off, even one after the other, was much less uncomfortable though she did gag a bit if the man she was sucking pushed too deep.

When the watch changed and Gladys came for her S was in much better shape than the last time. The hot bath and Gladys's tender ministrations were just as welcome, though. She drifted back from the bathroom to the guard room in a state of gentle euphoria, her body glowing from the bath, her mind more or less blank. She picked up the rattan from the rack where Gladys had left it, handed it to her and draped herself across the table in readiness. She was puzzled when, instead of the fire of a caning, Gladys pulled her up from the table and shook her head.

It took a moment or two for S to register what it meant. Gladys's eyes were shining and her face was lit by a huge smile. She hugged S and kissed her happily, taking the cane and tossing it back into the rack. When it dawned on S that she was not going to be caned she felt a surge of joy. She had given satisfaction and Gladys was pleased with her! Kano too, perhaps. She hugged and kissed Gladys in return, then moved to face the new squad of soldiers, her shoulders square and her eyes bright.

The next forty-eight hours became a dream, a fantasy. S polished boots, made coffee, did piles of dishwashing. She sucked cock after cock. They felt her and fucked her, on the bunk, from behind bent over the table, kneeling on all fours. She marvelled at how different each fuck felt, big, smaller, quick and slow, rough or gentle. She orgasmed almost to exhaustion and was brought back to recovery by Gladys's lovely hot baths and massages. She slept in fits and starts, seldom for long because of the demands on her body. She even fell asleep once or twice when one or another of them was fucking her. She was caned a few times, but never more than three or four strokes at a time.

Gladys carried her away from the guard room at the end, literally cradling S in her arms and carrying her off to a hot bath and blessed sleep. Next morning they set out on their journey to Prince Adenkano's rural estate.

* * *

S was weary after her time in the guard room, even though a shower and a good breakfast helped somewhat. Gladys, naked now except for small squares of cloth hanging front and back from a chain around her hips, had to help her up into the back of the Land Rover which was to transport them to wherever they were going. She hugged Gladys and told her how sorry she was for getting her into this trouble, but Gladys hushed her and told her it would be all right in the end.

A couple of armed guards had climbed into the back of the Land Rover with them and sure enough, hardly half an hour into the journey, one of them spoke loudly and gestured. At once Gladys was on her knees, pulling at his fly. He waited until she had hauled his cock out and got it erect with kisses and licks before shoving Gladys away and pointing to S.

The momentary eye-contact between the two women was enough to give S support. She knelt, taking Gladys's place between the soldier's knees, and moved her mouth down on him. He was not especially big, nor especially eager. He was doing this as much to show his power over the women as to get pleasure.

S turned the tables on him by using every little trick she had learned since her training at Seigneur's mansion had first begun. She cupped his balls and squeezed them gently, and pressed her fingers against that sensitive area between his sac and his anus. She stroked his length with encircling fingers as her lips slid over his engorged glans, swirling her tongue around his satiny hotness. She took him as deep as she could then sucked hard as she pulled back until he was almost out, making mewling and slurping noises as though she was wildly excited by what she was doing.

It took the soldier only a few minutes to come and S swallowed hard, giving his shrinking cock a few last licks before tucking it back into his trousers. To her chagrin, her performance had obviously impressed the second guard, who was waiting his turn with his cock already out and rampant.

The journey took several hours, mostly over rutted and unmade roads, but the soldiers made no further demands on the two women in their charge. The estate they eventually arrived at was big and looked very well run. Behind the large, single-storeyed house in which the estate manager lived stood the workers' quarters, forming three sides of a large square, most of which was taken up with a vegetable garden. A small river meandered beside the road along which they had driven, and fields of maize, millet and other crops stretched into the distance.

As soon as the Land Rover came to a halt in a swirl of red dust the two soldiers leapt out and lifted S and Gladys to the ground, making sure to have a good long feel of their breasts as they did so. The estate manager was already waiting for them on the wide, shaded verandah at the front of the house. To S's surprise he looked European, the first she had seen since arriving in the Principality. For some reason it made her feel self-conscious, and she placed a hand shyly over her pubis.

One of the soldiers escorted the two women to the bottom step of the verandah, saluted, and handed the manager a thick envelope before returning towards the vehicle. Before the manager could open the envelope a noise of loud squabbling filled the air. The two guards and the driver were shouting and gesticulating in a fierce argument, and the driver kept pointing towards the two women and shaking his fist at the guards.

With a curt 'Stay there!' the manager walked briskly over to the three shouting Africans. He quieted them with a shout and a rapid conversation ensued. It was in some kind of local dialect and S could not understand a word of it, but it was obvious from the gestures that she or Gladys, or perhaps both, were being discussed. After a few minutes the manager turned and came towards them.

'You, white girl,' he said. 'Is it true that you sucked off those two guards on the way here?'

The way he said it made it sound as though she had *chosen* to fellate them and S blushed hotly as she nodded, unable to speak for a moment.

'Well the driver says it isn't fair, and he wants a go too.' He paused. 'Well, get on with it then!' he added irritably when S did not move.

God, it was so humiliating! The driver did not even bother to get inside the vehicle, but just lounged against its side in full view of the others as S crossed towards him and knelt between his booted feet. He took a lot longer than either of the two guards had, and S had to work really hard to bring him off. Even then he managed to add to her humiliation by pulling out of her mouth while he was still coming, and spurting onto her face and breasts.

His loud laugh, and those of the two guards, made S want to shrivel up with shame, and the look on the manager's face when she returned to the verandah did not help.

'There is a pump around the back of the house,' he said. 'Go and wash the dust off yourselves. Clean yourselves up then report to my office. Use the back entrance.' Without further ado, he turned and walked into the house, tearing at the envelope as he went.

The pump was one of those old-fashioned cast-iron ones, with a wide spout and a long pumping handle.

Gladys let S go first, levering the handle with strong arms. The water was icy and felt wonderful, taking S's breath away and making her skin tingle. There was no soap, but S scrubbed herself all over with vigorous hands and quickly felt more alive than she had for several days. Working the pump handle for Gladys soon had her warmed up, and both women were giggling happily by the time they were finished. When they discovered that there was nothing to dry themselves on they found it hilarious, and chased each other around in the sun like little girls until the air dried them.

They were still breathless with suppressed giggles when they presented themselves at the back door. An enormously fat woman working in the kitchen directed them to the manager's office, her eyes popping at the sudden appearance of two giggling women, one small and white and stark-naked, the other tall and chestnut-coloured and virtually naked as well.

The manager's house seemed even bigger inside than it had appeared to be from the outside. The kitchen woman's directions had not been very coherent, and they went astray several times. Eventually, though, they came to the right door. Gladys knocked nervously, and the women entered at the shouted command to come in.

The manager was sitting with his feet up and he regarded the women coolly as they came and stood in front of his desk. The opened envelope was on the desk by his feet and in his hands was a sheaf of papers.

'You are Gladys, I believe?' he said after a long pause. To judge from his accented English S guessed that he was probably French.

'Yes, sir.'

'And you must be the one called S.'

'Yes, sir,' S responded in her turn. She wondered what was written on the wad of papers he had in his hand.

'You behaved like a slut with your escort,' he said in a matter-of-fact tone. 'Right out in the open where anyone could see.'

S was stung. 'But you said! You told me to –!'

'Silence!' His feet were off the desk and he was upright so suddenly that both S and Gladys jerked back with shock. He leaned forward, placing the knuckles of his big hands on top of the desk. 'In my establishment you will not speak without permission. The only words you may utter are to answer a direct question or to ask permission to speak. Is that clear?'

He was a big man, built like a wrestler, with a mane of thick black hair, heavy eyebrows above dark eyes and a hooked nose, and thick, sensual lips. At that moment he looked very frightening. Both women nodded frantically, not daring to speak.

'Good.' His voice was quieter as he sat down again. 'You have been imposed upon me for apparent lack of discipline. You, S, seem to have very little understanding of your station in life. Speaking to His Highness out of turn indeed. And then entertaining your escort so lewdly on the way here. Quite reprehensible.'

S almost blurted out a protest. It was so unfair. She had only spoken to her Master because her heart was breaking with longing for him, and she had only 'entertained' the two guards because they made her. Worse, the manager himself had ordered her to fellate the driver. It wasn't fair!

'And you, Gladys,' he continued calmly, 'are as much to blame as this slut. More. You have belonged to His Highness for, what, six years now.' He

65

consulted the sheaf of papers as he spoke. 'You should know better by now. Well, I shall begin as I intend to continue. I have experience in training the Prince's women to know their place. Your duties will begin tomorrow morning, but in the meantime you will be beaten to remind you who is the Baas here.'

He pronounced it 'Baas' and not 'boss', in the South African manner. He opened a drawer in the desk and took out a strange-looking, dark grey object.

'Do you know what this is?' he asked, placing it on the desk in front of him. It was perhaps two and a half feet long, and heavily wrinkled on the surface. S heard Gladys gulp and felt her shudder.

'Please, sir, I know, sir. It is the tail of an elephant, sir!' S could never have imagined hearing her lovely Gladys sound so scared.

'Exactly!' The manager sounded pleased. He flexed the object in his hands. 'I have found over the years that an elephant's tail is just about perfect for good discipline. Some people use a bull's pizzle, probably for symbolic reasons. I prefer this. It does not mark up too badly, but it hurts like hell. Does it not, Gladys?'

Gladys was shivering now, and there were tears hovering on her lower lashes. She had clearly experienced the elephant's tail in the past.

'Yes, baas,' she whispered, her eyes huge with fright.

The manager pressed a bell-button on his desk. A factotum, dressed incongruously in a morning suit, appeared and led the two frightened women off to a side room, where they waited for what seemed like hours.

S began to speak, to ask about the elephant's tail, but Gladys clapped a hand across her mouth to silence her, in case there should be anyone within hearing distance. After that they whispered into each other's ears, and S became even more scared.

The punishment was organised as a public entertainment for the estate workers. After sunset the incongruous factotum reappeared carrying two long leather straps, each an inch wide. He bound Gladys's wrists in front of her with the first one, then did the same to S. From his pocket he produced a chain leash, divided at one end. These ends he clipped to the two women's pubic rings, then hauled them briskly out through the back of the house, jerking the leash so that the naked women often staggered and had to scurry to keep up.

Outside in the vast yard fires had been lit and what looked like a number of barbecues were in progress. The firelight lit up people's faces with gold-orange flickerings. There were many people. But the dominant feature of the yard was a large metal frame, illuminated by a high-mounted spotlight.

The factotum led S and Gladys to the frame. He made them raise their arms above their heads and inserted a big iron hook through the straps he had bound around their wrists. He moved to a bulky control box fixed to one of the supports of the frame and pressed a button. There was a loud whirring noise and S felt her arms being stretched upwards. When she was on tiptoe, her face close to Gladys's, she felt something stiff being passed around the small of her back. It was a leather belt, six inches wide and long enough to pass round both women's dangling bodies.

The factotum cinched the belt tight so that S and Gladys were squashed together face to face, body to body. There came another whirring noise as the winch attached to the hook through their wrist straps pulled them higher. It stopped when Gladys was on tiptoes, but since S was at least six inches shorter her feet were right off the ground.

The two women looked into each other's eyes. S was terrified. Gladys was scared too, but she managed a gentle smile. 'Be strong, darling,' she whispered before closing her eyes and tensing for what was to follow.

The manager himself began it. He strolled into the circle of the spotlight, talking to the crowd about why these two women were here and how discipline was paramount. Then he swung around without warning and lashed at Gladys's helpless rump.

S felt the shock of the blow almost as much as Gladys because of the way they were strapped so tightly together. Gladys bit her lip to stifle a scream and her body convulsed, writhing against S. Before she could even think, S too felt a stripe of fire right across the fullest swell of her buttocks. She could not stifle her scream as Gladys had, and her legs kicked with the agony of it.

The manager walked around them, whipping each shuddering backside in turn while he made his speech about discipline to the audience of estate workers. The strokes after the first two were less hard, but still hard enough to make the two women writhe and flail their legs about. The manager gave an order and a man ran over and strapped a long belt around the women's legs, above their knees. He pulled it so tight that one of Gladys's knees was forced between S's, squashing their bodies even closer together.

The beating was less hard now, and through the pain S became aware of something unbelievable. The rhythmic jerking the whip caused was making her vulva press and rub against Gladys's thigh and, incredibly, she felt herself becoming aroused! It was too awful, but she could not prevent it. Indeed, without her even being aware of it her pelvis had begun to rock against Gladys's body, increasing the wild sensations until S was gasping as much from arousal as from the pain of the elephant's tail.

Even when the beating stopped S continued to rock, close now to orgasm. When she realised that Gladys was rubbing her pelvis against her own leg in exactly the same way, it sent her over the top. She came violently and visibly, and not even the manager's loud laugh put her off. Gladys was coming as well now, and even the audience of estate workers began to giggle at the sight of the two dangling women wriggling and gasping and pumping their hips.

Consciousness of the fire in her backside returned to S when her orgasm was over and she began to whimper. Her wrists were also aching from the straps suspending her, and her arms felt numb. Through a haze, she felt the straps around their thighs and waists being removed and the winch lowering them to the ground. Both women were so weak they simply crumpled to the ground when the hook was removed from their wrist straps.

Some people picked them up and carried them to a room in the workers' quarters. They lay the semi-conscious women face-down on two truckle-beds, and within minutes both of them had fallen into an exhausted sleep.

S awoke to bright daylight. A cheerful, round-faced girl was smearing some kind of ointment over her backside. She hissed with the sting of it, but the girl prevented her from wriggling away by pressing a strong hand on her back. Another girl was ministering to Gladys in the same way.

S craned her head around to peep at Gladys's bottom and then her own. To her astonishment there seemed to be relatively little damage. At the time it had felt as though the elephant's-tail whip had been slicing lumps off her buttocks, yet there were no cuts and no blood. True, her buttocks were criss-crossed with angry stripes which stung dreadfully as the girl rubbed the ointment on them, but there was hardly even a raised weal. It was amazing that a beating could cause such pain with so little actual damage.

The girl tending to S's backside said something in a language she did not understand. Gladys translated.

'She wants you to get up on your knees. No, keep your head down on the bed. Get your legs apart.'

S looked at Gladys in puzzlement as she obeyed the instructions. Gladys smiled wearily.

'She wants to see whether white women are built the same way as us,' she added.

The explanation became unnecessary when S felt the lips of her sex being pulled open and fingers begin to explore. The examination was thorough, detailed, and very embarrassing. Fingers pulled her wide and tested the texture and resilience of her labia. Her clitoris was teased into erection. Her vagina was probed, and then her anus.

The embarrassment became excruciating when the girl said something to the one tending Gladys then called loudly through the door. As though they had been waiting for a signal a whole gaggle of girls and women crowded into the room. Every one of them wanted to check for herself that white women really were normal.

The examinations went on for an eternity. All these women had witnessed the beating last night and seen her flagrant display. Now they wanted to see if they could make S come. The nature of their touches

70

between her legs changed. They were no longer examining her but deliberately stimulating her over-sensitised womanhood.

The situation was desperately humiliating, but that only seemed to make matters worse. As fingers probed her gaping vagina, and others teased her straining clitoris, and yet others probed her anus and stroked the insides of her thighs, S sobbed into a slow, overwhelming come which made the women teasing her giggle and brought tears of shame to her eyes.

Six

The estate manager had said that S was here to learn her place, and within only a few days she knew that he really meant it. She was, of course, kept naked, although Gladys was allowed to wear the little square flaps of cloth she had worn on the journey to the estate and which more or less concealed her sex and backside. S was given the most menial tasks. She scrubbed floors for hours every day. It was her task to visit all the workers' quarters every morning and take the night soil to the cesspit, then wash out the buckets with a hose.

She carted the vegetable peelings from the kitchen to the compost heaps, or mixed them with left-overs and maize into pig-swill. The buckets were large and weighed heavy, and the snuffling, snorting porkers scared her but she knew better than to protest.

She was not allowed to sit down with the estate workers at their communal meals but ate standing in a corner, facing the wall and eating with her fingers rather than with a spoon as the others did. Contact with Gladys was kept to a minimum and since she did not speak the local language, and none of the other workers spoke English, she began to feel very lonely.

As a final humiliation, she was made to sleep on the floor in the kennels. The first time she was pushed into there by a grinning supervisor, S was terrified.

The dogs were huge and there were a lot of them. She backed against a wall, trembling with fright as they sniffed at her, certain they were going to leap at her throat at any second. She could have cried with relief when, their sniffing and licking over, the dogs proceeded to ignore her.

Exhausted from a day of back-breaking labour, S lay down on the floor in a corner as far away from the dogs as possible, curling herself into a ball for warmth as well as protection. There were no blankets, and the African night gets very chilly. Before long S found herself crawling across the floor of the kennel and snuggling down among the dogs for warmth. Apart from the one which licked her face with a big, sloppy tongue, the dogs took no notice of her arrival except to make room for her to creep in amongst them.

Apart from that humiliating mass-examination the morning after the public beating, nobody touched S for several days and nights. It changed when, as she was scrubbing the kitchen floor, one of the kitchen porters came up behind her and thrust his hand between her legs so suddenly and so roughly she screamed and knocked over the bucket of soapy water.

The water splashed over a pair of highly polished black boots. S looked up into the face of a very angry-looking estate manager.

'What the hell do you think you're doing!' he bellowed, his face reddening.

S blanched at his ferocity. Stammering, she tried to tell him what had happened, that it was not her fault, that the porter had hurt her, that she would please clean Baas's boots. If she thought he would be merciful she was wildly wrong.

He said something to the porter in rapid local dialect. The porter grinned and grabbed S by the arm. As the porter pulled her towards a table, his intentions obvious as he scrabbled at his fly with his free hand, the manager turned to walk away.

'Come to my office when he has finished,' he said over his shoulder. 'My boots need cleaning!'

Too shocked to resist, S allowed herself to be pushed backwards on to the table. The porter grabbed her ankles and pulled them so high and wide her knees were buried in her armpits. He grunted something and nodded towards where his already hard cock was bobbing eagerly. S reached down and guided him. He came into her with a single thrust that made S groan aloud. He fucked her without finesse, with no concern for anything except his own pleasure, rutting in her with frantic speed, jerking her body like a fish on a spear. Even so, S came before he did, whimpering at his force, her vagina writhing and pulsing. When he crammed in really hard and began spurting his heat into her she cried out and bucked against him, forcing him even deeper, her greedy vagina gulping in his emissions.

The estate manager was still wearing his boots when S entered his office a few minutes later. Her face and chest were still flushed red from the frantic activity which had just taken place in the kitchen, and she was unable to look him in the eye. He indicated a wooden box on the floor beside his desk, containing cloths and brushes and tins of polish. She knelt at his feet and began work, hoping against hope that this would be her only punishment and that he would not feel the need to get out that appalling elephant's tail.

She cleaned and rubbed and brushed his boots as though her life depended upon it, her breasts

75

bouncing with her efforts. He said nothing at all until his boots were gleaming so brightly S could see her face on them. Then he directed her to go to a chest standing by the wall and bring him a particular pot. It was plain white with no label, betraying nothing of its contents.

Next he ordered her to drape herself across his desk and get her feet apart, and S knew that he was going to fuck her. She heard the top of the pot being unscrewed. She felt him smearing something greasy around, and even into, her anus. She suddenly realised what his intention was and leapt up.

'No, please, baas. Not that! No one has ever –' Her pleas were cut off by a stinging slap across her face.

'Get down! Spread!' His voice was hard.

S obeyed, trembling. She managed to whimper, 'Please don't hurt me . . .' as he smeared the greasy substance further into her. She clung to the furthest edge of the desk as he parted her buttocks and came up close. She could feel the roughness of his trousers against the backs of her thighs. Then she could feel his hot glans pressing against her tense rose-hole.

It was not easy for him, even though S tried to relax herself as much as she could. She was a virgin in that place and her instincts were to tense and tighten. Slowly, grunting, he forced entry. Once his glans had pushed past her sphincter, the rest was easy for him.

He came into her in a rush, grabbing her hips with hard fingers, his engorged cock cramming her, seeming to crush all her internal organs up into her stomach. Like the porter who had just used her, the estate manager paid no attention to anything save his own pleasure. He simply took her, at his own speed and for his own pleasure, rutting hard.

After the first half-dozen thrusts it did not hurt so

much, though it was still far from comfortable. S felt awfully stretched, and hoped he had not torn her. His rutting was making the fronts of her thighs bang against the edge of the desk, and soon that became almost as painful as the thick penis thrusting in and out of her.

He shouted aloud when he came, bucking wildly, flooding her with his emissions, oblivious to her gasps and whimpers. He stayed inside her for a while after his climax, running his hard hands over her flanks and reaching round to squeeze her breasts. She could sense him slowly detumescing; it felt strange. Even when he became soft and small he had to pull himself out because she was so tight.

Then, with a mocking smile, he compounded S's humiliation by ordering her to fetch a bowl of water, soap and a towel, and clean him up. There could be no finer way of driving home to S her lowly status. She washed him gently and carefully, partly because she was scared of hurting him and earning a spanking, but also because she felt a strange kind of tenderness towards the soft, vulnerable organ she was tending.

The incident with the kitchen porter and then with the manager brought a new element into S's life on the estate.

The manager, whom she only ever heard called 'baas', sent for her three or four times a week and had her bend over his desk so that he could take his pleasure in her backside. After a while S got almost used to it, though it never gave her any actual pleasure. What did, in the strangest way, was washing him afterwards. She began to find his soft cock and drained testicles almost appealing; pretty even. Once, without thinking, she gave his cock a little kiss when she'd finished drying it. She might even have taken it between her lips for a gentle little suck had he not pushed her roughly away.

The manager only ever used her bottom, as though he only liked women for what they had in common with boys. It was not so with the estate workers. Although there were a lot more women on the estate than men, and pretty well all of them were young and available, during the week or so after the kitchen porter fucked her, most of the men wanted to try the new girl out.

There were about twenty of them, but mercifully they never came for her all at once. In fact they were rather casual about it. S would be in the middle of carting out the night soil, or mixing the pig-swill, or one of her many other tasks, and a hand would grope her bottom or grab a breast. The man in question would gesture, and S would stop whatever she was doing and move to the spot he had indicated.

They mostly took her on her back on the ground but some were more imaginative. Several enjoyed fucking her up against a wall, lifting her off the ground as they shafted her. One, who became something of a regular, liked to get her bending over with her hands braced against the rail of the pig-pen, and take her from the rear while he gripped her hip-bones and rutted very deep in her vagina. Others wanted her on all fours, doggy-style, and still others preferred to use her mouth.

It was the one S came to think of as the pig-pen man who taught her a valuable lesson. The first time he fucked her she was very tired, and so she just stood there and let him have her. She was astonished when, after he had come, he got angry and gave her a very thorough spanking. S could not understand the words he shouted but some instinct for survival told her what the matter was. The next time he came for her she sighed and wriggled and pushed back against him as though what he was doing was the most wonderful thing in the world.

She learned to fake it with all of them, although sometimes her orgasms were all too real. She even pretended wild delight when the manager used her backside. She found it made them easier on her, and she did not get spanked quite so much – although some of them spanked her just for fun.

One of the first things S learned on the estate was that more or less everyone had the right to tip her over their knees and spank her bottom, even the lowliest of scullery maids, girls who were clearly younger than S, hardly more than teenagers. All it needed was for her to make the most trivial of mistakes, drop some peelings or spill some water, and over she would go. They only ever used their hands to spank her, but it still smarted dreadfully and her buttocks seemed to be permanently bright pink and glowing.

S came to accept it all as only her due. Her Master had sent her here to learn her place, and her place was as the lowest of the low. If Kano wished her to cart buckets of night soil and feed pigs and scrub floors, then so be it. He had accepted her as his voluntary slave back in England and brought her out here to his Principality, and he had only sent her to the estate because she had not pleased him.

It was only right, therefore, that she was at the beck and call of anybody and everybody, to spank or fuck her any time they fancied it. She would learn true servitude, and he would take her back, and she would be happy again.

Through these musings, S developed a sort of calm contentment. She did not enjoy being bent over baas's desk while he rutted in her back passage. She did not enjoy it when some chit of a kitchen maid spanked her bottom for some trivial lapse, nor when some man or other decided he wanted to fuck her. She did not enjoy it, but she accepted it calmly. She even accepted sleeping in the kennels with the dogs – and the regular nightly visits of the kennel-man.

He started visiting her about ten nights after she started sleeping among his dogs. The pattern was always the same. He would enter the kennels very late at night, after she was asleep, and nudge her awake with his boot. No matter how tired she was, S had to roll over and get onto all fours, her knees wide and her back arched to make herself accessible. He always took her that way, from behind, holding her by her hip-bones and rutting frantically. He never took long and seldom gave S an orgasm but she accepted it as his right and her duty. She even accepted as her due the fact that he always gave her a really hard slap on her backside when he had satisfied himself and withdrawn from her.

All of it was bearable, even justifiable since her Master wished it. What she found really hard was never getting the chance to speak with Gladys.

She saw her friend around the place quite a lot, but since their duties did not coincide it was only ever at a distance. She quickly realised that Gladys's situation was not much better than her own, though her work was less menial and she seemed to be treated with at least some respect.

S frequently saw Gladys being beckoned by a man, or sometimes two or three, and going off somewhere relatively private with them. She sympathised, but was also oddly pleased that at least they were not going to fuck her out in public, as they nearly always did with S herself. She never saw Gladys going into

80

the baas's office and so was glad for her. It also seemed that only the men had the right to spank her, for S never saw Gladys over the lap of any of the women.

Gladys's sleeping arrangements, too, were different, and S did not know whether to be envious or grateful. Whereas S slept on the floor of the kennels, snuggling down in the midst of a pack of dogs, Gladys spent each night in one of the estate workers' dormitories. Thus she was able to sleep in a bed, but since it was always one of the men's dormitories S doubted whether Gladys ever got much sleep.

One afternoon, when they had been at the estate for perhaps a month, S became aware of a strange and rather frightening tension in the air. As she scrubbed the kitchen floor the place was much quieter than usual. People were whispering rather than shouting, as they normally did. Nobody touched her, and even when she accidentally knocked a pan off a bench no one spanked her. It was very strange.

She found out what it was all about as darkness fell. All the estate workers assembled in the yard, S along with them. They stood in a large circle around the awful frame she and Gladys had been hung on for the whipping on their first day here. The wait was no more than fifteen minutes but it felt like an age. Then the whispering crowd fell silent and all faces turned towards the three figures who approached.

She saw that the leading figure was the manager, baas. From his hand dangled his awful elephant's-tail whip, and S felt a chill at the sight of it. Behind him came two more figures, one male, the other female. Both of them were naked and had their wrists bound. It was only as the figures got close to the light that S realised, with a gasp of horror, that the female was Gladys.

What had she done wrong? Why was she going to be publicly beaten? What had the man done?

Gladys and the naked man, whom S did not recognise, stood with bowed heads under the frame as baas addressed the audience and made a speech. It was in local dialect, and S did not understand a word of it, so she was none the wiser about whatever offence had been committed.

Baas pressed a switch on the box that controlled the winch and the big hook slowly descended. At a command, several men hurried forward. They moved Gladys and the man close together, face to face, raised their bound wrists and looped them over the hook. The winch buzzed again, and their arms were pulled up high. The long strap was buckled around their waists and cinched tight, squashing Gladys's full breasts against the man's chest.

Then it became different. Instead of simply winching the two figures off the ground and starting to beat them, baas signalled a pretty young girl from the crowd and gave her some instructions. As two of the male helpers each took hold of Gladys by a leg and pulled her wide, the girl knelt behind Gladys and began to do something between her spread legs.

S could not quite see what the girl was doing, and moved to find a better vantage point. She gasped when she saw what was happening. The girl was not touching Gladys at all, but was stroking the man! For a while the fluttering of her delicate hands around his genitals had no effect and so, casting an anxious glance at baas, the girl scrambled down and began to lick and suck him, her head at an uncomfortable angle because of the awkwardness of their relative positions.

Even in these extreme circumstances the man could not resist such treatment, and soon he came erect. At

82

once the girl pulled her mouth off him and, taking his thickening cock in one hand and spreading Gladys's love-lips with the other, stuffed him in. S was stunned. The manager was going to whip them while they were having what appeared to be a compulsory fuck!

When the man was fully embedded, and even beginning to move a little, Gladys's legs were wrapped around his and her ankles strapped tight. Only then were they hoisted up off the ground.

The beating was not hard. It seemed to be intended for the entertainment of the audience and the humiliation of the victims. Baas gave a shove which sent the bound and dangling couple rotating slowly. As each bare rump swung round he gave it a stripe with his elephant's-tail whip, so that first Gladys would buck against the man, then he would buck against her. Each time, the man's cock would be thrust deep into Gladys's helpless cunt. Baas timed it so that their bucking grew quicker and quicker as his strokes became harder to increase his victims' writhings.

They came at the same moment, wailing and writhing, then screaming as baas gave each of them one final, very fierce stroke with his whip. It was the wildest, most frightening, yet also the most erotic thing S could ever have imagined witnessing. Gladys drooped against the man she was strapped to, sweat beading her body and her head lolling against his chest. Her ankles were not released until the man became soft and slipped out of her, his shrunken cock glistening with her juices. Then they were lowered to the ground and unstrapped.

S loitered, hoping to get a chance to ask Gladys what on earth she had done to deserve such treatment, but it was in vain because both Gladys and the man were led off somewhere and S had no choice but to go back to the kennels and snuggle down among the dogs for the night.

She had begun to think of the dogs as her friends, for they accepted her presence among them happily, allowing her to cuddle up to them for warmth and never even growling at her. In fact some of them had even become quite protective of her, as a couple of men found out to their cost.

Like everybody else on the estate they knew that S slept in the kennels, and one night, after a few jugs of beer, they had decided to have some fun with her. S was already asleep when the two men crept in. She was lying between Kino and Kia, her two favourites, both big German Shepherds. If the men had not made any rash moves they might have got away with it, for although Kino and Kia as well as several of the other dogs woke and pricked up their ears, they were used to the smells of the estate workers. But when one of the men grabbed S by the arm that cuddled Kino and tried to drag her up, pandemonium broke out.

With a ferocious growl Kino was at them, followed instantly by Kia and most of the other dogs, all barking and snarling wildly. With howls of terror, the two men crashed through the kennel door, the dogs boiling through the gap after them. S did not know what had happened to cause the sudden uproar, and crouched in terror in the farthest corner as she heard the dogs howling away into the distance.

None of the dogs returned for a long time, and S crouched in her corner wondering what on earth had been the matter. At last the moonlit doorway darkened and she recognised the shape of Kino entering. He came straight up to her, looked at her for a second, licked her face several times, and lay down between S and the door, his ears cocked and his nose twitching.

The big dog was obviously in an 'on guard' position and, although she did not know what had caused the ruckus, S felt a wave of gratitude. She slid out of her crouch and lay down beside him with her arm across his big shoulders and her face nuzzling the thick fur of his neck. She quickly fell into a contented sleep, feeling warm and protected.

She woke early as usual and the events of the night flooded back to her when she saw that the kennel door was wide open and half the dogs were missing. She crept around nervously, collecting the night soil, certain that she would be in big trouble with the kennel man and possibly even the baas himself. When mid-morning came and she still had not been sent for, her nerves turned to curiosity.

There seemed to be an odd atmosphere about the place. Some of the kitchen girls gave S hard looks as she collected peelings and stirred the pig-swill, but most of the men seemed to be sharing some kind of joke, and suppressing laughter. S became even more puzzled when, just after the mid-day meal, the kennel-man's Jeep rattled up in a cloud of dust and all the men crowded out of the kitchen to watch, grinning and whispering excitedly.

Kia was in the back of the Jeep keeping guard over two bedraggled men who looked very sorry for themselves. The baas emerged through his back door at the noise and stood watching as the kennel-man called Kia to heel and snapped an order at the two men. They climbed stiffly out of the Jeep. To S, who still knew nothing about what had gone on, it looked as though they had been in a fight, for their clothes were torn and bloody and one of them had what looked like a large bite-mark on his forearm.

Once again, everything that was said was spoken in the local dialect, so S understood nothing of it. What was obvious was that the men were in some very serious kind of trouble. The baas ranted at them for several minutes, then waved them away. Later S caught sight of them limping off down the road with bundles over their shoulders.

But that was of far less importance to her than the fact that neither the kennel-man nor baas had yet sent for her. She kept herself as inconspicuous as she could all afternoon, trying to make herself invisible. Her heart sank when one of the kitchen girls approached while she was scrubbing pans after the evening meal.

'Baas want you,' the girl said, her eyes big and holding a hint of mockery. 'Baas want you now.'

The estate manager was not alone when S tapped on his office door and entered at his call, already trembling. On either side of him as he lounged in the swivel chair behind his desk stood the kennel-man and somebody S recognised as one of the field supervisors. She had seen him, but never come into direct contact with him before. He was huge and ugly, with no neck and biceps that were bigger than her waist, especially as he now stood with his arms folded tightly across his broad chest.

On baas's desk lay the elephant-tail whip.

S instantly adopted the supplicant position, head bowed, hands behind her back, feet wide apart, praying that her servile pose might ease things for her, but already knowing that there was no real hope. She was obviously going to be punished; all she could hope for was to make it as easy as possible. The long, tapering shape of the whip lying across the desk burnt itself into her mind.

'Head up. Hands behind neck. Elbows back.' The manager's commands were barked coldly. Even as she obeyed S was aware of how this new pose thrust her breasts out towards the three watching men, almost as though they were being offered to them. The field supervisor licked his lips at the sight.

'Do you know why you are here, girl?'

'Yes, baas. The dogs got out, baas.'

'Yes, indeed. The dogs got out. Mr Bilimbo here –' the manager waved a hand towards the kennel-man, whose eyes were fixed on the steel ring at the join of S's thighs – 'Mr Bilimbo has had to spend hours rounding them up, and Joshua has lost two good men.'

Joshua, the huge field supervisor, was also staring at S's crotch. She knew that whatever her punishment might be she was going to have to pleasure these two men afterwards, and felt a flutter of arousal in the place they were staring at.

Since it was Mr Bilimbo and Joshua who had been 'inconvenienced', as the manager put it, it was they who would give S her punishment. She held out her hands as ordered and the kennel-man bound her wrists with a leather strap. The estate manager tossed Joshua the elephant-tail whip and handed Mr Bilimbo a long leash, which he clipped to S's pussy ring.

They paraded her out to the front of the manager's house, all the way round the yard and the workers' quarters and even around the barns and the pig-pens, making sure that as many of the estate workers as possible knew what was about to happen. Before long a whispering, giggling crowd was following along behind them.

S could feel all the eyes on her back and almost taste their growing excitement. Clearly, whatever her punishment was to be, it would be a public entertainment. The excitement of the crowd, the persistent tugging of the leash on her pussy ring, the sight of the awful elephant tail swinging from Joshua's beefy hand, the certainty that she was going to be both beaten and fucked; all these combined to send S into a trance-like condition in which she was more aware of the throbbing in her belly and the tension in her breasts than even the swinging of the elephant tail.

Mr Bilimbo and Joshua led S to the only large tree near the estate yard. Joshua threw a rope over one of its thick lateral branches about fifteen feet above the ground. Mr Bilimbo attached one end of the rope to the straps around S's wrists. Joshua hauled at the other end, and in moments S was off the ground, dangling pale and helpless as the audience gathered around.

Her trance vanished when the first stroke landed. They had not tied her ankles and as she screamed her legs flew and kicked, and her body began to rotate on the rope that held her suspended. The blows landed quickly and indiscriminately, on her backside and thighs and breasts and belly. Joshua and Mr Bilimbo took turns, tossing the elephant tail back and forth, neither holding back on the force of their blows.

It was like being dipped into molten metal as S kicked and span and screamed, and then stopped screaming because she had no breath left. Dimly, in the background, she heard laughter and applause from the audience. Then the rope suspending her was cut and she fell in a heap to the ground, and Joshua was on her. She wailed as he began fucking her, partly from the agony of the ground against her seared flesh, but mostly from the ferocity with which his cock speared her.

How many of them shafted her was impossible to tell. S knew that both Joshua and Mr Bilimbo fucked her several times, in several ways, but there were others. A lot of them. She regained consciousness with the sun well up the next day. She sighed gratefully as a couple of the dogs licked soothingly at the whipmarks which striped her from her armpits to her knees.

Seven

The next time S was woken by the noise of the dogs was several weeks later, and it was terrifyingly different. She leapt awake with a scream when the dogs suddenly started howling and barking and throwing themselves madly against the kennel door. Then she heard other noises, loud cracks, a rapid rattling, shouts, screams. She fought her way to the door and turned the handle to open it, but somebody must have barred it from the outside because it would not shift.

The dogs were going mad. S tried to find a chink in the walls to peer out of, but it was a very well-built kennel and there were none. The only way to see out was a narrow, unglazed transom high above the door. S jumped up to grab at the opening and began to haul herself up. All her hard work over the last couple of months had made her arms quite strong and, with one foot perched precariously on the door handle, she was able to lift herself high enough to see out.

What she saw made her gasp with horror. Men with guns were running all over the place, shouting and firing into the air. Those estate workers who were not running away were lining up against the walls of their quarters with their hands on their heads. The baas was lying face-down on the ground, still in his pyjamas, a pistol in the dust near his outstretched hand.

S dropped to the ground, her eyes wide with fright. She cowered in a corner. It was a raid! The estate was being attacked! S had heard about guerrilla wars in Africa, but Kano's Principality had seemed so peaceful and prosperous, and to judge from the crowds which had lined the route when he first brought her here he was immensely popular.

The noise of shouting and gunfire died away. S tried to quiet the dogs, terrified that their noise might bring the raiders investigating. They were very excited and it took a lot of hugging and 'shh-ing' before she managed it. They were still very tense, though, and several of them continued to pace and prowl in the confined space. S put her arms around Kino and Kia and crouched between them in the corner. She could feel the big dogs trembling with tension, and all three of them stared towards the door for a long while.

Eventually S heard the noise of engines and the slamming of vehicle doors. There was more shouting, but no gunfire this time. Then the engines revved loudly and gearboxes grated, and she heard the vehicles moving off. She waited several minutes then, her heart thudding, hauled herself up to the transom again.

A cloud of red dust in the distance told her that the vehicles were now a long way off. S peered nervously around the compound. The only movement was some birds wheeling in the sky. Baas was no longer lying on the ground. It was unnaturally quiet.

She dropped back down to the floor and sat with her back to the wall, thinking hard. The raiders had gone, but had they left any guards behind? What had happened to baas and all the others? Were the raiders just bandits, or was she caught up in some kind of civil war? The one thing she knew for certain was that she had to find a way out of the kennel. If she did not she would starve, or worse still the dogs would get hungry and eat her.

S got up and tried the door, knowing as she did so that it was not going to budge. She moved around again checking the walls, but there were no chinks or loose boards. Finally, she looked up at the transom. Although it was at least a yard wide it was no more than about twelve inches high. Getting out through there would be no easy task, and what would happen if she got stuck? But it had to be done; there was no other choice.

She sighed, gulped a couple of deep breaths, and jumped up. The wood of the frame was rough and S scratched her breasts and shoulder-blades as she hauled herself through. There was nothing to grab onto on the outside and by the time she had wriggled through to her hips S realised she had no choice but to let herself drop to the ground. She landed on her back and shoulders, and the fall knocked the breath out of her. She lay for a few minutes to recover, then started to move gingerly. Surprisingly, she seemed to be no more than shaken, barely injured apart from some scratches.

A thick wooden pole had been wedged against the kennel door to keep it shut, and the first thing S did was to heave it away and swing the door open. Somehow she had expected the dogs to charge out howling and barking. They did come out, of course, but pacing rather than running, their ears pricked, their heads high and swinging from side to side as though searching. They fanned out and went trotting off in different directions. All of them, that is, except Kino and Kia, who stationed themselves on either side of her as though they had appointed themselves her personal bodyguard.

Feeling a lot more brave with her two beautiful

dogs beside her, S set off to explore. The workers' quarters were deserted, what little furniture they had held wrecked in what looked like random violence. She scanned the fields out to the horizon, but could detect no movement other than the breeze in the crops. She checked the vehicle shed, which was empty except for a few oil smears on the ground. The raiders had obviously stolen the Jeeps and the two lorries. S felt an odd pang of regret when she found that they had also stolen the pigs, for the pens were deserted and silent.

Kino started to behave oddly when they crept into the mealie store, snuffling and pawing at the huge pile of grain. S screamed with fright when the pile suddenly heaved up and two faces appeared. The dogs barked and the faces looked scared. Then S began to giggle with hysterical relief. Rather than scowling bandits with guns, the faces turned out to belong to two of the young kitchen maids. With tears of laughter half-blinding her, S reached up and helped the girls heave themselves out of the mealie-pile.

Then it struck her. If these two had managed to hide, perhaps others had too. Her heart leapt. Maybe, just maybe, Gladys had also managed to escape!

'Gladys!' she screamed, pointing at the mealie and grabbing one of the girls by the arm. 'Gladys?'

The girl shook her head and S ran out of the storage shed and into the next one. This one housed maize and she threw herself at it, yelling for Gladys and heaving great sacks aside as though they were feathers. Nothing. Nothing in the next shed either, nor the next. For fully half an hour S ran around like a demented animal, soon too breathless to call out but still with enough frenzied energy to crash through doors and heave aside bales and sacks and piles of vegetables.

S could think of nowhere else to search. They must have taken her. Exhausted, the last possible hiding place searched, S sank miserably against one of the struts of the water tower and began to sob with loss and sudden loneliness. How could she survive without Gladys? It was unthinkable.

Then, through her despair, S heard strange noises from above her head. They seemed to come from the big metal tank, scrabbling and clunking noises. She leapt up and ran out a short way so that she could see the top. Slowly a hinged lid creaked open. A face appeared, then another, then another. One man and two women. And one of the women was Gladys!

S's lungs emptied themselves in a great sob of relief and joy, and she had to fight to get her breath back. It was one of the girls from the mealie pile who had the presence of mind to grab up a ladder that was lying on the ground a few yards away. When a wet and shivering Gladys reached the ground S flung her arms around her so enthusiastically they both tumbled to the ground in a storm of laughter and flailing limbs, kissing wildly and hugging the breath out of each other.

There were now six of them, five girls and a man who seemed even more frightened than they were. They found baas on the floor in his office. He had been badly beaten and every room in his house wrecked. It was Gladys, always calm and capable, who suggested that they stay there for the rest of the day, patch up the baas, and sort out what they could. Then they could get a good rest and set out for safety in the morning.

The two kitchen girls rustled up a meal, and so used was S to her role as slave to the servants that it never occurred to S not to scurry around fetching and carrying for them. Nor, when she dropped an empty pan, did she hesitate to go down over the girl's knee for a spanking. After all, it had happened many times before.

Then there came a banshee scream of rage. S was kicked off the girl's lap and sent sprawling. When she managed to take in the scene a real cat-fight was in progress. Gladys had the girl by her hair with one hand and was slapping her face with the other. The girl put up a fight, scratching and trying to bite, but she was no match for an angry Gladys. Soon she was whimpering against a wall, her wide-eyed companion close beside her as Gladys raged at them, picking up a big wooden spoon and shaking it at them like a battle club. Both girls began to whimper and dropped to their knees, pressing their hands to their faces and touching their foreheads to the floor. Gladys took S by the hand and pulled her to her feet. The girls had not moved by the time they reached the door and Gladys turned. She called something to the two terrified girls, put an arm around S's shoulders and led her off.

'I told them you belong to me now,' she whispered later, her mouth close to S's ear as they lay in bed. 'I said you are my woman and if they so much as look at you hard I will tie them down on a red-ants' nest and fill their cunts with honey. Ha! I think I got them scared. Now, come here and do that again. Yes, that. Ah, yes!'

S did not know whether to giggle at her beloved friend's wild threat or shiver at the very thought of it, but that ceased to matter as she moved down again and began to kiss and lick.

'Don't you think I should have some clothes or something, please, Gladys?'

It was morning. They had patched up the baas, who was too weak to travel, and were getting ready to set off. Gladys and the other three girls were all wearing the usual little aprons, front and back, and looked entirely natural for this part of the world. The man was wearing cotton trousers and a torn T-shirt. S, however, was still absolutely naked. It had not mattered back at the palace or here on the estate, and in fact S had got so used to it that it only occurred to her at the last minute. The others would not look out of the ordinary walking through this countryside as they were, but a naked white woman would attract attention, to say the least.

They found some khaki trousers for her, and a bush hat beneath which her hair, which was very long by now, was pinned and piled. When it came to a shirt Gladys giggled and pointed out a difficulty, or rather two of them, to which she gave a playful slap from below to bounce them.

'Your titties stick out too much for you to be a boy!' she laughed. 'We find you something big and baggy!'

To the very baggy shirt Gladys found she added a leather shooting jerkin, which effectively concealed S's breasts, then they set out, bundles over their shoulders. When the path they were following began to become stony S realised that they had forgotten all about footwear. Even though her feet had hardened during the last few months, walking was still a bit uncomfortable – but not nearly as uncomfortable as wearing clothes. S had been naked since before she left England, and even though what she had on was loose and baggy it still felt close and constricting, and as the heat of the day grew she began to sweat freely. Soon, she was mopping her face with her sleeve and longing to feel a breeze on her skin.

Once off the estate they stuck to side paths and even animal trails, anxious to avoid contact with settlements and people, just in case the rebels were nearby. They kept going all day and S was exhausted by the time Gladys, who seemed to have become the accepted leader, called a halt not far from a large water hole.

They found a clearing surrounded by thick scrub and thorn bushes about a hundred yards from the water hole. Gladys set the man and the other girls to gathering wood and making a camp while she and S went down to the water to bathe and to bring back water in a goatskin bag.

It felt wonderful to strip off the constricting clothes. S squealed with delight as she plunged into the beautifully cool water. Gladys hushed her and looked around dramatically, as though she expected enemies to emerge from the surrounding bush. S blushed and whispered an apology, but her spirits were not dampened and she swam and rolled in the water until she felt as fresh and clean as she ever had in her life.

She washed her grimy clothes while Gladys went to another part of the water hole to fill the goatskin, and then both women strolled back to the campsite feeling relaxed and happy. The others had done well in setting up camp and already had a virtually smokeless fire going. While they went off for their turn to bathe, S and Gladys began to prepare a meal. It was sparse – mealie porridge and chopped vegetables, with some salt for flavour – and they had only brought one cooking pot with them, but to S it tasted of heaven – even though the pot became their communal serving dish and they had to eat with their hands.

Afterwards, when they had drunk from the

goatskin and rinsed their hands, S picked up the cooking pot and carried it down to the water hole to clean it. It was just sunset, and the sky and the surrounding bush looked beautiful. She was just finishing her cleaning when a word was spoken behind her. It was a very familiar word.

S turned to find the man standing there, his hand rubbing lewdly against his crotch. She sighed and put down the pot, looking around for a relatively flat spot to lie down on. She did not fancy this at all, but obediently lay down on her back and spread her knees – after all, he had the right to fuck her if he wanted to; they all had on the estate. He grinned, pulled out an erect but not very large penis, and got between her knees.

He had hardly got into her before there came a bellow of rage and he was flung backwards. Gladys had him on his back and was punching him furiously as he cowered beneath her. Gladys was a big, strong woman and the man did not stand a chance. Yelping with both pain and fright, the man wriggled away and ran off, not even pausing to do up his trousers.

Gladys was grinning in triumph as she turned to the astonished S.

'I tell him he's a worm!' Gladys laughed as she gathered S up into her arms. 'I tell him he don't get to fuck you no more. You are mine 'til we get back to our Prince. If he wants a fuck he use the others. You are mine, all mine! The others leave you alone!'

Being told by Gladys that she was 'mine, all mine' set off such a wave of emotion in S that she could not hold back tears. Her place at the estate had only been bearable because her Master and Gladys required it of her. She had accepted being spanked and fucked by anybody who felt like it as no more than her duty, but, she now realised, she had been lost and lonely all the while. Lost in her slavery and its demands. Lonely for her Master and, more immediately, for her beloved Gladys.

They lay together close to the dying fire. Their bodies touched, moved, became entwined. S felt Gladys's hands moving on her body. Her own hands moved. The other woman's breasts felt wonderful, so full and firm, the ringed nipples like nuts. She kissed them, licked their whole surface and the deep valley between. She suckled on each nipple in turn, delighting in the flavour and the way they hardened under her tongue. She kissed and breathed down over the firm belly and licked into the shallow dimple of her navel, then moved further down to where she wanted to be.

Gladys's hard thighs moved apart willingly and S delved, her lips and tongue and fingers moving instinctively, voluptuously. Oh, it had been so long!

Somehow, as S moved so did Gladys. The fading firelight glimmered on their entwined bodies, on the two heads moving between splayed thighs as each woman worked to pleasure the other, and thus get pleasure in return. They were lovers of old and each knew how to keep the other on the brink, to wind up the ecstasy until it was almost painful before allowing release. This time, though, they were both too worked up to hold out long and they writhed into simultaneous orgasms, licking and drinking each other frenziedly until they both collapsed, sated and fulfilled. They slept in one another's arms and awoke with the dawn, feeling wonderful.

The feeling vanished when they realised that they were alone. At some time, for some reason, the man and the three girls from the estate had crept away before the dawn. No, it was well past dawn to judge by the elevation of the sun, so it could have been after dawn, but they were not there anyway. Why had they gone? What was the matter?

Gladys was instantly on guard. She put her fingers to her lips to keep S silent, gestured her to get her clothes, and crawled on all fours towards the ring of bushes which surrounded the little clearing. S grabbed the clothes she had left draped over some bushes to dry and scrambled into them. She quickly followed Gladys, crawling on all fours as Gladys had done.

Surrounding them was nothing less than a military encampment, and a very well-disciplined one by the look of it. There were about a dozen vehicles parked neatly, with small groups of armed men lounging around near them, while some more were patrolling the area on sentry duty. Gladys took hold of S's arm and gestured her to keep silent. She mouthed the word 'rebels', and tugged S back into the clearing.

Motioning S to stay where she was, Gladys crept from side to side of the clearing and peeped through the bushes. Her face was very serious when she came back.

'They are sure enough rebels,' she whispered. 'Some are by the water hole and the rest are out there where the grassland begins. We've got no way out.'

'But can't we crawl out through the bushes?'

'No. If they not hear us, they see us when we get out the other side.'

'But –'

'Hush up! Let me think.' Even though she was whispering Gladys's voice was fierce.

There was a long pause before she spoke again, and what she then said had S open-mouthed with shock. Gladys's plan sounded mad! S began to splutter a protest, but Gladys cut her off.

'Look,' she explained patiently. 'If we stay here they will soon find us. If we try to sneak away they will catch us for sure, and what do you think will happen to us then – before they kill us I mean! No, this is the only way.'

S nodded doubtfully, already breathless with nerves about what Gladys proposed.

The effect on the rebels lounging in the camp when two figures stepped out of the bushes waving and calling was astonishing. Some dived beneath trucks to hide; others grabbed their weapons and rushed for cover as though they were being attacked; yet more simply sat and stared in amazement.

The women approached the camp waving and smiling happily, which S found the hardest bit of all, for inside she was terrified in case it all went wrong. It did not take long for some of the rebels to recover from their surprise, and soon a dozen rifles and submachine guns were directed at the women.

Gladys called loudly, first in local dialect then in English. At first warily and then, when they were sure they were not under attack, swaggering and laughing the rebels formed a circle around the women and shepherded them towards the only tent that had been erected in the camp.

The man seated at a camping table inside the tent was dressed in perfectly pressed military fatigues. He was a big man, broad and obviously very tall. He concealed his surprise when the two figures were shoved into the tent, and scowled at them fiercely.

'Ah, General! We find you at last! Wonderful! Wonderful!' Gladys almost went too far in her pretended joy. 'We escaped from the palace. We have come to join the revolution against the great oppressor.'

There was a tense silence. With no more than a single glance at S, the seated man looked Gladys over carefully. He picked up a swagger stick, reached forward and lifted the front of Gladys's loincloth. She kept still as he inspected her. He leaned back in his chair, letting the loincloth fall back to cover Gladys's sex again.

'I can see from your barbaric decorations that you have indeed been a possession of the so-called Prince. I have heard that he puts rings on all his women. So perhaps it is true you have escaped from him. But that does not explain the boy here.' He waved his swagger stick towards S. 'The so-called Prince does not keep boys.'

'Oh no, General. This not a boy!' Gladys whipped S's bush-hat off so that her hair tumbled down around her shoulders. 'This English girl. Prince's slave just like me. Show the General!'

With trembling fingers S unbuttoned her shirt and slipped it from her shoulders together with the jerkin. The General's expression changed as she exposed her breasts to him. His eyes glittered and he sat straighter in his chair.

S fumbled with the buckle of her belt. The baggy trousers she wore fell down around her ankles as soon as the belt was released. She dropped her hands to her sides and remained still as the General's eyes drank in her nakedness. For a moment his face became a mask of pure carnality as his eyes flicked from the steel pussy ring resting on her vulva to the rings piercing her protuberant nipples.

S felt a shiver run through her. What this big man was thinking was starkly obvious, and it scared her. Yet at the same time she felt a lurch of heat deep in her belly. Gladys had told her they needed to be nice to the rebels to get away with the trick they were trying. Being nice to this man was clearly going to take an all too familiar form. S felt the lurch in her belly change to a slow throbbing at the image which invaded her mind.

Stepping clumsily out of the trousers puddled around her ankles, S stepped forward until she was within reach. He examined her nipple rings, flicking them with a thick fingertip. Then his hand moved down to her larger, heavier pussy ring. He hooked his finger through it and began tugging, rhythmically and none too gently.

'I can see from these rings that you have indeed been in the possession of the so-called Prince,' he said, continuously tugging and releasing her pussy ring until S was blushing and beginning to pant. 'How did you, an English woman, a member of our colonial oppressors, come to belong to him?'

Coached by Gladys, S had worked out a story to cover just such a question. She told the man that she had been in a bar, on holiday in Cairo. Somebody must have drugged her drink, because the next thing she knew she was tied up and stark-naked in some kind of crate on the back of a lorry. Then she had been sold at an auction to the Prince's factotum.

'Yes, sir,' she said in answer to his question. 'They beat me a lot. With canes and paddles and things. It was awful until Gladys helped me escape.'

He had changed the motion of his hands. Now, as his index finger tugged at her ring his other fingertips were teasing between her labia. It was the most exquisite of torments. She had to concentrate hard on what she was saying, to keep her story believable, but what he was doing between her legs was most awfully distracting.

'So you are not the white woman he brought here a few months ago? The whore who paraded through our streets, flaunting her nakedness before our oppressed people clad in gold and jewels?'

Despite the effect of the fingers he thrust into her at the moment he asked the question, she managed to keep her presence of mind.

'Oh, no, sir,' she panted. His fingers were moving deeper into her vagina, their motion becoming wildly disturbing. 'She was not a slave like me. She is stuck up and superior. I hate her!'

The man continued to tug at her pussy ring and move his fingers in her, and despite her efforts at self-control S succumbed into a half-suppressed orgasm. He laughed when he felt her body pulsing and her juices flowing over his hand.

'Well,' he said, releasing her and wiping his hand on a rag. 'I don't know about your story, but since you are here I am sure you can be useful to me. My men's morale is important.'

S and Gladys glanced at one another. They both had a very good idea what he meant.

Eight

The General made no secret of the fact that his own morale was his most immediate concern. Releasing S he let his eyes wander over Gladys. A shaft of light poured through a narrow gap in the tent flap and caught her in its gleam. She looked magnificent, her full, high breasts shining dark copper in the light, her head high, her lips smiling and sensuous. The General scribbled a note, tore the sheet from the pad on his camping table and handed it to S without even looking at her. His eyes were fixed on Gladys, and he was licking his thick lips.

Obeying his grunted order S hurried off to find the sergeant-major she had been sent for – whoever he was. She had no idea where she was going or who she was looking for, only that the General was beckoning Gladys towards him even before S got out of the tent.

If the sight of two figures emerging from the scrub had astonished the assembled rebel soldiers, that of a stark-naked white woman hurrying towards them waving a piece of paper froze them. But not for long. By the time S got near to the first group, waving the note and calling 'Sergeant-major? Sergeant-major?' they were more than ready for her.

They crowded close. Their bodies were hard and their hands were everywhere. S tried to wriggle between them, still calling for the sergeant-major.

They were laughing and grabbing, dozens of them. S squealed as she was suddenly spun off her feet. She was swung round in the air, arms and legs everywhere. Even as she was dumped down on the ground, her legs hauled wide, she still managed to shout for the sergeant-major.

Her calls died when a soldier stepped between her upraised feet and pulled open his trousers, releasing an already erect penis. He was leering as he lowered himself towards her, his thick cock held in the fingers of one hand. S screwed her eyes shut and took a breath in readiness for his invasion.

Then, instead of the man plunging forward and impaling her, he suddenly whipped backwards as though catapulted and in his place appeared a huge man in a beret and khakis, looking very angry. Instantly, all hands were off her and, as the now silent men backed away, S scrambled inelegantly to her feet. Fortunately, the newcomer seemed to be angry with the men rather than with S and she managed to bob him a sort of curtsy and offer him the note, hoping against hope that he was in fact the sergeant-major.

Now that she was standing, S realised that this man was even bigger than he had at first appeared. The top of her head hardly came level with his shoulders. His neck was as thick as her waist, and his perfectly pressed khaki uniform was stretched taut over hard muscle. The hand which took the note from her looked big and powerful enough to break her in half with a flick of its fingers.

If this man was an example of the rebels who were trying to usurp Prince Adenkano, the task she and Gladys had set themselves – to spy and gather information about numbers and plans, then escape and carry them back to their Master – was going to be much, much more difficult than even S had imagined!

The sergeant-major read the note swiftly then pointed towards the tent, giving S a shove to hurry her on her way. She was grateful for his sudden appearance as she watched the hungry-eyed rebels opening a path for them; there were an awful lot of them, and she could virtually smell their lust.

The General was busy when S and the sergeant-major entered the tent. They both backed out hurriedly. The General was on his back on a groaning camp-bed with Gladys astride him, her breasts bouncing and her belly and thighs writhing as she rode his straining cock.

They waited outside the tent, S feeling she was in the shadow of a hill as she stood beside the sergeant-major, blushing for her friend. The General was very noisy, his grunts becoming shouts and swearwords as he rose towards his loud and obvious orgasm. S felt herself blushing hotly at the vision of what was happening inside the tent, of Gladys bucking and writhing, of the General jerking and pumping deep inside her. Most of all, though, she blushed at what she was thinking about the huge man by whose side she stood.

A couple of minutes after silence had fallen in the tent the General came out. He was looking pleased with himself, strutting proudly, a satisfied grin on his face as though he was some kind of victorious gladiator. Behind him, through the gap in the tent flap, S caught sight of Gladys. She too grinned, and shrugged her shoulders as if to say: 'This is going to be a piece of cake!'

S glanced over her shoulder to where the rebel troops had bunched and gathered. She shivered at the realisation of just how many 'pieces of cake' there were likely to be before she and Gladys could get the information they needed and escape back to their Master.

The sergeant-major was called Nkwame. It very quickly became obvious that it was he rather than the General who controlled this troop of insurgents. To his sheer size was added such a natural air of authority that not even the toughest-looking of his men dared hesitate at any order he gave. Even the order that they were to leave S and Gladys alone.

He put the two women to work once the General had finished with Gladys, and such was sergeant-major Nkwame's authority over his men that not once was either of the women touched except with greedy eyes. For S it became almost surreal. Stark-naked, in broad daylight, she moved unmolested among sixty or more men gathering wood and dried dung to feed the fire in a field kitchen, then peeled yams and other vegetables and fetched water to cook them in.

The men made no secret of what they would be doing to her had not their sergeant-major forbidden it, and to Gladys too if they got half a chance. An atmosphere of raw lust grew and grew as the day progressed. Whether it affected Gladys or not S could not tell, but it certainly got to her. It was as though there was some kind of telepathy at work, for every time she caught one of the men looking at her she could almost feel his hands grasping her and his cock rearing. By the time sunset approached she knew that if one of them had so much as fondled her backside she would have come on the spot.

Gladys seemed in better control than S when the sergeant-major called the two of them together just before sunset but S noticed that her nipples were standing out like nuts, so perhaps she was a bit worked up after all. The sergeant-major got the two naked women to stand on the back of one of the trucks, facing his men. He ordered them, in excellent English, to adopt the military 'at ease' position, feet apart, heads up, hands behind backs, shoulders square. S knew that the soldiers crowded below them were getting the most revealing of views, and her arousal cranked up yet another, almost unbearable notch.

Sergeant-major Nkwame then made a long speech in a dialect S could not understand. As he spoke it was clear that he was talking about the two women on display, and that his men's excitement was growing. In a sidelong whisper Gladys translated some of what he said.

'He is saying that we have volunteered to join their glorious revolution,' she whispered. 'He is saying we must be treated with respect. He is saying that from tomorrow we will be happy to reward the men who do best at their drills and in battle. He is saying that for tonight it will be the luck of the draw, whatever that means.'

What it meant became clear when the sergeant-major jumped up onto the truck and stood between the women. He was holding a steel helmet in his hand, high up so that neither Gladys nor S could see into it. He snapped some words towards S.

'He is telling you to reach in and take out a number,' Gladys whispered.

By God! The luck of the draw meant no more and no less than that they were being raffled! Her face burning at the knowledge of what was about to happen, S stretched up and reached into the helmet. It contained a number of large plastic discs. She pulled one out with shaking fingers and handed it to the sergeant-major without looking at it.

He held it up and called out a number. Whoops came from the back of the crowd of soldiers, and at once four grinning, laughing men began to push their way towards the front. S stared appalled as they shoved through the crowd and reached up for her. She was not being raffled to a soldier, but to a group of them! As they dragged her from the back of the truck and carried her off, holding her above their heads like some kind of hunting trophy, she saw Gladys reaching into the steel helmet and heard the sergeant-major call another number. She could not see any more for she was bundled into the back of yet another canvas-draped truck.

Then, weirdly, the men paused. S scuttled to the far end of the truck and crouched, looking at the men through huge eyes. It was not so much that she was scared, though she was – there were four of them after all! – as that the whole bizarre situation after hours of being worked up by their stares and obvious intentions had nearly sent her over the top. Even as she crouched in the corner of the truck she could feel herself tingling and oozing with arousal.

One by one the soldiers climbed into the truck, effectively blocking off any chance of escape even if S had thought about it. Slowly, for they knew they had all night, the men took off their clothes and hung them from the struts holding the canvas cover of the truck. They were not putting on any kind of performance but stripped entirely casually, which only made the whole thing all the more erotic.

They were soldiers, young, fit and hard-bodied. S looked from one to another as they stood before her. She felt a shudder run through her at the sight of the four erections that swayed above her, but it was a shudder of something very different from fear!

No words were exchanged. One of the soldiers

pulled a bed-roll from a rack near the truck's roof and spread it on the floor beside where S was still crouching. He lay down on his back, his body gleaming in the failing light. At the junction of his widely splayed thighs his cock pointed imperiously to the roof. He made a gesture and S scurried around to kneel between his feet. She grasped him with both hands and bowed her head.

He was almost too big for her mouth but he tasted clean and tangy and delicious. S sucked at him in a kind of fever. She had been so worked up for so long that even if he was only in her mouth it was relief of a kind. Then she felt hands on her hip-bones as a second soldier joined the action. He thrust into her vagina so suddenly and so beautifully hard that S wailed aloud in rapture, and began coming on his first thrust.

Like the man in her mouth, he was big and took his time. During her time on the estate, when anybody and everybody had the right to fuck her whenever they felt like it, S had learned various little tricks to make the men who used her think they were wonderful, and she was especially adept at simulating wild passion for them. But such tricks were far from necessary now! She groaned and slurped and gulped as the man in her mouth erupted, anxious to swallow it all but distracted by the sheer power of the man fucking her from behind. When he too burst into a volcanic orgasm she felt she was going to faint from the sheer power of her own release.

When the two men pulled out of her, S was rolled onto her back on the bed-roll. Instantly, her legs were grabbed and pushed high and wide. She was still coming from the first man when the next began to fuck her. She felt rather than saw someone kneel astride her shoulders. Her head was lifted. Something

113

silky-hard bumped against her lips and she opened her mouth willingly.

There were four of them. They were young and fit. By the time morning came S was no more than a dish rag, and even the soldiers were exhausted. It had become like the wildest dream imaginable. They were insatiable. They took turns on her, each seeming to spark off the lust of the others, and each taking longer as he fucked her for the third or fourth time. As she limped weakly to the water hole to clean herself up, S wondered whether she had just lived through one long, fantastic orgasm or a hundred one after the other.

Gladys was already bathing herself. She too looked exhausted. 'How did you get on?' she said as S slipped into the water beside her. Her eyes rounded and she giggled. 'I don't think these boys have been near a woman in years!'

S relaxed as she eased into the water. A hot bath would have been much, much better, but bathing at all after her hectic night felt luxurious.

'There were four of them,' she said after a while, her voice slightly troubled. She knew now that she had acted like a complete whore and felt the stirrings of shame. Her body had bucked and writhed and pulsated as though she was a creature possessed; she had taken everything they could give her, rabidly, wanting more. She suddenly burst into tears and Gladys was hugging her tight.

'It's all right, child,' whispered the older woman as she held S to her strong body. 'I had five. Sometimes a woman can't help herself. Did you come an awful lot?'

S nodded, her face crushed into Gladys's shoulder, ashamed at the wanton way her body had reacted to the soldiers.

'There, there, child.' Gladys kissed S on her temple. 'Me too. It is the woman's way. There are a lot of men about and we have to survive.'

Suddenly she started giggling. 'Just imagine, little love,' she gasped, falling backwards into the cool water and dragging S with her. 'Lots of them and only one each of us, and I'll bet they're more shagged out than we are.'

The sight of the four naked soldiers lolling asleep in the back of the truck as she had climbed out to come to the water hole came back to her. They had been! She began giggling as well. Soon the two women were laughing wildly at the ridiculousness of their situation, tears streaming down their faces as they wallowed in the water.

There was a new boldness on their bearing as they strolled hand in hand back towards the camp, water streaming from their bodies in the morning sunlight. S did not duck her head now when she caught a soldier looking at her, but looked back at him openly, as if in challenge.

Sergeant-major Nkwame was a thoughtful man as well as a strict disciplinarian, and he told the two women to go and get some sleep in the back of a Land Rover while he drilled his men. Although they were both physically tired, neither of the girls could sleep at first. There were some sleeping bags in the vehicle and they each slipped into one, whispering together about the things they had to find out before making their escape.

The number of soldiers and vehicles would be easy; all they had to do was count. What kinds of weapons they had would be more difficult, for neither of them knew much about guns. Hardest of all, and perhaps even impossible, would be finding out whether there were any other groups of rebels, whether they would be joining forces and, most important of all, what their plan of attack was.

'Only the so-called General will know that, I suppose,' said Gladys, snuggling down in her sleeping bag and yawning.

'Well that shouldn't be too hard then,' S whispered, yawning in her turn. 'He obviously fancies you like crazy. All you've got to do is play up to him, tease him along a bit, and he'll probably tell you anything you want.'

Gladys smiled at the notion, but then frowned. It might not be that simple!

As it turned out, it was S rather than Gladys who had to play up to the General.

The shaking of the Land Rover woke the women at around mid-day. As he had promised, sergeant-major Nkwame had rewarded the two men who had done best at drill. They fucked the girls lying side by side on the floor of the vehicle, accompanied by raucous shouts from outside as the vehicle bounced and rocked with their efforts. It did not take long.

Afterwards the girls were called out to help serve up the mid-day meal. Once again the sergeant-major's discipline held, and not a single soldier touched them despite the fact that they all knew exactly what they had just been doing and that the girls had to lean so close to the men when they dished out ladles of meat and vegetables. Dozens of times S found herself squeezing so close between two soldiers that either of them could have merely turned his head to nuzzle her bare breasts.

It changed when S was called over to the field kitchen, given a large tray bearing covered dishes, and sent to the General's tent. The General clearly did not have to keep his hands off; even as S placed the tray on his camp table he was feeling her thighs. She made to hurry away but he hooked a finger into her pussy ring and kept her beside him while he ate.

His food was the same as that of his men except that his was served on china plates rather than into mess tins, and he had a fork as well as a spoon. Using only one hand he ate with gusto. The other hand was busy with S. She stood silently facing him with her legs apart, trying not to react to what he was doing between them. His table manners were awful and he slurped and guzzled at his food, cramming in one mouthful almost before he had finished chewing the last one.

Halfway through his meal he pulled his hand out of S with an audible squelch and waved towards a low cabinet near his camp bed. It contained at least a dozen bottles of whisky, one of which was half-empty, and a single glass tumbler. S placed the opened bottle and the tumbler on the table near him then, in response to his gesture she poured until the tumbler was more than half-full.

He did not speak until he had finished his meal and S had poured another half-tumbler of whisky. Then he leaned back expansively in his chair and looked her over from head to foot.

'So,' he said, belching loudly and hooking a finger into her pubic ring to pull her closer. 'This poor little representative of our former colonial masters was drugged and kidnapped, eh? Something of a cliché, don't you think?'

The expression in his eyes was sharp and calculating, and S suddenly felt that he was a lot more shrewd and dangerous than his table manners had suggested.

'My father and his father and his father before him, back through generations, were victims of your kind,' he said, his voice languid but his eyes hard. 'The colonialists were always thieves and liars. They took our land and our women and robbed us of our dignity.'

His face had become cruel, but S felt that the gleam in his eyes as he stared at her breasts suggested something other than anger at his country's colonial history. Gladys had told her she had to 'be nice', so that is what she would be.

'Oh, sir!' she said when he reached up and grasped her by her breasts, pulling her towards him. 'You're so strong!'

When he pulled her down on to his lap she curled herself against him, gazing up at him winsomely, snuggling, parting her knees when his hand descended. He hurt her a little as he fingered her but she still managed to smile coquettishly as she wriggled on his hand.

It worked perfectly. Any sign of anger or cruelty on his face was transformed to naked lust as S kissed him beneath his chin and wriggled her bottom against the erection burgeoning in his trousers. Within minutes she was beneath him on the camp-bed, her ankles locked behind his knees, her hands clawing at his back, her face buried in his chest as he took her so hard she thought the wooden bed must surely break.

He was very big, and her moans were not entirely faked.

The General kept S with him almost until sunset. His 'conquest' had put him in an expansive mood, and he revelled in the admiration S poured on him.

'Oh, sir, you're so big!' she cried. 'Ah! Ah! Harder! Harder!'

He swelled with satisfaction when, after he climbed off her that first time, she writhed around like an eel and began sucking him even before he sat down. He was soft and tasted of her own juices but S knew enough of sex by now to understand how much a man likes the feel of a woman's mouth on him.

She managed to get him talking, but it was mostly about colonial times and how powerful he would become once the country was freed from the blood-sucking Prince. She learned little or nothing about his actual plans for attack. She told him he was her hero and how wonderful he was and then he fucked her a second time, just as hard as the first but for far longer, and now S did not have to fake her orgasms.

He sent her off to the water hole to bathe after that, and then she helped Gladys serve the soldiers' evening meal. While the men ate the two women sat on the ground by a truck near the tent. They heard raised voices.

'They're having a row,' Gladys whispered to S. 'It's about you. The one who calls himself the General is saying he wants to keep you in his tent. For his own use. The sergeant-major is saying the men will not like that. He is saying they will not like it if they don't get their share. He is saying the General can have you during the day, but the men must have a chance also. He says that he is ready to draw lots for us like last night, and the men will be upset if he does not.'

S hugged her knees and felt a hot shiver run down her spine. Before she had answered that fascinating advertisement a few months ago she had been a dull, frustrated secretary to a provincial solicitor who was too dull to know what frustration was. Now, she was sitting naked in the middle of a rebel camp in the African bush listening to other people arguing about whether she should become the General's private whore or be shared out as a raffle prize by his troops!

The lurch of hot wetness she felt between her legs at the thought said all that was needed.

Nine

The plastic disc she pulled out of the steel helmet read 'GS42'. There came a whoop from the edge of the crowd of soldiers, and S watched her companions for the night scrambling towards her, grinning wolfishly. Dozens of other men groaned and made gestures of disappointment, but S was grateful that she would only be having to deal with four of them. Then again, she would have to go back to the General's tent first thing in the morning.

She smiled brightly as greedy hands reached for her, pretending she was delighted at what was about to happen.

Sergeant-major Nkwame was scrupulously fair in conducting the nightly raffle, and S and Gladys each went to a different truck each night so that all the men got their turn, in groups of between three and six. In the mornings he always allowed them a few hours' sleep in his Land Rover, and during the day the only soldiers who were allowed to have them were the two who had done best at whatever drill or exercises he put his men through. He never touched either of the women himself.

The regime – little sleep and a great deal of sex – was exhausting for both women, but was compounded in S's case by the fact that she had to spend from mid-day until evening every day in the General's tent.

For the first few days he was so pleased at having what he called a 'colonialist' in his power that he was very demanding and took delight in humiliating her. He required her to kneel underneath his table and fellate him while he ate his meal, and would frequently reach down and tweak her nipple rings. She was not allowed to make him come, though; she had to save that for after his meal, when he would lie back on the camp-bed and order her to get astride him.

The one time she made the mistake of getting him to come in her mouth he pulled her out from under the table by her hair. She was stunned to see that instead of looking pleased at how well she had sucked him, he seemed furious. He shoved her aside so forcefully that she sprawled across the ground, arms and legs all over the place. When he told her to get up and get across the table, she saw that he was already unbuckling his wide leather belt.

'Whores like you need discipline,' he said coldly. 'And I know how to apply it.'

Was she a whore? S could not have said at that moment. She had certainly fellated him very actively and with all the skill and enthusiasm she could muster; she had even enjoyed it in a way. But did that make her a whore?

Any such thoughts vanished as the first blow landed and she shrieked aloud at the force of it, the camping table rocking beneath her weight. She clung on, hoping that by keeping still and taking it she might allay his fury. The belt was wide, perhaps three and a half or four inches, and so the pain was diffused a little. Even so, the fire that spread across her flinching, squirming buttocks was appalling.

She had no idea how many strokes he gave her – twelve, fifteen, twenty. It did not matter. All she knew was that when at last he stopped beating her and left her drooped and sobbing across the table, the fire in her buttocks slowly turned into a throbbing ache, an ache which was somehow transferring itself inwards, to become an insidious pulsing in the pit of her loins and the tips of her breasts.

S came to a sort of awareness when she registered a fierce order, spoken sharply as though it was being repeated. She pushed herself up from the table, wincing, and saw that the General was lying on his back on the camp-bed, naked, his engorged penis straining upwards. The sight of it, and the knowledge of what was about to happen, sent the pulsing in her body into overdrive.

A tiny part at the back of her brain told S that she was doing this because she had to, but her body said differently. She climbed astride him stiffly, wincing from the pain in her backside, but once she impaled herself on his erection her movements became fluid and instinctive. She began coming long before he did, the muscles of her sheath writhing on his thickness, her cervix pounding against his bulb.

Maybe she really was a whore, said that tiny, retreating part of her brain as she fucked him. And without doubt it was *she* fucking *him*. Her pelvis and sheath had taken on lives of their own, rioting on him. She rolled her head and wailed. She mauled at her own breasts and clawed at his hard chest. Her splayed thighs beat down on his hip-bones as she ground on him, taking his whole length then pulling back to feel him sliding in her, then crashing down again to feel the pressure of him on her clit and pubic bone.

He laughed afterwards, after she had bucked and wailed when he shot into her depths, then collapsed

123

onto his chest exhausted, her vagina still rippling on him as he slackened and subsided until he slipped out of her.

The beating became a daily part of the General's fun with S. It pleased his pride to have his naked, supplicant 'colonialist' woman bend over for him to belt the trembling globes of her pale backside. It did not mark her much and the effects wore off quickly, for it became more of a ritual than a punishment and he seldom beat her as hard as that first time.

They both knew that, somehow, the beatings aroused S as much as they did the General, and that her orgasms when she climbed astride him afterwards, and impaled herself on his rampant prick and fucked him to a finish were always absolutely genuine. The General too gloried in the ritual humiliation almost as much as in the glorious fuck which always followed, and was spurred on by her submissiveness to find other ways of demonstrating her servitude.

He made her ask to be allowed to suck him off – with, he laughed, 'that "Pretty Please" you English sluts always say'. He made her say 'thank you, master' after each separate episode of their afternoon sessions. She even had to thank him for belting her backside and letting her ride him afterwards.

It was the fourth or maybe the fifth afternoon that he found a new means of proving his mastery over this compliant colonialist slut. S had knelt beneath the table, dutifully sucking for about half an hour, and was now bent across the table. He fingered her offered sex, as he always did before beating her. Then he did something new. S gave an involuntary yelp as his hand moved and a thick fingertip thrust up to the second knuckle into the tight pucker of her anus.

She tried to escape, her buttocks squirming and flexing against the sudden invasion, but he pressed a strong hand into the small of her back to keep her down. It became like a dream to S. She felt his fingertip manipulating her, heard his words through a fog, heard him laugh. Blushing to her core, she went off to find Gladys.

'He says you have to give me an enema.' Her voice was cracking as she hugged the older woman. 'I think he's going to do me in . . . in there. In my bum. Oh, Gladys, it's too much! He's ever so . . . ever so –'

'Hush, child.' Gladys kissed away S's hot tears. 'We got to do this. *You* got to do this. Keep him happy. Give him what he wants and we'll learn his plans. You can do it, girl!'

Half an hour later, strengthened by Gladys's kisses and encouragement, S re-entered the General's tent. Gladys had flushed her out, cleaned her up and, to make things easier, greased her liberally inside and out.

At his gesture, she knelt sideways across the bed. She flinched momentarily when she felt his hard fingers parting her buttocks. She tensed when she felt his exploring finger but forced herself to think of Gladys's warm voice saying, 'Relax, girl, relax. You can take it.'

The finger went deep, but what followed went deeper. Her eyes bulged as he pressed against her. She forced herself to relax her sphincter, to allow him in. He felt so much bigger there than in her mouth or vagina. He took his time, gripping her hips and pushing in with little jerking motions. It felt as though every one of her internal organs was being crammed up into her stomach. Then he began to fuck her and her mind span away.

Every sensation was multiplied to such extremes

125

that they became a whirlpool, a kaleidoscope of physical reactions fighting mental ones, neither winning. When he came S screamed, partly from the force of him but partly, to her shame, from the fact that she also orgasmed. He was in the wrong place, was stretching her anus, was doing what she knew was forbidden – yet she was coming as hard as she ever had in her life. When he at last pulled out of her she was crying silent tears; tears of humiliation at his power over her, but also tears of shame at the way her body had reacted.

Maybe, she thought as she sagged down onto the bed, maybe I really am the whore he calls me!

After perhaps a week, S's efforts to flirt and convince the General that he was the world's greatest lover and that she was awed by the glory of his penis began to pay off. She still had to do her duty under the table, but he no longer jerked so fiercely at her nipple rings. He still spanked her with his leather belt, of course, but not so hard now. And although he made her ride him still, he used her rear entrance most days too, and she learned to relax and make it easier on herself. More importantly though, he began talking to her.

He told her about the time, long ago now, when he had been a student at the London School of Economics. He was bitter about the way some of 'the colonialists' treated him and his fellow Africans, but had become convinced that white women were all sluts at heart. Why, he had fucked any number of them during his time in London and they had gone mad for his 'hammer' – and was not S herself living proof of this? Since he was rutting energetically in her rear entrance at the time, S could not really answer his question.

He had returned to the Principality as an

126

enthusiastic young man with a head crammed with ideas. All around, former colonies were gaining their independence from the oppressor; soon it would be their turn. He joined the Civil Service but found promotion to the upper echelons was restricted to the colonialists whom he was learning to hate more than ever.

'But I'm not a colonialist,' whispered S, circling her pelvis on his thick shaft and feeling him begin to twitch and pulse. She lifted his hands to her breasts and cupped them there. 'You don't hate *me*, do you, master?'

She knew he liked her to call him master, but she always thought of it with a small m. Her real Master was many miles away and she would get back to him soon, somehow or other, and everything in life would be wonderful again. She shrugged off such lovely thoughts and concentrated on fucking the General as expertly as she possibly could. She had to win this man over if she and Gladys were ever to find out what they needed and get away.

'How are you going to attack the palace?' she asked in a false little-girl voice.

The company had moved on the previous day and, having helped to erect the General's tent, S was now snuggling against him, her bare backside – freshly beaten – wiggling against his growing erection as his hands reached around and toyed with her breasts.

'Don't you worry your head about such things,' he said. 'Women, especially you colonialist whores, are for fucking, *not* for strategy!'

His voice took on a cold, almost suspicious tone and his body tensed. Instantly aware that she had come close to making a mistake, S wriggled around to face him, and became kittenish. She fluttered her eyelashes and reached down to stroke his already half-erect penis.

'Ooh, master! That's a much nicer idea.' She kissed his bare chest. 'I'm not really a colonialist, you know, but you do make me feel like a whore!' She stroked his cock. 'Are you going to fuck me now?' she whispered.

He did, rolling her onto her back and allowing her to guide his thickening cock into the soft, moist folds of her sex. He took his time, riding her slowly because she had fellated him to a finish less than half an hour ago. These days he was not too rough with her breasts, but always took delight in digging his hard fingers into her freshly beaten buttocks, making her gasp and squirm.

S came long before the General did, clamping her legs around his back and pumping her sex against him to get him deeper. Part of her was ashamed at the way her body responded to him, but he *was* big, and when he moved slow like that, staying deep and sort of circling, then pulling back and thrusting hard, only to circle again, there was no possibility of resistance. When she screamed out the filthy words he liked to hear, and her pelvis bucked against him, he laughed and spurted into her undulating vagina.

It was at those times that S realised that, at some level, she was indeed the whore he called her. She did not like him. She was only here and letting the General and his men do anything they liked to her out of dire necessity. Yet when he fucked her and when his troops fucked her in whatever truck she had drawn in the nightly raffle, her body nearly always went wild.

Gladys counselled and consoled her as they lay together one morning in the back of the Land Rover, exhausted from yet another shattering night keeping up the morale of the rebel troops.

'It's all right, little love,' she murmured, kissing S on the brow and eyelids. 'A woman comes. It is what her body does. If you didn't come you would be all dry, and sex would make you sore. You are not a bad woman just because this sweet cunt gets hot and wet on a prick. It is natural. See!'

She slipped a finger into S as she spoke the last word, and S moaned. Her body seemed so hyper-sensitive these days, so unbelievably ready, that even Gladys's finger had her panting in only moments.

'It's natural,' Gladys repeated as S squirmed on her hand. 'You are a real woman, built to be fucked. Don't fight your nature. Just keep your wits about you so we can find out what we need and get away from here.'

Having her wits about her was just about the last thing S was capable of as her pelvis rocked against her friend's hand. The soldiers last night had been very vigorous and her senses were still spiralling down from the heights they had driven her to. Now Gladys was holding her and kissing her and caressing her with insidious intimacy, and S felt as though she had been coming non-stop for a lifetime. Gladys kept on kissing her even after she swooned, overcome by new thoughts and overwhelming sensations.

After she asked about his plan of attack on the palace, however, the General was much more reticent with her. Even though she behaved as humbly as possible and gave him the best sex she could, and virtually screamed the things he liked to hear – 'Oh, fuck me! Fuck me harder!'; 'God, you're so big! Shove it up me!'; 'Fill my cunt with your hammer! Shaft me to death!' – he remained suspicious of her. She never made the mistake of asking such a question again.

But then one afternoon he caught her looking at some papers he had left on his table, and all her attempts at innocence were to little avail.

The papers were innocuous, stuff about food supplies, but the General's anger was cold and implacable. As he towered over her, his face a mask of rage, S detected something else in his eyes, a hint of triumph, as though she had fallen into some cunningly laid trap.

He ordered her to find sergeant-major Nkwame and fetch him to the tent. There was a rapid discussion in dialect, during which Nkwame was clearly dubious about what was being said, but eventually bowed to his superior officer's orders. He went out of the tent and shouted some orders in the sort of voice only sergeant-majors ever seem to possess, and in moments four of his troops hurried in. They were carrying ropes and several long poles.

The sergeant-major remained silent as the General fired off a series of rapid instructions. The soldiers grabbed S and spread her on her back on the ground. Each man took a wrist or an ankle and, pulling them wide and tying them firmly to the ends of the poles, stretching S into a helpless human X. The General was still maintaining his act of extreme anger, but S could see something else in his eyes – something which told her she was in for a very hard time.

At another shouted order, the four soldiers each took the end of one of the poles and lifted S bodily from the ground. They carried her out of the tent and across an expanse of bare ground to one of the many acacia trees that grew around the camp.

They laid her out, still on her back, at the foot of the tree. S had never felt so exposed and helpless in her life, yet at the same time she felt a surge of heat in her belly at the way the four soldiers looked down at her. They had all fucked her at some time as a result of the nightly raffles, but their hot eyes – eyes that gleamed with the same lust as the General's – betrayed their eagerness to fuck her again, this minute, given half a chance. One of them, bolder than the others, pressed his hand against her splayed pudenda and she groaned at the invasion of his fingers, ashamed at how wet and ready she was.

The fact that minutes later, in response to the sergeant-major's furious instructions, the whole squad of rebel soldiers was gathered round and looking down on her nakedness only made her arousal worse.

The General made a brief speech to his men. This, he told them, was a colonialist whore whom he had caught spying. She had come among them on false pretences, flaunting her body to try to learn the secrets of their glorious rebellion. Now all was revealed, and she was to be punished for the whore she was.

S listened to the harangue with growing dismay. What he said was all true, but he could not possibly have known it. She was going to be punished for nothing more than his pleasure, for his enjoyment at seeing a 'colonialist' writhe and hearing her scream. The lust in his eyes betrayed it. Why? It was not fair! She had given him everything he wanted, done everything to please him . . .

She knew she was going to be hung up and beaten and had reconciled herself to it; she had been beaten before and would be again, she was sure. She would survive it. She steeled herself as a pair of brawny soldiers approached, then gasped in horror. Instead of picking up the pole to which her wrists were tied, they went to the other one, the one holding her splayed ankles. With ease, they lifted her high and hooked the pole over a stout branch, leaving her swinging upside-down and disorientated. She made to raise her tethered arms, but the two grinning men grabbed the pole her wrists were bound to and tied it to a stake driven into the ground, pulling her arms down until her helpless body was stretched tautly between the branch and the ground.

The General approached her, a wicked grin on his face. He knelt close to her head and crammed a cloth gag into her mouth, fixing it with another piece of cloth knotted tightly around her head.

'We don't want to spoil things with silly screaming, do we?' he chuckled, and S felt a chill of dread replace her earlier state of arousal.

He used a dog-whip, its handle no more than a foot long and an inch or so thick, but its thong a yard in length and tapering to no more than the thickness of a shoelace. The very first cut across her backside sent S into such paroxysms of agony that she nearly dragged the stake out of the ground. Had she not been gagged her screams would have frightened every animal within miles.

It was the worst beating she had ever known, worse than the rattan, the riding crop, even the elephant tail. It felt like the cut of a white-hot knife, as though her flesh had been sliced. A second blow fell almost immediately, this time across her breasts. She snorted, wild-eyed, almost swallowing the gag in her shock. The third was across her backside again, right where her buttocks merged with her thighs. More followed, setting her writhing in her bonds, her eyes bulging and her face puffy. Then one stroke fell vertically down between her thighs, exactly along her crease, whipping right through to set fire to everything between the pucker of her anus and her navel, and mercifully she fainted.

Ten

S swam up from a dream of clouds and pain and
lustful eyes. She tried to close her legs and found she
was unable. She tried to struggle up but a gentle hand
held her down, and a voice murmured. It was Gladys,
and her face was close, her eyes soft and loving.

'Hush, child,' she breathed, kissing S on her
temple. 'He was a bad man and went too far, but Mr
Nkwame sorted him out.'

It took another couple of days for S to learn all
that had happened – days during which Gladys
nursed her tenderly, for the whip had indeed bruised
her. Her backside was perhaps the least badly hurt,
but her breasts and between her legs were very sore.

It seemed, from Gladys's account, that the General
had got carried away when he was whipping her and
had begun flogging her in earnest, as though he really
hated her. It was then sergeant-major Nkwame had
intervened. He had bellowed at the General, dragged
him off, torn the whip from his grasp. There had been
a fight of sorts, though Nkwame was so big and
powerful it had not lasted for long, and then the
General had been deposed. The troop of rebel
soldiers had gone along with their sergeant-major.
Apparently, the General was not very popular
anyway it seemed and had been driven away by a
mob of his troops.

The reason S was unable to close her legs for a day or two, despite Gladys's tender nursing, was because the General had concentrated a rain of blows between them before Nkwame had dragged him off. Gladys had fixed a short spreader-bar between her knees.

'It was like he was trying to cut you in half!' Gladys said as she smoothed cream on to S's skin. 'He evil man!'

It took several days more for S to recover to Gladys's satisfaction – a satisfaction which was tested by Gladys using her lips and tongue to assess S's reactions. As the weals across her breasts slowly healed, Gladys kissed her and sucked her nipples. If S hissed with pain Gladys became solicitous. When she stopped hissing and began instead to gently pant Gladys knew that the wounds were nearly healed.

S had not actually been cut between her legs, although she was very sore and sensitive. Nevertheless, Gladys paid a great deal of attention to that area, kissing and licking and nuzzling there with unbearable tenderness. Both women knew that this was much more for pleasure than as part of the healing process, and well before Gladys allowed the spreader-bar to be removed S had experienced any number of slow, voluptuous orgasms.

'Besides, girl,' Gladys giggled on one occasion, looking up with her chin and fingers glistening. 'Coming is good for a girl! Helps get the blood flowing, and take away the soreness of a tanned bum!'

When at last the spreader-bar was removed and S could get her legs together and climb off the bed, she walked stiffly, supported on Gladys's arm. Some of the whip marks were still visible as thin, dark lines across her breasts and behind, but Gladys assured S that they would not form scars.

'You'll be all nice and pretty again before we get back to the Prince,' she said.

Getting back to the Prince, their Master, had become a major problem. It was now several weeks since the two women had surrendered to the rebels, and according to Gladys, when the convoy had moved a week or so ago it had actually been away from, rather than towards, the capital and the palace.

'Besides that,' she added with a worried frown, 'with what we've been doing they might say we was supporting the enemy.'

S was aghast. 'But they couldn't!' she whispered in horror. 'We didn't want to – to do it! They made us!'

'Oh yes! How many of them fucked you since we been here? All of them?'

'Well, yes, I suppose so, but –'

'And did they have to drag you off kicking and screaming, or did you pick out your raffle card like a good little girl?'

S blushed at the irrefutable truth of Gladys's implication, and at the recollection of night after night in bouncing trucks spent pleasuring straining rebel cocks, and time after time kneeling under the General's table or riding him on his camp-bed.

'Yes, me too,' Gladys continued with a shrug, a hint of bitterness in her voice. 'So who is going to believe that we was not willing? We don't know much about their plans yet, and they haven't killed us or even marked us up much!'

The more Gladys talked the more hopeless their situation seemed, until S was weeping miserable tears. They were interrupted by a messenger. Sergeant-major Nkwame was waiting for S in what had been the General's tent. He looked at her shrewdly as she entered, noting her red eyes and the stripes across her breasts.

'Do not be afraid,' he said at once. 'I may have taken his place but I am not like him. I do not take pleasure in inflicting discipline for its own sake.'

He was sitting casually on the only chair, so broad in his shoulders he seemed to fill the whole tent. His voice was quiet and very deep, and somehow reassuring. He bade her come close and examined the marks on her breasts and thighs, before telling her to turn round so that he could inspect her back and bottom. S felt a hot shiver run through her, and her nipples hardened. He was so overpoweringly male, and she was very close to him and stark-naked. When she felt him trace one of the stripes on her backside with a thick fingertip, she held her breath.

He was the only one among the whole troop of rebels who had not fucked her; had not even touched her in fact. Indeed, it had been he who had kept his men off S and Gladys and given them those hours of blessed sleep in his Land Rover each morning. And it had been he who, as Gladys told it, had bellowed his rage and grabbed the General off her, flinging him aside like a rag when his whipping of S had gone too far.

Yet it was also he who had organised the evening raffles which sent the two women off to spend hectic nights servicing three, four, five, even six lusty soldiers. He knew, also, about her afternoon duties with the General, for he had frequently reported to the tent while S was under the table suckling and slurping.

But he had never touched her until now, as his fingers traced the marks on her buttocks with the lightness of feathers. Surely, she thought, now was the time. They were alone; she was naked and posing her body for him; the bed was just over there. When he told her to go back to the Land Rover and get some sleep, she was surprised and, she realised with a blush of shame at her own wantonness, disappointed.

The raffle was held as usual that evening. Gladys chose first, and a quartet of whooping soldiers led her off towards a Bedford truck with a crumpled right-front wing. With her beautiful face and voluptuous figure Gladys was very popular, and four pairs of hands were all over her long before the group reached the truck. S felt a pang of conscience that for nearly a week now, since the whipping, Gladys had had to serve the troops all by herself. One woman and all those men! The poor girl must be exhausted!

S turned and reached up into the steel helmet to choose her own plastic disc, to find out which truck she would be going to and how many men she would be entertaining for the night. It was odd, because there seemed to be only one disc in the helmet. She fluttered her hand around to make sure but, yes, there was only the one disc. She drew it out and read the number aloud, as usual. Instead of the familiar whoops and grabbing hands, all that happened was a communal groan of disappointment, and all the soldiers turned and began to drift away.

All except one.

S looked at sergeant-major Nkwame in confusion. The number on the disc was not one she recognised, and she thought she knew them all by heart by now. Then something in his eyes gave her a flash of realisation. She looked to her left. There, twenty yards away, stood the Land Rover. Its number matched that on the disc in her hand. S felt a sudden hotness in her chest.

The huge man standing beside her had cheated. Somehow, while everybody was watching Gladys going off with her four excited soldiers, he had removed all the discs from the helmet except the one that signified his own vehicle. He was not whooping as the ordinary soldiers would have done. He was not even smiling. Without a word, S turned and walked towards the Land Rover, conscious of his eyes on her naked back.

He helped her up into the back of the Land Rover and buckled the canvas flaps at the back so they would be concealed from prying eyes, while S spread the sleeping bags on the floor. He leaned over the front seat and flicked a switch on the dashboard. A dim courtesy light came on, illuminating the back of the vehicle with a low, warm glow.

'It will run down the battery by morning,' he said, his voice low. 'But I have waited a long time for this and I want to be able to see you.'

Knowing what her role here was, S reached forward for the buttons of his shirt, but he pushed her hands away.

'No. Lie down.' His voice was hardly more than a hoarse growl. 'No, keep your legs together. Put your arms above your head. Lie still.'

Removing his clothes was difficult because of the lack of headroom in the back of the Land Rover, but even on his knees or sitting down struggling with his military boots, his slow undressing took S's breath away.

Despite his size, his movements were precise and neat. As he folded the shirt he had just removed S became entranced by the play of soft light across the muscles of his chest and back. He might well be very big, but there was not an ounce, not even a gramme of fat on him. The simple act of reaching down to his boot laces set off ripples of sheer power under his gleaming skin. When he tugged off his immaculately pressed uniform trousers S shut her eyes, both hopeful about and scared of what might be revealed.

There was a long, long silence. S sensed movement, heard breathing. Then she felt it, the breathing, on her skin. It was so unexpected that for a moment she stiffened with surprise. Then her senses surrendered. His breath was soft and warm on her temple. His lips touched her skin more softly than the wing of a moth. He did not touch her with his hands, nor even his tongue, only with his breath and the lightest skim of his lips – but with those, he touched every swell and curve and declivity of her body, from her temples and forehead to the soles of her feet.

He did it slowly, as though he was breathing in the bouquet of a rare wine, and the effect on S became something deeper than mere torment. She fought hard to keep still as he explored her, desperate to move, to be touched, to open herself. By the time his hands touched on her knees, parting them, she felt she had been on a plateau of pre-orgasm for a million lifetimes. When she felt the heat of his body descend on her and the first pressure of his cock against her swollen entrance, she convulsed into a come which had her almost fainting. Her pelvis bucked forward and her oozing, greedy sheath sucked him in. Although he was the one on top, she was the one doing the fucking, her hips pumping wildly, her legs clamping around his back, her body taking on a life of its own, the life of a tigress.

'You need to trim your nails,' he murmured later, as they lay entwined. S was still spiralling down, her body curled into his, small and warm and oh, so sensitive to the touch of her skin against his. S could not suppress a giggle at the sheer comfortableness of the remark. She snuggled back and wriggled her bottom into the bend of his torso and thighs.

'You cheated, didn't you,' she breathed, feeling a delightful stirring against the cleft of her buttocks.

'I had to. You kept on missing my number.' His big hand smoothed gently over her breast, nudging her nipple ring but not tugging on it as the General always used to. He moved closer still, letting her know that he was getting harder. She felt so deeply comfortable, and clenched her bottom against him. It became almost flirtatious, except she was not a girl outside a club seeing whether she fancied the man – she was naked, in his arms, and he had just fucked her until she was dizzy, but somehow it still felt like a flirtation.

His number had been in the raffle every night. She snaked around, keeping her skin close on his, her arms holding him. She nestled against his chest, breathing against his hard muscles. She teased him. She whispered that he could have had her any time he wanted, but he told her that would not have been fair on his troops. Nuzzling against his hard pectoral muscles and slipping a hand down towards his groin, she asked whether Gladys had ever drawn his number in the raffles. No, and he had not fucked Gladys either.

He was very erect again. S curled down and around and took him into her mouth. He kept still. She cupped the heaviness of his testicles in her hand and kissed and licked his length. Somehow, she was doing it more for herself than for him. His hardness, his scent of masculinity, his gentle strength, but most of all the sheer physicality of what was happening took her over.

He was circumcised, and she rolled her tongue avidly around his thick glans and the ridge where it gave onto his shaft, and most of all over the cleft of its single eye where salty droplets were already forming. He tasted clean and heady and S became lost in what she was doing. This was for her pleasure, not his.

She gave a little mew of disappointment when he pulled her greedy mouth off his erection, but it turned into a moan of delight when he lifted her, moved her round as though she weighed no more than a leaf and thrust his cock into her vagina. He held her by her ribcage, his hands so big his fingertips were on her shoulder-blades while his thumbs pressed the under-swells of her breasts. Using just the strength of his arms, he eased her up and down on the length of his shaft. She had no control. She was above him but he was handling her as though she was no more than a puppet, moving her up and down on his throbbing prick. She was no more than a marionette with a vagina, a doll designed for fucking.

She sobbed when she started coming, and he laughed. Then he crammed her hard and erupted into his own orgasm, grinding her on, flooding her with gouts of pulsing heat. To S it felt as though he was coming directly into her brain and her body cramped and convulsed as if she was being electrocuted. Not since Kano had she come so violently, so overwhelmingly. So beautifully. Her tears when Nkwame lifted her off his slackening prick were as much at the thought of her beloved Kano as for the voluptuous orgasm which was still rippling around her nerve-ends.

S was hardly capable of registering when sergeant-major Nkwame left the back of the Land Rover after sunrise and a weary Gladys crawled in to lie down beside her. He had kept her going practically all night, insisting that she used her mouth on him during the times he was recovering between fucks – and he had fucked her an awful lot.

141

Her hips felt stiff; her jaw ached from hours of licking and sucking; she felt sore and swollen between her legs, for Nkwame was big as well as very energetic. When Gladys hugged her and slipped a tender hand down onto her breast, all S could do was moan, 'No, don't. Please, darling. I'm really tired.'

Now that the General had been banished Nkwame was in sole charge of the band of rebel soldiers, and maintained just as strict discipline over his men as before. Apart from that, little changed. The two men who had done best in the morning drills and exercises still took S and Gladys into the back of some truck or other to enjoy their 'reward' after the mid-day meal. The nightly raffles continued, as did the girls' blessed morning rest in the back of the Land Rover.

It was Gladys who first noticed that there seemed to be a pattern to the results of the raffles. There were ten trucks, plus Nkwame's Land Rover, and not only did neither of the girls ever draw the same truck twice running, but the draw seemed to go in rotation so that the crew of each truck took turns, as it were. S knew that Nkwame was capable of cheating in the raffle, and when she told Gladys they both found it wryly amusing. After all, they were going to get fucked by some crew or other every night so it was only fair that Nkwame rigged the draw so that his men got equal shares!

Nkwame himself suddenly seemed to be getting rather more than equal shares. It had taken several weeks for his number to come up, and even then he had cheated. Now, it seemed to come up every second or third night. Only two evenings after her first exhausting night with him, S drew Nkwame's number again. She blushed at his sidelong grin when she read out the number, certain that he had cheated again.

When he stripped his uniform off in the back of the Land Rover S felt that familiar surge of heat and wetness in her belly. His body was magnificent, his mahogany skin taut and glossy over hard muscles. His penis was only half-awake but was already as thick as her wrist. As she reached for it with delicate fingers S found herself wondering how on earth she had taken such a thing the other night – and how she was going to take it tonight.

He lay down on his back, reaching out to cup and fondle her breasts as S began to caress his increasing hardness. She leaned down and began to lick the length of his shaft, feeling him stiffen. He came fully erect as she slid her soft mouth onto him. She could not take much more than his glans into her mouth, but licked and sucked with all the skill she could muster, cupping his heavy balls in one hand while she stroked his steely shaft with the other.

She shifted her position when he moved a hand down between her legs, parting her knees as she knelt. His big hand was sensitive and delicate as it worked upon her swelling labia and throbbing clitoris. The fingers he inserted were thick and hard, but gentle. By the time he lifted her head off his cock and turned her around for the next stage, S was more than eager.

She got astride him, holding his hardness with both hands as she lowered herself onto him. God, he was big! She could feel him in her ribs! She lost track of everything except the intensity of her bodily sensations as she started to ride him. She ground herself down hard, crushing her pelvic bone against his before rising up until she felt the thickness of his glans stretching her entrance, then crushing down again until he filled her.

She felt his hands on her breasts and wanted him to squeeze harder, to pull at her, to bruise her. She wanted his cock to double in size, to tear her apart. She fucked him more and more wildly, oblivious to everything except the orgasm that was building, growing, rising inexorably in her blood and senses.

She did not know that she screamed when she came, only that her brain seemed to explode with red-gold fire and that every muscle in her torso went into spasms of voluptuous greed. When Nkwame came in his turn, S was too weak to do anything save accept his thrusting and pulsing and groan with every spurt of delicious heat, and lie against his chest, their sweat mingling.

The next time was with S on her back, her legs hooked wide by Nkwame's powerful arms, his muscular body bucking and flexing as he shafted her. Later, he took her from behind, her knees spread and her head and shoulders drooping onto the floor of the Land Rover, protected from grazes and splinters by the thin sleeping bag on which they had lain. He fucked her repeatedly during the night and then again as the dawn broke. This time her body was too weary to do more than simply open to him and let him pump at her, and groan as he orgasmed deep inside her yet again.

Gladys thought S was exaggerating her state of exhaustion until it was she who picked out Nkwame's number three nights later. Her eyes were enormous when S climbed wearily into the Land Rover after her own night with three soldiers in the back of a Leyland one-tonner.

'God!' she whispered as S slipped into the sleeping bag beside her. 'The man's a monster! Nobody's ever done me like that before. He's got a truncheon. And he must have done me six times at least.'

S hugged her in sympathy, neither knowing which

was the more exhausted, S after a night with three 'normal' soldiers or Gladys after her night with just Nkwame. What they did agree on, when they went to bathe in the river after their morning's sleep, was that being fucked by Nkwame was the most shattering experience either of them had ever known.

Their conversation was interrupted by the rising noise of vehicles approaching. They climbed out of the river and crept to the line of bushes. Being braver than S, Gladys was the first to part the shrubs and look through.

'There are hundreds of them!' she gasped.

While they had been bathing a fresh convoy had arrived to join Nkwame's troop. There were not actually hundreds of soldiers, but the two groups together did form a considerable force. There were now some thirty trucks, some of them mounted with heavy machine guns. Men in fatigues, with belts of ammunition crossing their chests and rifles hanging from their shoulders, were hurrying about all over the place. Right in the middle of the space Nkwame called his parade ground, on which he had drilled his men, stood a dust-covered Jeep. Nkwame was stiffly saluting the man sitting in its passenger seat. In contrast to Nkwame's broad, muscular frame, this man was tiny, his arms thin and stick-like, his head seeming too small for the wire-framed spectacles he wore. Small as he was, there was an air of authority about him. Even though he did not even reach Nkwame's shoulders it was instantly obvious who had the power here.

It was more than an hour before S and Gladys heard Nkwame shouting for them, by which time the camp had settled down somewhat. Nevertheless, the reaction from the newcomers when two naked, nervous women emerged from the shrubs fringing the river was raucous. Men came running, leapt out of trucks, whooped and gestured as they walked towards the table at which the new commander sat. S knew that had it not been for the obvious discipline this new leader, and Nkwame too, exerted, she and Gladys would not have got six paces before these men were all over them.

The soldiers formed a gangway leading towards the table at which their leader sat. It was a corridor of pure lust, and S had never been more conscious of her nakedness and vulnerability as she walked along it holding Gladys's hand for comfort. Gladys, on the other hand, kept her head high and her shoulders back, defying the ogling men to intimidate her. Her back was straight, her glorious breasts bounced and trembled as she moved, her hips swayed.

S did not understand any of the cat-calls and comments the soldiers made, but their gestures were blatantly obvious. The discipline of these newcomers was clearly not as strong as that of Nkwame's men, and S felt herself go hot at the prospect of what would happen if their leader were to let them loose.

This new leader appeared even smaller and more insect-like when the women stood before him than he had at a distance, especially in comparison to the giant figure of Nkwame standing just behind him. His face was pinched and his eyes, even through the thick lenses of his spectacles, were cold. He wasted no time.

'I disapprove of whores!' His voice was surprisingly strong coming from such a slight frame, and was as cold as his eyes. 'I disapprove of women who parade themselves as naked Jezebels for the temptation of men! You will be punished, clothed, and confined to sergeant-major Nkwame's custody until further notice.'

Both S and Gladys stared at him open-mouthed

with shock. He waved a hand and before they could even begin to protest several men grabbed each of them and they were dragged away.

Eleven

They were hauled across to a large acacia tree and pushed against its thick trunk on opposite sides. Their arms were pulled around the trunk and tied with ropes, each rope passing round the back of the neck of the other woman, so that they were holding one another close against the rough bark. Next, a rope was passed right round the tree at the level of their waists and tied tight. Then their legs were pulled wide and around, and each woman had her ankles tied to those of the other, the bark of the tree harsh against their bellies and breasts.

It was an extraordinary position to be bound in. S saw the soldiers gather in a jostling circle around the tree, staring and some even rubbing their hands over their crotches. She knew that she and Gladys must make a powerfully erotic sight with their arms and legs wrapped around the tree and each other.

Two burly soldiers stepped out from the circle. They were tugging at their thick leather belts, and for a moment S was sure she and Gladys were about to be raped. One of the soldiers went behind Gladys while the other came around to her side of the tree. From the corner of her eye she saw him swing the belt high. He brought it down across her backside with a crack that made even some of the watching troops wince.

S's body tensed as though she had been electrocuted and her scream was almost as loud as the crack of the belt on the flinching globes of her backside. She heard another loud crack and felt Gladys's arms tense around her neck as she too was beaten. The strokes came alternately, first on S's squirming flesh then on Gladys's, as the two soldiers set up a rhythm of fire.

The position they had been tied in forced their bellies tight against the treetrunk, and with each fearsome swipe across her bottom S found her spread sex-lips pressing against the rough bark. The effect was hardly believable, for as the fire of the beating spread across her back and bottom another fire began to grow inexorably in her belly.

Soon, the tears streaming down her face were from shame at her lack of control as much as from the pain of the beating. The belt became almost an irrelevancy as her body twitched and writhed of its own accord. Even after the beating stopped S's pulsating torso kept on pumping against the rough trunk, oblivious to everything except the ferocious orgasm that was coursing through her sweating body.

She only became aware of her surroundings when she was suddenly cut free and fell onto her back on the hard ground. The soldier staring down at her still had his belt in his hand. With the speed of a snake, he whipped it down between her legs, sneering 'Whore!' as she screamed and clutched at her new agony, yet another unbidden orgasm shaking her.

S was a blank as she limped behind Gladys towards Nkwame's Land Rover. The soldier was right, she *was* a whore. She must be to behave the way she just had! The fire burning over the skin of her back and buttocks became nothing compared to the shame that flamed her cheeks to crimson.

Sergeant-major Nkwame was waiting for them by his vehicle. He had one of his shirts dangling from each hand. He avoided looking S in the eye, and her sense of shame at her wanton behaviour redoubled. The shirts were old-fashioned army khakis, with a few buttons at the neck and long tail-flaps which reached down to their knees. The sleeves were much too long, and both women had to roll them up to free their hands. They climbed into the back of the Land Rover in mutual silence, both stiff and sore from their beating.

They lay on opposite sides of the vehicle, for once not touching and comforting one another. S wondered what would befall them now this new, frightening leader had taken over. Although the regime under the so-called General and then sergeant-major Nkwame had been exhausting, at least it had been predictable and the soldiers had behaved with some discipline. This new leader appeared harsh and puritanical, yet his men had behaved much more raucously than Nkwame's when they had seen the naked girls. Would he have the same control over his troops as Nkwame?

The answer came when S peeped her head nervously through the canvas flaps at the back of the Land Rover. Nkwame, standing outside, shrugged his shoulders at her blushing request, and waved towards some bushes a hundred yards away. Gladys was asleep, so S scampered across the space alone, hoping nobody would notice her.

She was still squatting, the khaki shirt bunched up around her waist, when the soldiers appeared. There were three of them and they stood over her, grinning and rubbing their crotches until she finished. S dabbed herself dry with a handful of grass and stood up, blushing. She knew there was no point in trying to resist and walked quietly to where one of the soldiers pointed.

It was a small clearing among the thorn bushes, lush with thick grass. S could not understand what they were saying, but their gestures were blatantly clear. She reached down to the tails of the old army shirt, pulled it off over her head and hung it on a bush. When she turned to face the three soldiers they had all lain down their rifles and were tugging at their belts.

Despite their hurry to strip off and get at her, the soldiers became fascinated by S's body rings. They stared at them, and their fingers reached out and tugged at the steel in her nipples. They pulled harder than was comfortable, stretching her until she was conical and almost pulling her off-balance. They were even more fascinated by her pussy ring and tugged and tweaked it for an age – an age during which the effect on S was almost as wild as the episode at the tree had been.

She shut her eyes, feeling their hands on her, feeling the insistent tugging, knowing what was certainly about to happen. By the time she was borne down to the ground, spread on her back and felt her legs being raised high and wide, she was halfway there. As the first of them impaled her throbbing centre she began to come.

They took turns on her, each eager and too quick in his lust. Thick shafts pierced her and made her sob and gasp, and set her hips bucking and her legs clamping around them, only for them to spurt and pull out too soon, so that by the time the third of them entered her she was a wild thing, clutching at him with clawed fingers, pumping herself against him, screaming when she felt him begin to come, the muscles of her vagina writhing and milking him.

Afterwards, as she lay oblivious, the muscles of her belly and thighs still rippling from the aftermath, they rolled her over so that she lay face-down on the grass. One of them pulled his belt from the waist-loops of his discarded trousers.

They took turns to beat her just as they had taken turns to fuck her, the lashes whipping down on her pale flesh like bolts of lightning. It was as though they were angry with her, and S entered into a surreal state. She knew that they were beating her, that fire was searing her buttocks and thighs; she knew when they stopped whipping her with the awful belts and dragged her head up so that she could pleasure them with her mouth; she knew that she sucked each of them in turn and swallowed their essence. But she also knew, and this was what dominated, that she was in the midst of as powerful, awful, wonderful, shameful orgasm as she had ever experienced in her life, even with Nkwame.

The last soldier to come in her mouth gave her such a shove when he finished that she fell over onto her back. It was a while before she recovered enough to scramble up. She found the shirt she had been given to wear and pulled it on. The men were long gone. She walked stiffly back to Nkwame's Land Rover hoping that Gladys would not be ashamed of her when she told her what had happened.

Being confined to the back of Nkwame's Land Rover and subject to the new leader's puritanical rule did not prove much protection for the two girls. Whenever either of them went out to answer a call of nature, several soldiers would quietly sneak into the bushes around them and have their fun. Although the evening raffles were discontinued the girls' nights were at least as active as before, for as soon as Nkwame went off duty for the night men in twos and threes would creep into the vehicle, and it would bounce and sway for a while, and then furtive figures would slink away only to be replaced by another group of eager soldiers.

The only benefit so far as S and Gladys were concerned was that these new soldiers were much less careful about what they said. Indeed, some of them actually boasted about what the rebels' plans were.

As Gladys reassured S, 'You give a man a good time and make him think he's wonderful, he'll tell you anything.'

And they did. S took to sauntering towards the bushes when she needed to answer the call of nature, knowing that a group of men would soon be following her. She flirted with them and fluttered her eyelashes in admiration, caressed and sucked their manhoods with wild enthusiasm and worked hard at being what Gladys called 'a good fuck'.

One result was that she became very popular, though that very fact soon led to disaster. As usual, when she went into the bushes around mid-afternoon a number of eager men followed. They waited impatiently until she finished her business, and then moved in. There were half a dozen of them, and more seemed to be sneaking up. They got her on her back across a thick fallen treetrunk and came at her two at a time. She was already wet in anticipation when the first of them drove into her vagina, bucking like a beast, but her moans were cut off when a second man pulled her head back. His thick penis bumped against her cheek then her lips, and she opened her mouth for him. She had been taken by two men at a time before, but never in this position, her neck arched painfully back as her throat was ploughed, her spine grating on the treetrunk as the other soldier fucked her, wild in his lust.

The one fucking her came convulsively, and was

instantly replaced by another, just as wild. She gagged and choked when the man in her mouth climaxed, but hardly had time to swallow and catch her breath before another pair of hands grabbed her head and another thick glans pushed against her lips.

S was in the middle of a convulsive orgasm when it happened. She had no idea how many of them there had been, only that her neck ached and her back was in pain and neither mattered compared to the overwhelming pulsing in her thighs and belly as her sheath sucked at the cock ploughing it. She was so far gone that the shock of the men's sudden withdrawal took a few seconds to register. Then she became very scared.

Standing above her, looking down with furious eyes as S lay helpless across the treetrunk with her sex and mouth both still agape from his men's invasions, was their puritanical leader, the man who had called her a whore of Babylon, and had her beaten and confined. His eyes were bulging with rage and his body was stiff with anger. He shouted orders. The men who had grabbed her and thrown her into that shameful position, and then taken turns to slake their lust on her, instantly hauled her up.

They carried her aloft, her limbs all over the place like some rag doll, out from the bushes right through the ranks of parked trucks, and dumped her on the ground in front of their leader's tent. She barely managed to scramble to her feet before the leader himself arrived, still looking outraged. Luckily, the soldiers who had enjoyed her had not pulled her shirt off, so at least she was not naked as she stood before him, quaking with fright.

The small man who seemed to have so much power ranted for a long while, not at S but at his men, and in the local language so that the trembling girl could not understand more than a word here and there. Finally he turned towards S, his eyes cold and contemptuous. S found herself blushing as the man looked at her, then colouring even deeper as he spoke, his voice little more than a hiss.

In cold, well-modulated English he told S she was a whore and a slut. He sneered at her for being an insatiable temptress intent on sapping the strength of his men with her body. For a minute S was stung by the unfairness of what he said, but then had to admit to herself that there was an element of truth in it. She had flirted with his soldiers and worked to give them a good time, so in a way she *had* tried to be a temptress.

Her eyes flicked to the soldiers standing in a wide circle around them. Her blush felt as though it reached her ankles when she realised that there was not a single one of them who had not fucked her at least once during the past weeks, and most of them several times. The thought distracted her so much that the man bitterly berating her had to shout to regain her attention.

'You will go from here,' he was saying. 'I must protect my men from harlots such as you! I would have you flogged except that you seem to enjoy it, but you will be stripped and banished from here with nothing save my contempt! Sergeant-major! Deal with this slut!'

As the small, disdainful leader turned away the huge sergeant-major appeared at S's side. The contrast between the two men lived in their expressions as well as in their size, for Nkwame's eyes were sympathetic as he took S by her arm and led her away.

The assembled soldiers had fallen silent as Nkwame led S over to his Land Rover, although there was a chorus of cat-calls when he held out his hand and S pulled off the shirt and gave it to him. It had felt strange to wear the shirt after being unclothed for so long; now it felt awkward and embarrassing to be naked again. She was uncomfortably aware of a multitude of eyes on her back and bottom as Nkwame led her out of the camp.

When they had gone a hundred yards or so he spoke for the first time, quietly and without turning his head.

'I do not agree with this. No, don't look at me. I don't want them to suspect I am talking to you.'

S had been lost in fright and despair at the prospect of being sent alone and naked into the African bush, but her heart began to lift a little as Nkwame spoke.

'About half a mile from here you will find a knoll, a small hill, with three acacia trees and some scrub. Hide yourself there and wait. Now go. I will make sure nobody follows you.'

S found the knoll and concealed herself among the scrub at the base of the innermost tree. The wait felt like an eternity. The ground on which she curled herself was hard and gritty. As the sun finally descended she heard the snuffling and grunting of small animals coming from among the bushes. A snake slithered past, its head waving from side to side, but it ignored her and moved on and she was able to breathe again.

Somehow, despite her state of nerves, S fell asleep. She started up in fright when a hand shook her by the shoulder, but fell back with relief when she saw Nkwame's face smiling down at her. He offered her a canteen of water and a wrapped package which held a wad of bread and meat, and S realised how ravenous she was. She drank greedily and chewed on the food as though her life depended on it – which it probably did, she thought ruefully.

Nkwame had a bag with him, a military knapsack stuffed with a shirt, a pair of boots, a big knife, and more food. S examined the knapsack's contents with wonder and gratitude. Without a thought, she threw her arms around the huge man's neck and kissed him enthusiastically.

What began as a hug and kiss of sheer gratitude very quickly changed into something deeper, more passionate. The strength of his body, his warmth, the taste of his lips and his masculine smell all suddenly combined to set S writhing against him.

Nothing was said. With one arm she clung around his neck, kissing him softly while her free hand reached down to his groin. At first he was surprised and unready, but soon he began to respond. She tongued his mouth, her belly throbbing as she clung to him, crushing her breasts against the rough material of his shirt. Her hand worked at his belt and then his zip, scrabbling for the organ she now needed more than anything else in the world.

She almost ripped his trousers in her eagerness to get at him. She writhed around as his penis filled her hand. She pulled him out from the restraining cloth of his trousers, and dipped her head towards him. He surged into fullness as her mouth found him, greedy, eager, revelling in his taste and hotness.

As her mouth slurped ravenously on his hot erection, Nkwame lifted S by her knees, moved her around, set her down astride his head. His mouth found her, his tongue searching, finding, sending her wild, as her own mouth worked on him as though she was a starveling, sucking and guzzling in time to the voluptuous motions of his mouth between her legs. His tongue flicked into her entrance then teased the nub of her clitoris before lapping at the entire length of her oozing slit, then probing her vagina again. She sobbed with passion as she moved her head up and down, engulfing his length with frantic lips.

She wailed when he suddenly heaved her off, then moaned with gratitude when he span her round and planted her down astride his loins, his cock sliding into her in a single, wonderful, welcomed, over-whelming thrust that had her coming instantly. He fucked her violently even though she was the one on top, his hands hard on her backside, and he came very quickly, flooding her with delicious heat.

She swooned down onto his chest, her strength spent but her sheath still clinging to the shaft that impaled her. He did not withdraw. Clasping her in his powerful arms, he rolled them both over until S was on her back on the grass, his body heavy on hers, his cock already stirring back to life. It felt wonderful as he grew inside her, and more wonderful as he began to move, gently at first, and with increasing power, until S was moaning and clasping him with frantic thighs, her hands clawing at his back and shoulders as she bucked and shuddered into yet another orgasm.

She came back to reality when he withdrew, lifting his warm weight off her, kissing her softly on her brow. He murmured some words, but she was too far gone to register them. She pulled the shirt over herself in lieu of a blanket and drifted into a delicious sleep filled with dreams of wondrous sensations and soft caresses and seeking lips.

'Hey, child! Come awake! We got to get away from here!'

It was Gladys. Somehow she had escaped from the rebel camp, and was shaking S roughly to get her alert. It was not quite dawn, though the sky to the east was beginning to lighten.

'Get that shirt on. Grab the bag,' Gladys hissed, her mouth close to S's ear. 'We got to run before they look for me. Come on. Come *on*!'

She practically dragged S to her feet and threw the army shirt over her head, then grabbed her hand and started to jog towards the horizon, away from the soldiers' camp. They ran for a long time, S gasping and stumbling, Gladys pulling her along. At last they fell into a clump of shrubs and lay panting and gasping, S in a far worse state than Gladys from lack of fitness and strength.

They hid there all the rest of the day and into nightfall, nibbling at the food Nkwame had given S and sipping from the canteen of water, but mostly watching out to see whether their escape had been detected. They saw the dust-trails of vehicles driving fast in all directions. Some even came close to where they lay hidden, close enough for them to hear voices shouting. But none of the searchers thought to check out the little patch of scrub in which they lay curled and breathless with nerves.

At full dark the two women sneaked out and began to walk. The night was chilly and there were lots of animal noises. S clung to Gladys's hand for reassurance; she had been out in the African night before, but never without men and guns around. This was much more frightening. She visualised lions leaping on her, jackals snapping at her throat. Nothing of the kind happened. Instead, Gladys marched her briskly forward into the night, chiding her when she stumbled, encouraging her when she complained of being tired, even teasing her into rueful giggles at one stage by commenting on how much stamina 'that sergeant-major Nkwame' had, and how he could 'make a girl real shattered'.

They stopped twice during the night to drink and nibble some food, and Gladys refilled the canteen from a tinkling spring. As the sun began to rise they found a hide-away among some rocks and thorn bushes and settled down to wait out the day. Through sheer exhaustion S at once fell into a deep sleep, despite the discomfort of the rocky ground. She was soon joined by an almost equally tired Gladys.

Twelve

Shouts and a hard stabbing pain in her side brought S stumbling awake. The sun was high and almost blinded her to the figures of several men looming over her, one of whom was poking her with the handle of a spear. Gladys was receiving the same treatment, and the two women clung together in shock and fright.

The men were tall and naked except for bands of animal fur around their biceps and calves, heavy necklaces of animal teeth, and huge bone earrings. They all carried spears and wooden clubs, and their bodies were decorated with intricate patterns of cicatrices.

'Killibaso,' Gladys whispered. 'Very fierce. Keep still. Do what they say.'

The men moved around the two huddled women, occasionally poking one or the other of them with a spear handle. At a fierce gesture the two women stood up and moved off in the direction the men indicated, keeping very close together, the men close behind herding them along.

As they walked, their pace dictated by sharp jabs from spear butts, Gladys was able to tell S a little about what was happening – and in doing so made S much more scared than she already was. These were men of a tribe called the Killibaso, a nomadic people who lived by cattle herding. Nobody knew much about them except that they refused to change from their old way of living, had a ferocious reputation, and were alleged to drink blood. What made the situation worse, Gladys added, was that she did not speak their language.

'Just go along with them,' she hissed. 'They can't be as bad as all that. They haven't hurt us yet.'

The terrain through which they were moving was broken and hilly, but the men set a pace which soon had even Gladys panting and stumbling. There was no let-up, though, until they crested a low ridge and saw below them a crude but surprisingly large camp. It comprised little more than two circles of piled thorn bushes, one huge and containing a mass of browsing cattle, the second smaller and crammed with tumbledown shelters, fireplaces and people. It was towards this one that S and Gladys were shepherded.

Their arrival caused a sensation. The men herding them ululated in high-pitched tones which carried over the long distance to the camp. In minutes people were pouring out through the only gap in the thorn fence and scampering up the slope towards them, and soon S and Gladys were surrounded. Holding hands and expecting the worst the two women shuffled, heads bent, through the crowd and into the camp.

Not a single one of these Killibaso people wore any clothing, not even a loincloth, but all of them were festooned with necklaces, bracelets, anklets, and nose- and earrings, and the women and girls all had multi-coloured beads woven into their hair. They were unnervingly quiet but their faces seemed curious rather than menacing.

The two captives were shepherded to a small clearing in the middle of the camp. People crowded close around them, and inquisitive hands reached out for their hair and the military shirts they were still wearing – but they were tentative hands, seeking rather than prying. Gladys's description of this tribe's reputation had prepared S for the worst, yet somehow they seemed gentle rather than frightening, as though they found the two women interesting but little more.

Since she was white, S was more interesting than Gladys to the people crowding around, at least to judge by the number of hands that reached for her hair or touched her face and hands. Some of the hands rubbed her cheeks as though they suspected that the whiteness of her skin might rub off. Other hands plucked at the material of her shirt, then pressed against it to feel the body beneath. When somebody lifted the back of the shirt, S squealed and pushed it back down again in a reaction of instinctive shyness which made her feel rather silly and embarrassed.

Just then a gap appeared in the crowd and a tall man grasping a long staff in one hand came through. He had a russet-coloured blanket draped across his shoulder, dozens of necklaces festooning his chest, and a thick gold ring through his left nostril as well as a pair of stone earrings so heavy they dragged his lobes nearly down to his shoulders. Apart from that he was as naked as the rest of the Killibaso, but even so seemed to exude an aura of enormous dignity.

He stood in front of the two women and looked at them for a long time, his eyes piercing and shrewd. The crowd became entirely still and silent. At last he spoke, his voice quiet but assured. He looked questioningly from Gladys to S and back again. When they both looked blank he spoke again. This time Gladys understood him and replied. At the same time she dropped to her knees and bowed her head, pulling S down with her.

As the man continued to speak S turned her head to ask Gladys what was going on, but Gladys hissed at her to shut up. There came a pause and Gladys spoke herself, keeping her head bowed. To judge from the rhythm of the exchanges, an inquisition ensued, the man asking long questions and Gladys hurrying to respond. Suddenly, Gladys turned to S.

'Take your shirt off,' she hissed. 'Stay kneeling down and get your shirt off!' At S's horrified expression, she added '*Do* it! He is the Chief of the tribe. His word is the law. He wants to know if you are a real human being and the same colour all over! Do it!'

S knelt up and hauled the shirt off over her head, acutely aware of the gasps from the crowd pressing all around as she revealed her pale nakedness. She expected dozens of hands to reach for her as she bowed her head again, but no such thing happened. Instead, Gladys acted as interpreter in what became an almost balletic process of inspection and exploration.

S stood up when Gladys told her to, and kept absolutely still as the Chief of the Killibaso tribe stepped forward. He ran his hands briskly over her shoulders and arms, pinching her flesh to check its firmness. He pulled her lips apart to inspect her teeth. When he squeezed her breasts S winced involuntarily, for his grip was very hard.

He seemed fascinated by her nipple rings, leaning close to examine the piercings and flicking and tugging the rings themselves for long moments. He called something and a young woman stepped out of the crowd to stand beside S. She was the same height as S and her figure was similar. The man reached forward and slapped the undersides of the girl's breasts, then did the same to S, as though he was comparing them. He gave yet another tug at S's rings then gripped the other girl's nipples between his fingers and thumbs and pulled at them. It must have been painful for the girl but she accepted it stoically.

He launched into a loud speech, gesturing towards S's breasts and then the other girl's, bouncing and tugging each of them in turn. After a while he turned towards Gladys and a rapid conversation ensued. S could not tell what was being said, but felt by the changing expressions on Gladys's face that it was yet another and this time more intimate inquisition. At one of Gladys's responses the man suddenly stooped and reached for S's crotch.

Over the last weeks her hair had regrown down there and her pubic ring was more or less concealed. His fingers soon found it though, scrabbling through her bush and scratching her a little. He hooked a finger through the ring and pulled on it, snapping a remark to Gladys.

'He says to get your legs open. He want to check you out.' Gladys had not shifted from her kneeling position and she had to crane her neck around to look up at S. The girl beside her had already adopted a new position, her feet wide apart and her knees bent so that her crotch was pushed forward. S at once followed suit, finding the position awkward and difficult to maintain. It became even more difficult when the man leaned down and began to tug persistently on her pussy ring as he explored her crease with hard fingers. He released S for a moment to feel the other girl, then returned to probe S even more deeply.

To her chagrin S found that even in this strange and outlandish situation the action of the man's hand between her legs was making her wet. She became so distracted that Gladys had to repeat the next translated instruction. Quickly, S turned and bent to touch her toes. She blushed at the realisation of the view she must be presenting to the man, but the thought only served to increase her state of involuntary arousal.

The man rubbed his hands over her lower back and then down over her buttocks. He squeezed them and prodded them mercilessly. He pulled them apart, and S gave a hiss of shock as he suddenly probed the pucker of her anus. He felt the length of her legs as though he was inspecting some animal or other, then turned and addressed the kneeling Gladys directly. Since she had not been told she could move, S remained in her uncomfortable and undignified position.

After what felt like a very long while Gladys told S that she could stand up. 'He says thank you for being polite,' said Gladys to S's astonishment. 'He says he has seen ghost people before – he means whites – but only from far away. He says he is sorry for you that you have no colour, but is pleased that you are built like a real person.'

S glanced at the man and blushed. He had checked very thoroughly that she was 'built like a real person'!

'He says he thinks your rings are pretty and has ordered that his Killibaso women will have them.' Gladys paused and had to suppress a giggle as she continued. 'He also want to know if you can take a man like a real woman can. I told him yes. I said you are a real woman even if you *are* a ghost person.'

There was a pause as Gladys considered how she could phrase what she had to say next.

'He says that as a token of his gratitude for your kindness in letting him see a ghost person up close he

168

will lend you some of his young men for your pleasure.'

It took a moment for the significance of what Gladys had said to sink in, then S gasped with shock. She span around to face Gladys, her mouth agape. She was stopped short by the fact that Gladys was obviously struggling to suppress her laughter.

Gladys was barely able to control her giggles as she explained all to an alternately incredulous and embarrassed S. It was apparently a religious belief among the Killibaso that women were the life-source, linked to the mother spirit of the earth. In honour of this, men were required to serve their physical needs. Since S was a ghost person, she had clearly not received such service before and the Chief was offering it as a gift of gratitude.

S found herself in the middle of a bizarre ceremony. All the men in the camp lined up in front of her as the women and children backed away to form a wide circle. Gladys had hissed at her that it would be regarded as an insult to the tribe if she did not go through with this, and now she was standing naked, looking at a line of equally naked tribesmen, and required to select some of them 'for her pleasure'!

It became more than bizarre. The men began to dance, their line waving backwards and forwards, their feet stamping in unison. The light gleamed from their limbs and torsos, their chestnut-hued skins glossy as though burnished. S felt disorientated; she had been displayed for other people many times; never had people displayed themselves for her.

She had to choose. How could she choose? The men danced back and forth, back and forth, their rhythm almost mesmeric. Distractedly, not really capable of thinking about what was going on, she pointed to one of the men, who whooped and ran out of the line to stand grinning behind her. After a minute she pointed to another man, younger than the first, and blushed as he too whooped and ran to stand behind her, his penis already pointing to the sky in anticipation of what was about to happen.

S was totally disorientated by what was going on. She was picking out men from a dancing line, men who were going to fuck her because their Chief wanted to show his tribe's gratitude for her politeness. The whole concept was staggering to a woman who less than six months ago had been a shy secretary in provincial England.

She picked out a third man, then, in obedience to Gladys's urgent whisper, a fourth and a fifth. It seemed that five was regarded as a lucky number by the Killibaso. Then Gladys's voice broke through S's distraction.

'The Chief says can you change one,' she called, her voice urgent. 'He says you are very pretty for a ghost person and he would be honoured if you would pick him.'

S looked at Gladys bemusedly. This was all becoming too confusing.

'Send one of them away!' Gladys's tone was anxious and insistent. 'Send one of them away and pick the Chief. Only five are allowed, and you didn't pick him. Pick him now!'

In a daze, S gestured to one of the men she had previously chosen, then pointed to the Chief. He stepped forward with a wide grin. The man she had rejected looked angry for a moment, but the Chief pushed him aside and took his place in the line behind her. S looked wildly at Gladys, wondering what on earth to do next. The matter was taken out of her hands and, literally, into the men's.

All five of them, including the Chief, moved close

and began to caress her with gentle hands. They were not the touches of men seeking to get pleasure from exploring a woman's body, but those of hands wishing to give pleasure – and knowledgeable in how to do so. At first S was desperately aware of the fact that she was standing up, in the open air, surrounded by watching eyes as five pairs of hands played on her senses. Soon though, everything disappeared except the intensity of her reactions.

They used their fingernails, with tantalising delicacy, to scratch insidiously at the inner parts of her elbows and up towards her armpits. They caressed her calves and the backs of her knees. Their hands smoothed over her neck and shoulders. They ran over her spine and buttocks with the delicacy of butterflies.

Then, just as she was beginning to become breathless from the excitation of it, they stopped. As one, the hands left her and the men moved back. They were replaced in an instant by a posse of laughing, giggling girls, who grabbed S and pulled her off to one side. They brought scented water and washed her down, leaving no part untouched. They rubbed her dry with soft cloths, then combed her hair with wooden combs, all the while giggling and kissing her. Like their Chief, the girls were fascinated by S's body rings and spent a lot of time touching and examining them, whispering wide-eyed among themselves then bursting into fits of giggles and tweaking one another's nipples.

It was almost sundown by the time the girls finished with S, then a group of older women arrived bearing bowls and trays. One of them spread some kind of animal skin on the ground and gestured S to sit down. The rest of the women knelt around her and began to feed her with tit-bits from their bowls. She was not allowed to do anything for herself, but had to submit to being fed from the fingers of half a dozen different women. The food was delicious, small pieces of roasted meats, crisp vegetables, pieces of tangy fruits.

At first S felt awkward and silly leaning this way and that to accept pieces of food from other women's hands, but then the experience took on an oddly luxurious nature. It began to feel as though she was a princess being served by humble retainers; one of the women even dabbed her mouth and chin clear of grease from the meat after each mouthful.

The illusion was dented somewhat when she was offered a drink in a bent and battered enamel mug. The drink was a cloudy copper colour, and tasted rather like very sweet sherry. There was rather a lot of it but they kept putting the mug to her lips, so S drank it all. It felt warm as it went down to her stomach, and by the time she had finished it all S felt quite light-headed. Then the men came for her again, the Chief and the four others.

They had decorated themselves with new, more extravagant jewellery and their bodies were painted with elaborate designs. They looked both eager and respectful as they took S's hands and led her back to the centre of the clearing. A thick pile of animal skins had been spread. They lay her down upon it, and spread her limbs wide.

S gave no resistance because Gladys had ordered her to go along with whatever happened. But what was happening felt as though it was out of some wild fantasy.

The men spread her on top of the bed of animal skins, a soft bed, thick with fur. They eased her arms and legs wide until she was no more than a living X. Then they began to caress her body and limbs with

172

bunches of feathers. At first the sensations were only confusing, as though they merely intended to tickle her. Then they became more purposeful, stroking her neck and arms, her feet and legs, her shoulders and temples. The sensations set her skin tingling and she drifted into a sort of dreamy voluptuousness. It felt wonderful.

The feather brushes ignored her breasts and belly, places which became more and more eager for their touch. S was on a cloud of luxury but at the same time began to feel a growing, increasingly urgent need swelling inside her.

When her body began to move towards the insidious brushings the men began to use their hands as well as the feathers. Now they did not neglect her breasts, nor the vulva which undulated towards their touches. Five hands and five bunches of feathers caressed her increasingly sensitive skin, setting off sparks of delicious sensation in every part of her body. They were soon joined by five tongues and pairs of lips, kissing and licking her from her brow to the soles of her feet.

Two mouths began to suck and nibble on her breasts and S sighed with the luxury of it. When another mouth descended between her spread legs she groaned and pushed herself towards it. Her eyelids drifted open and she became aware, as though from a distance, that what looked like the whole tribe had gathered around to watch what was happening. It did not matter, though, as the tongue between her legs set off shards of brilliant sensation in her nerve-ends, and other mouths drew on her swollen nipples.

At some stage one of the men entered her. She had no idea which one. It did not matter. All that existed in the universe at that moment was the glorious sensation of a hard cock thrusting deep into her, and the star-burst of her instant, slow, shattering orgasm – an orgasm which seemed to go on and on and grow and grow as the men fucked her in turn, each more concerned with her pleasure than their own; each competing with the others to rouse her as high as possible.

S was hardly conscious of when one man pulled out of her and another took his place, nor when her head began flailing from side to side, nor of the applause from the watching crowd when she wailed and bucked and clamped her arms and legs around the man fucking her in a fit of such heightened orgasm it had her body jerking like a fish on a spear and almost threw the man off her.

When S swam into consciousness next day Gladys was beside her. Her body ached and between her legs felt puffy and swollen. Gladys had a strange expression on her face as she handed S her shirt, one of mixed solicitude and amusement.

'They gave you a hard time,' she said, her voice warm but struggling to control a chuckle. 'But you saw them off, child! You surely did! You was still going like a civet when the last of them cried off!'

S was too woozy to appreciate the full connotations of Gladys's vivid phrase at the time, but she did later and frequently blushed in private at the image of herself 'going like a civet' until she had exhausted five eager men!

'Anyway,' Gladys continued, her tone more serious. 'The Chief gave me a message for you. He says that he would be honoured if you would become his wife. He says he will give you a lot of babies and make sure his other wives do not beat you too much.'

As S gazed up at her open-mouthed with shock, Gladys suddenly giggled and hugged her.

'It's all right, though,' she laughed. 'He says that if you are not willing to have his babies he will let us have some guides to take us back to Master!'

The very thought sent a glow of happiness through S, a happiness which grew as Gladys helped her to the nearby stream to bathe her exhausted body then organised a breakfast of fruits and mealie porridge and ewers of cool water.

While they were eating the Chief appeared. He was smiling, his posture erect and proud. He stood above them as they sat with bowls in their hands. S suddenly felt very embarrassed. She could not drag her eyes away from the join of his thighs, nor her mind from the thought that last night – only last night! – she had taken not only him but four other men as well, and fucked them to a finish. What had been in that drink the women gave her? She did not know whether to feel proud or ashamed, but the tenderness between her legs reminded her that she had not escaped entirely unscathed.

The Chief and Gladys spoke together for a few minutes, his voice at first firm and jovial but then increasingly disappointed at what sounded like Gladys's refusals. At last he shrugged his shoulders in resignation then turned to address S, giving her a brief bow before speaking. Gladys translated.

'He says you are a powerful woman. He is sorry you will not become his wife because you will one day breed strong warriors. He hopes the man you select to be your mate will be worthy of you and always be hard in his cock for your pleasure.'

Blushing, S could not help noticing that the Chief's own cock was distinctly swollen.

'He says he is going now to arrange our escort party and wishes us a safe journey,' Gladys continued. As the Chief turned to walk away she gripped S by the wrist. 'In their world it is polite to show thanks!' she hissed urgently.

S looked at her in confusion. 'But what – how?'

With a single brief glance Gladys indicated what and how, and raised her eyebrows questioningly.

'Oh! Oh!' said S as the realisation of what Gladys meant dawned on her. 'But I can't, honest I can't. I'm ever so tender down there and . . .'

'There are other ways!' Gladys's voice was even more urgent as the Chief moved further away. By the time S understood what Gladys was referring to the Chief was some distance away and talking to a group of his warriors.

However, when the Chief returned with a party of three tall, spear-carrying men, the matter had been settled between Gladys and a blushing S.

'I have told him that you wish to show respect and gratitude to him in the manner of your people,' Gladys told S after a brief exchange with the man.

Without a word, S moved to kneel at his feet, her hands reaching forward. He was already naked so there was no preamble, no fumbling with clothing to reach his manhood. Hot with self-consciousness, wishing she could do this somewhere private rather than out in the open under the gaze of several other obviously interested men, yet also strangely aroused by the whole situation, S began to caress the Chief.

Despite his exertions of last night he became erect very quickly. His scent was fresh and clean, but none the less heady, as S moved her mouth onto him. His heat, his taste on her tongue, his aroma on her breath, became hypnotic. S lost all sense of anything save what she was doing to the cock filling her hands and mouth. There was no Gladys; no watching warriors; no sound of lowing cattle in the background; nothing save the satin-on-iron hardness of the instrument her greedy mouth was working on.

He was not nearly as big as Nkwame, nor even the General. For a tiny instant S wondered whether she should have offered him the place the General had preferred. But what she was doing now was clearly more than acceptable. He kept still as she worked on him, her hands fluttering, her mouth slurping. It took a long time, for she had pretty well drained him last night.

When he did at last come it was brief and easy to swallow, but he gave a great bellow of triumph and the watching warriors as well as every man, woman and child of the tribe within earshot whooped and ululated with joy. S gave him a few more licks and sucks to finally finish him off, only stopping when she felt him give a final shudder and put a hand on her brow to push her away. A strange feeling of deep-lying power had replaced her earlier embarrassment. Last night she had taken this man and four of his tribesmen to exhaustion; now, she had milked him dry yet again, until it was he rather than she who called the thing to a halt.

There was a new lift to her head, a new sway to her hips as she rose from her knees and walked over to join Gladys. Now she was ready for their journey away from the Killibaso and back to Prince Kano. The expression in Gladys's eyes confirmed her new understanding. She was, as Gladys had said repeatedly, a real woman – and as a woman she could out-last, out-do and out-fuck any man, anywhere!

Then her beloved Kano flashed into her mind and she suddenly felt guilty and ashamed. Had she been disloyal to him? Had she behaved like a whore? Would he understand and forgive her?

The thoughts nagged at her as the small party of

Gladys, S and their three escorts walked away from the village of the Killibaso, scarcely thirty hours after they had entered it.

Thirteen

The three guides treated the women with great respect. They knew S was tired after last night and set a gentle pace, with frequent breaks to rest and drink water. Around mid-day they found a sheltered spot by a small stream and gestured the women to lie down while they gathered wood and built a small fire.

S was asleep almost instantly, and was awakened nearly two hours later by the aroma of roasting meat. The men had created a substantial meal of meat and fruits which they served to the women on slabs of hot, unleavened bread.

'What I heard about these Killibaso was wrong,' said Gladys between mouthfuls. 'They look fierce but really they're nice. And I didn't see anybody drinking blood!'

Then she began to giggle.

'Mind you, girl,' she said at last, almost hiccuping with laughter. 'Wanting to fuck you to show respect and thanks is a bit different from what we're used to!'

Suddenly both Gladys and S were howling with laughter at the incongruity of it. The three Killibaso guides looked on in amazement as the women screeched and clung together and pounded each other's backs and shoulders, tears streaming down their faces, their lungs gulping for breath. When at last the women regained some control the men had drawn back from them and were looking nervous, as though they thought S and Gladys had gone a little mad.

The guides treated the women with even more deference during the afternoon march than they had in the morning, as though they were now rather frightened as well as respectful. S felt strangely uncomfortable being treated this way by three tall and naked warriors. Everything she had experienced in recent months told her that it should be she who was showing respect, she who was scampering around to assist the men rather than the other way round. It became even more disorientating at the evening camp.

The men had got a fire going and cooked a meal. They had gathered great bunches of long grass to make beds, and erected shelters of brush. Then, just as the women were settling down for the night beneath their shelter, two of the guides appeared at its entrance. Having just bathed themselves in the stream S and Gladys were as naked as the men, but somehow that seemed more natural than to be wearing their shirts. The men had discarded their spears and stood in front of the shelter looking oddly shy, lacing and unlacing their fingers nervously. One of them, the boldest, made a hesitant and protracted speech to Gladys, who looked first surprised and then amused. When the man finished she turned to S with a wry smile on her face.

'He says he is very sorry but Mankolobu, his Lion Chief, has ordered them to keep us warm.' Gladys could hardly contain her laughter as she explained to an increasingly incredulous S. 'He says he knows you are a powerful woman and he is not enough for you, but he will be shamed if you do not give him permission, and not be able to hold his head up. And by the way, the other one is for me!'

Gladys's eyes locked on S's, their expression a mixture of lust and hilarity. Her eyes flicked across to 'the other one', the younger of the two men to judge from appearances. He was staring at the ground and shuffling his feet shyly.

'Come on!' she whispered, grabbing S by the arm. 'We can't shame them. Besides,' she grinned suggestively. 'My one is pretty, and unlike you I slept alone last night!'

The guides had erected three separate shelters. Reluctantly, S stood and walked towards the second of them, the guide following her closely. From the corner of her eye she saw Gladys's hands reach out and pull the other guide into the shelter she had just left. The noises began almost at once.

S's own guide, the warrior who had been ordered to 'keep her warm', was by now as nervous as his companion had been. In the inadequate light of the dying camp fire she stooped to get into the brushwood shelter and lay down on the thick mattress of grasses which had been piled inside. Last night had been hectic and demanding and she was not really ready for this, but Gladys had wanted it so there was no real choice.

They had no language in common, but by his demeanour and his eyes S's warrior seemed to be seeking permission for everything that followed. It was as if his whole reason for existence was to please her. By now, S was so accustomed to the sharp order or the click of the fingers when a man required her to spread her legs for his pleasure that this new circumstance was both confusing and heady.

The guide did not jump on her as so many others had, even though she lay down compliantly at his gesture. Instead, he touched and kissed and caressed her oh, so gently. Her toes; the soles of her feet; her calves and the backs of her knees; her arms and neck. His fingertips and tongue were like the wings of a moth, quick, light, overwhelmingly teasing.

He began to kiss her breasts, so softly his lips hardly seemed to touch her skin. He was above her, concentrating hard on working to please her. His penis was fully erect, but he had not once tried to pressure her with it. She reached up and took hold of him, pulling him towards her mouth, lifting her head to make it easier. He gasped as her mouth closed over him, then kept very still as she suckled.

With the flexibility of an athlete he moved around and then his mouth was at her centre, his tongue lapping, his fingers pulling her open to gain greater access. She moved with him. His tongue flicked between her clitoris and the weeping entrance to her vagina, tracing the length of her tingling sex-lips. She undulated under his attentions, moving her mouth on his cock in rhythm to the touches of his probing tongue.

In a red-tinged dream she became aware that he had pulled his cock out of her greedy mouth and that his tongue had left her pulsing sex. There was a moment of lostness, then she wailed as he thrust into her, his hips crushing down onto hers, his body hard on her chest.

He took a long time, holding himself back and fucking her slow and deep while S writhed beneath him, surrendering to come after glorious come. He was very gentle yet disturbingly powerful, and kept her going and going until she was dizzy and aching. At one stage she found herself praying that he would come, but he did not, and was still fucking her when she drifted into exhausted sleep. She knew next morning that he had come at some point, and very copiously, for it was still leaking out of her, but she felt good as she nestled against his warm, muscular body, breathing in the cool morning air mingled with his musky scent.

Gladys also seemed to feel good to judge by the expression on her face when she crawled out of her own shelter next morning. Both women felt oddly coy as they bathed together in the stream, glancing at one another but saying little. Then, as though reading each other's minds, they burst into fits of giggles and clung together gasping and hiccuping with merriment.

'How long do you think it will take us to get back to the palace?' S asked when she was at last able to breathe again and get some self-control.

'Don't know,' Gladys replied after a moment's thought. Then she grinned impishly. 'But after last night I hope it's not 'til tomorrow!'

S stared at Gladys in astonishment, but the mischievous expression in her eyes was contagious and soon both women were laughing again. They were still giggling as they walked back to the camp site, their shirts bundled in their hands as they let the air dry their bodies.

Their guides had revived the camp fire and had already prepared a breakfast of mealie-porridge and an infusion of a tea-like drink made with leaves from a small pouch one of them carried. Both women were ravenously hungry after their hectic night, and even though the porridge had to be eaten with their hands out of a communal basin they positively wolfed it down, with no concessions at all to good manners. Between mouthfuls they gulped down swallows of the tea, which proved to be delicious.

The atmosphere among the group was relaxed and easy. The men talked among themselves as, the meal finished, they took the pots down to the stream to wash them and to bathe themselves. S found herself watching in fascination as the men splashed and cavorted in the stream, the early morning sun making their lithe bodies glow and glitter. A wry comment from Gladys brought her back to earth.

'You'll be licking your lips any minute.'

S coloured; Gladys had read what she had been thinking.

'They're beautiful, aren't they.' Gladys's voice had taken on a husky, slightly amused tone. 'I don't know what they feed them on, nor how their mothers bring them up, but my one last night surely gave me a good time.'

S found herself blushing more deeply at the realisation that what Gladys was saying reflected exactly her own feelings. Her man, too, had given her 'a good time' last night, and she felt a bit guilty about just how good it had been. Always, up until now, it had been she who was required to work to please her lover – Erika, Kano, baas, whoever. To be among men who believed the opposite, who believed that it was the man who should work to please the woman, was a bit unsettling.

It became even more unsettling when the party was ready to set off on its morning march. One of the men came up to where the women stood, their shirts on, ready for the journey. He spoke haltingly to Gladys, looking all the while at S. His posture showed deference, as though he was nervously asking some great favour. Gladys turned towards S, making an obvious attempt to stifle hilarity.

'He says he watched you using his Chief for the custom of your people yesterday. He says he is sorry he is not the Chief, but if you are prepared to accept second-best he is at your service.'

Gladys could barely contain a chuckle as she

spoke, but became serious and even a little irritated when S's face went blank with incomprehension.

'What he means, you foolish child,' Gladys continued, 'is that he thinks ghost-person women need to begin their day by drinking a man's seed. He thinks you need it to keep up your strength, and is offering you his own seed because the Chief is not here.'

S's face was still blank, but now from shock and confusion rather than incomprehension. She certainly comprehended the meaning of what Gladys was telling her, but was stunned by the connotations.

Gladys was still talking, but S was unable to register the words. The man responded to a gesture from Gladys and lay down on his back on the ground. Feeling as though she was being operated by remote control S moved to kneel beside him, her whole being focused on the join of his long, smooth thighs. What disorientated her most was not what she was about to do, but that she suddenly, urgently wanted to do it more than anything else.

Then she was not a robot but a body, her senses throbbing into life. She felt her breasts swelling and her nipples becoming almost painfully hard as she reached down and ran her hands across the man's hard-muscled belly. His skin was smooth and warm, as if it had been oiled. Her fingers snagged for a moment in the bush of thick hair at his loins, but then she had him, curling her fingers around his tight balls, dropping her head down to smell and taste him. He rose up towards her, his thick glans already showing a clear droplet of excitement in its single eye.

She leaned further forward, the tip of her tongue lapping up the almost tasteless dewdrop, then swirled her tongue around his thickness. He was iron-hard and already throbbing. An instinct told her to engulf him at once, and she did – just in time, for he burst into orgasm even as her lips closed over him.

It was not enough. It was too quick. She kept her mouth on him as she swallowed, her hand caressing his shaft and balls. She worked on him gently, instinctively employing every skill she had ever learned to keep him going. He began to soften a little after his orgasm but she only worked on him harder, wanting this, wanting to breathe him, feel him with her hands and tongue and lips. Drink him. She did not know it, but the hand that was not stroking his shaft snaked down between her legs and began an almost frantic circling of her engorged clitoris.

S was in full, voluptuous orgasm before she managed to bring the guide to a second eruption, making him groan with the effort of it. It was only when, an eternity later, Gladys tapped her on her shoulder and S realised she still had the poor man's shrinking cock in her mouth and was still fingering herself wildly, that she began to come down to earth again. It took a few minutes for the embarrassment of it to hit, but then and for the rest of the morning's march S was blushing inwardly as well as outwardly about her brazen behaviour.

Most of the time she walked with her head down, worrying about what her Master Kano would think when he found out, and worried as well that Gladys must surely think her a complete slut. At the same time as her mind was examining her shame, however, her body was tingling with life. Never had the scents of grasses and shrubs seemed so acute and heady. Never had the colours and shapes of the countryside through which they walked been so clear and vibrant. Even the movement of the air felt delicious on her skin, so delicious that halfway through the morning she shrugged off her shirt to feel it better.

Walking naked through this countryside felt glorious, and her shame and guilt inevitably left her. The breeze toyed with her hair and played across her torso. Her limbs felt long and beautiful. Her breasts seemed full and heavy, while her head was light and happy. When Gladys grabbed her hand S had to focus closely to understand what she was saying.

'I think it was something in the tea.' Her voice seemed to be coming through water. 'The tea must have had something in it. I have never felt so strange in my life. Like I'm hot for anything. Like I'm so sexed up I'm ready to burst!'

At Gladys's words a small window of reality opened near the back of S's brain. Yes, probably the tea had had something in it, something that had helped the guides perform so well and for so long last night, something that was now making her feel luxurious and disorientated. Then the memory of last night and this morning closed the window again. Her body felt the movement of the breeze; her blood moved to a languid beat. She smiled at Gladys and shrugged her shoulders, taking her hand and strolling along behind their three tall, muscular guides.

S herself did not feel 'sexed up', as Gladys put it, but somehow a bit more alive than usual, and more relaxed and aware. The rustle of the breeze in the long grass through which they were walking became almost musical. The gleam of light on the backs of their guides was fascinating, a kaleidoscope of mahogany and gold playing over their skins as their muscles moved.

Their bodies had, she decided, a cat-like grace which could only be called beautiful. They were all tall and slender, the muscles of their backs and buttocks perfectly delineated, their long legs moving easily over the ground. One of them had a small scar to the left of his spine, in the area of his kidney. Another had very obvious scratches on his shoulders and ribs, scratches which could only have been made by clawing fingers, and S suddenly wondered whether it was her hands or Gladys's which had put them there last night. Oddly, the thought was not as embarrassing as it might once have been. She could not tell from the back which one of them had been with her last night, and which had been with Gladys – and it did not seem to matter at all.

The Killibaso guides once again found a sheltered spot for the mid-day break, this time a copse of thorn trees and scrub around a limpid water hole. S spread her shirt in the shade of a tree and lay down, propping her head on one hand and watching languidly as the three naked men gathered wood for a fire and fetched water for cooking. She soon drifted into a gentle sleep, to be woken later by an odd noise, a cross between keening and yelping.

She raised herself onto her elbows and looked sleepily across the little clearing. One of the guides was stirring a small cauldron suspended above the fire, from which wafted the smell of some kind of stew. Another was sitting cross-legged and facing her, sharpening the blade of his spear with a stone. S swung her head around towards the left, the direction from which the noise seemed to be coming, and sat up straight in surprise.

The third native guide was five or six yards away, lying on his back, his body rigid and his face screwed tight with effort. Gladys was astride him, her face too screwed tight as her full breasts bounced and swayed to the frantic speed with which her pelvis jerked on his cock as she fucked him so wildly that her cries of pleasure were intermingled with audible squelching noises from between her legs, and a stream of her glistening juices covered the man's belly and balls.

S watched with amazement as Gladys rode the man, her face tense with effort and ecstasy, the muscles of her belly and thighs spasming through what was obviously not her first, nor even her second orgasm. Suddenly the man beneath her bellowed and his body tensed like a spring, and jerked so hard that for a moment it seemed that only his heels and shoulders were touching the ground as he thrust upwards. It seemed that his every muscle convulsed as he spurted, and an expression of sheer joy spread over Gladys's face as she mewled and cried out and her pelvis rocked on him for a long while before, smiling and gasping, her body curled itself down onto his in a satisfied collapse.

Feeling shy at having witnessed such a scene of abandon, S lay down again and pretended to be asleep. But she could not eradicate the vision of Gladys's writhing, grinding body from behind her closed eyelids, nor stop herself hearing the slowly subsiding panting coming from a short distance away. She felt an all too familiar throbbing down below and tried desperately to think of something else.

S said nothing to Gladys while, after a further nap, they ate their mid-day meal – mostly because she could not think of the words and was still being plagued by an incessant pulsing sensation inside her vagina, and fighting off the desire to stare at their guides' lolling cocks as they moved around. Beginning the afternoon march came as a mercy, and it was even more of a mercy when, about two hours before sunset, the men stopped and pointed towards the horizon, talking rapidly to Gladys.

When Gladys told S that the guides would be leaving them now because the Prince's capital was just over those hills in the distance, her emotions were very mixed. There was a wave of joy that she would soon be seeing her Master again, mingled with a sense of relief that she would not be spending another night with these strange and exhausting men. There was also just a hint of disappointment as the image of Gladys earlier flashed into her mind.

It was disappointment that turned to dismay and then embarrassment when Gladys spoke her next words, grinning wickedly.

'They say they would like permission to show their respect and thanks to two strong women, even if one of them is a ghost-person.'

Obviously whatever had been in the tea that morning, if anything, was still working on Gladys. Or more probably, S thought as she looked at her friend, it was Gladys's basic nature that was making her eager. It was obvious what the guides meant by showing their respect and thanks. One of them was already rearing towards full erection, and S felt her breasts tighten at the sight of it.

'Come on, child!' said Gladys when she saw S's hesitation and blushes. 'It's only fair. Besides, there's no need for anybody to know, and I can see you're as hot for it as I am!'

She nodded towards S's breasts, where her nipples were standing out like nuts, then further down to where S could feel the slickness of arousal already oozing from her. Even so, she tried to protest.

'But we've got to get to the palace,' she wailed. 'We've got to tell Master about the rebel attack.'

'Shut up!' Gladys was suddenly fierce and angry. 'Who is your watcher? Show respect! Do as you are told or I'll sort that pretty arse of yours out.'

Both stung and stunned by the sudden change in her friend Gladys, but led by what had become almost an instinct for obedience, S moved to the spot Gladys had indicated with an angry hand. It was in the midst of tall grasses, grasses which were sharp and prickly when she lay down upon them.

The first of the guides appeared even before she had fully reclined. He said something to her which she did not understand. Then he gestured, his face questioning, and S almost laughed when she finally understood what he meant. He was asking whether she wanted him in her mouth or between her legs.

It was wild! Unbelievable! But then her body took over and S knew exactly where she wanted him – and that she did want him; very much. As she spread her legs he kissed her swelling sex-lips, then parted them with tender fingers so that he could lick her. It was brief, tantalising, but then she sighed as his mouth was replaced by his hardness, probing for her entrance, finding it, sinking in on waves of hot wetness.

Unlike the man who pleasured her last night – S was sure it was not him – he did not hold back, but fucked her hard, almost as hard as her craving body desired, then flooded her with gouts of heat which set off explosions in her brain and breasts and belly. He was hardly out of her when the next one thrust in, but he came in only a couple of minutes. The third one was wonderful. That part of S's mind which was still capable of thought guessed that this one had already fucked Gladys, because his orgasm took a lot longer to arrive – long enough for her to swell through several orgasms of her own, and to buck against his loins and claw at his back in her frenzy.

Fourteen

The two women crested a small rise and the outskirts of the settlement beyond which the Prince's palace lay came into view. They hugged each other with happiness and hurried onwards, their hearts lifted by the thought that they would soon be back with their Master.

As they drew nearer they saw that there were a great many soldiers and military vehicles around the edges of the town. It did not concern them unduly; after all there was a rebellion going on. They strolled forward happily, hand in hand. When they got to within a hundred yards of the first group of soldiers their happiness turned to alarm as several dozen weapons were suddenly aimed at them, and shouts were mingled with the rattling of safety-catches.

In less than a minute they were surrounded by shouting soldiers and being prodded with rifle barrels. In the midst of a mêlée of confusion and sharp jabs from weapons, the women were herded towards a low white building. The soldiers shoved them through the door so violently that they sprawled on the floor and S banged her head so hard against the leg of a desk that she was dizzy for several minutes.

By the time she recovered her wits a man in an officer's uniform was shouting orders and soldiers were thundering into the room. She was lifted bodily from the floor. Her arms were wrenched behind her and handcuffs were snapped on her wrists. She was spun around and frog-marched out of the room. The soldiers hefted her up and tossed her into the back of a truck as though she was a sack of rubbish, knocking the breath out of her again. Gladys was already there, looking scared as half a dozen soldiers jumped up onto the flatbed of the truck, still rattling their guns threateningly.

The journey was short and bumpy as the truck raced over rutted tracks, sending up great clouds of red dust. At the end of it the women were grabbed and hauled out then, still being stabbed at by gun barrels, herded into what seemed no more than a prison block. S screeched as she was flung through a door to tumble headlong into a small cell. Its cinder-block walls had been whitewashed, the floor was beaten earth, the door was very solid, and the only thing in the room was a large enamel bucket standing in a corner.

It was terrifying, but what scared S most of all was that she had been separated from Gladys.

S crouched against the wall for what felt like hours, her feet drawn up beneath her, hugging her knees and shielding her eyes from the very bright light which glared down from the ceiling. From outside the cell she could hear noises, but they were so muffled by the heavy wooden door that she could not make out what they meant.

Several times there was a scraping noise as the cover of a peephole in the door was drawn back and somebody checked on her, but she was too dispirited to even look up. By now she should have been with her beloved Master, telling him the rebel secrets she and Gladys had worked so hard to discover; instead she was stuck in a chilly prison cell without even dear

Gladys for strength and comfort. S was not aware of it, but silent tears welled from her eyes as she pressed her forehead against her knees and waited for whatever would happen next.

When they came for her she was half-asleep. It was very sudden. The door crashed open, hands grabbed her hair and the collar of her shirt, and she was dragged backwards out of the cell. It was all so quick that she was hardly able to take in the corridor they dragged her along nor, until she stood panting in front of a large desk, the room she was thrown into. Several men sat behind the desk, all in military uniform. They looked very stern. One of them, the one in the middle, harangued her for several minutes, but S could not understand anything he said. At her obvious lack of comprehension, he grew angrier and angrier.

Suddenly he seemed to lose any semblance of patience. He shouted to one of the soldiers who stood on guard by the door, who jumped forward dragging a huge curved knife from a scabbard at his belt. S screamed and fell into a huddle on the floor as the blade flashed close. The soldier grabbed the hem of her shirt-front and slashed through it in a single cut, while another soldier took a grip on her hair and dragged S to her feet.

Realising that they were not going to kill her, but still terrified, S stood absolutely still as they cut the shirt off her piece by piece, tossing the shreds to the floor and kicking them into a corner. She faced the officer sitting behind the desk and tried to speak, but her voice would not come. He was still shouting at her. Then he was giving more orders to his men.

Suddenly she was grabbed up by many hands and, completely off the ground, was rushed back along the same corridor as before and hurled back into the cell

– but not before those selfsame hands had made very free with her nakedness. She grazed a knee as she fell, and crouched against the wall once again, rubbing the wound then licking it to stop the slight bleeding.

The peephole in the door opened a lot more often than it had before, every couple of minutes it seemed, as though all the soldiers in the place were anxious to get a good look at their naked European rebel captive. It did not help the time go any faster for the prisoner. She was dozing, her head resting on her knees, when somebody opened the door and threw a blanket into the cell. It was thin and smelt of other bodies, but it was better than nothing and she rolled herself into it with difficulty because her hands were still cuffed behind her back, and lay down on the hard floor, curling her knees up close.

Again the door of the cell crashed open, but this time what happened was not frantic. Although S was already awake one of the soldiers standing over her nudged her in the ribs with the toe of an immaculately glossy boot. There were three other soldiers with him, all equally smartly dressed, with scarlet flashes on their shoulders as though they were military policemen.

The one who had nudged her with his boot gestured for her to get up, which she did with difficulty, rolling out of the constricting blanket and easing herself upright with her shoulder-blades against the wall. Suddenly, S wished even more urgently that her arms were not locked behind her, for the soldiers' eyes were far from the unemotional stare of impassive policemen.

Two marched in front and two behind, one each gripping an elbow with hard fingers, as they pulled S along the same corridor as before. They took her to a large room, whitewashed like the cell had been, but this one containing several chairs and, of all things, a vaulting horse such as S had not seen since school gym lessons.

They halted her in the centre of the room and the soldier who appeared to be in charge barked questions at her; questions in the language she could not understand.

'No!' she sobbed. 'You don't understand! I belong to Kano. I am his woman. I've –'

Her plea was stopped by a hard slap across her cheek, so hard it would have sent her staggering had not her elbows been firmly gripped by the two soldiers behind her. More questions were shouted at her and all she could do was shake her head and cry that she was English and belonged to Kano, and please would they not hurt her.

She felt the handcuffs being unlocked and felt for a moment that, just perhaps, they understood. Her hope died when she was lifted bodily towards the vaulting horse and draped across it. Even as she tried to scream protests her wrists and ankles were bound to the legs of the horse, her back and bottom splayed and awfully vulnerable. The one who had shouted the questions at her crouched down so that she could see him when she craned her neck. He spoke more quietly now, but with the same deadly coldness as before. He stood up again with a dismissive shake of his head.

Then the first stroke landed. There was no warning at all, no signal to tense her buttocks before the blow landed. She screamed at the awful fire of it, and in her convulsions almost broke through the bonds at her wrists and ankles.

They beat her slowly, and every three or four strokes the one who asked the questions crouched in front of her and spoke again. She kept on saying, as long as she could, that she belonged to Master Kano and to please, please stop, but the men did not understand English.

After a long while, an eternity so far as S's agonised backside was concerned, the men's tone lightened. They began to josh among themselves as they laid on stroke after stroke. The man in charge kept on asking questions until S was too dizzy and agonised to answer, then walked away as though he could think of nothing more to do with this rebel.

His men could.

There were a few minutes of blessed relief from the beating, during which the conflagration in her backside began to die into only a dull throb, then S felt hard fingers parting her cheeks. There was no preamble, no finesse. She cried out as the man took her, her body helplessly open to him. He did not take long, but was followed straightaway by one of the others.

Afterwards she was unstrapped from the vaulting horse, her hands were cuffed behind her, and she was once more frog-marched to the tiny cell. She was left alone for another age, then suddenly a trap she had not noticed in the bottom of the door snapped open and a tray containing two plastic bowls slid onto the floor. One bowl held some sort of porridge while the other was filled with brackish water.

S looked up to where an eye stared at her through the peephole and gestured with her manacled wrists, but the guard did not come in to release her. She struggled up onto her knees and crawled over to the tray. Neither the porridge nor the water looked very appetising but S was painfully hungry and her throat was parched. Kneeling over the tray, S bent forward and began to lap at the porridge like a dog. It was salty and almost flavourless but she gulped it down gratefully, not caring in the slightest how messy her face got as she dipped into the bowl. The water was tepid but she drank more than half of it, rinsing the porridge off her chin at the same time.

Then, replete and exhausted, she went through the awkward process of rolling herself into the blanket and fell instantly asleep despite the brightness of the light beating down on her.

It seemed only minutes later when she was jerked awake by strong hands whipping her blanket away and sending her rolling across the floor. She was still shaking her head and blinking her eyes with shock as the guard spread her legs. He was very big and he took his time, holding her down by her shoulders while he rutted. With her hands cuffed behind her S could not avoid thrusting her hips up towards him, making his penetration even deeper.

The hard floor grated against her shoulder-blades; she clamped her eyes shut because of the brightness of the overhead light; but in reality all S was conscious of was the man moving in her, filling her, setting off tremors of excitation in her sheath which reverberated out to every nerve-end then rocketed back to set the muscles of her vagina writhing against his thick hardness as it shafted her.

She bucked and wailed when he came, then wailed again when he pulled out immediately, so quickly there was actually a squelching noise as he left her. He was gone in an instant, and S was left to recover herself and fight off the swells of shame at herself that she had orgasmed so uncontrollably under such rough, impersonal circumstances.

Again she slept, until another guard came in. This one wanted her mouth and in a daze she gave it to him, her lips and tongue working instinctively to pleasure him. Later, they came to drag her off for more questioning.

This time she was hung from a metal bar

suspended from the ceiling, her ankles tied to shackles screwed into the floor so that her legs were spread wide. It was a different inquisitor now, a thin-faced man in his forties, wearing an immaculate uniform and carrying what looked like some kind of truncheon.

'Please! Please! I belong to Kano!' S was sobbing even before the first of the blows she knew would follow struck her. 'Don't hurt me! I am Kano's woman!'

It made no difference. She screamed as the first lash of the belt landed on her behind. It was wielded with a will by the guard standing behind her, as were the next two strokes.

The new inquisitor moved to stand in front of her shuddering, spread-eagled body. His eyes were very cold. He spoke, his voice as icy as his eyes, and gave a signal when once again S did not understand his words. Another stroke lashed down, and he smiled as S's body thrashed and writhed in her bonds and her scream echoed around the walls.

He spoke again, in what sounded like a different language, but once again S did not understand. He gave another signal, and one of his soldiers tied a gag tightly around S's mouth. His eyes were still glacial, and S realised that now, even if she understood what he was saying she would not be able to answer.

This time, at exactly the same moment as the belt lashed down across her buttocks, the inquisitor raised his truncheon and pressed it against her sex. He kept it there as she writhed, insinuating its bulbous tip between her labia, smiling all the while.

He spoke again, this time in what sounded like French. He was moving the truncheon against her now, and when yet another lash of the belt set her body jerking he pressed it hard so that it almost entered her.

It became a wild dream. The movements of the truncheon against her helplessly spread labia set off sensations in her which she wanted desperately not to feel, sensations which the fire in her backside only seemed to exaggerate. The truncheon kept up its insidious rubbing and the belt crashed down yet again across her soft, shuddering bottom.

The inquisitor spoke again, this time in English. S's head jerked up at the sound, but at the same moment the inquisitor pressed harder with the truncheon.

'You are a rebel whore,' he said. 'You have come to find out our dispositions and defences!'

S shook her head wildly at the accusation, her eyes bulging as she gurgled behind her gag. He spoke English! He could understand her if only they would let her tell them the truth, and stop beating her.

The rubbing of the truncheon against her sex had become more insistent as the inquisitor looked at her, his eyes now amused as well as icy.

'You are a rebel whore, and deserve everything you get!' The belt slashed down onto her backside again just as the truncheon rubbed harder. S tried to shake her head in denial but what was happening between her legs and to her flaming buttocks took her over. The inquisitor pulled the truncheon away and raised it until it was close in front of her face. It was slick and shiny with her juices.

'You may deny being a rebel whore, but a whore you certainly are!' He laughed as he waved the instrument before her eyes – eyes which filled with tears of shame. He was right. She must be a whore; how else could she have got so close to having an orgasm under such treatment?

The inquisitor walked away, saying something to his soldiers. They took their time about releasing her, first her ankles then her wrists, and their hands made free as she collapsed down from the bar she had been suspended from. They laughed riotously when one of them grabbed her as she fell, his hand hard in her crotch, and she sobbed and clung to him and came wildly on the rough fingers that penetrated her.

Later S lay in her cell staring at the whitewashed wall but not seeing it. She knew now that she was an object beyond redemption. She longed to find her way back to her Master Prince Adenkano, but knew too that she was not worthy of such a privilege. Her body was too wanton, such easy prey.

The inquisitor's guards had carried her back to her little cell, then taken turns on her. And she had orgasmed over and over again, crying out when their hard hands crushed her breasts, sobbing as one hard cock replaced another between her flailing legs, slurping greedily when one or another of them chose to use her mouth.

The guards took her out frequently for beatings, though the inquisitor was never present now. They hung her from the bar and laughed as they thrashed her, then laughed louder as they took turns to fuck her back in her cell.

She reached a mental stage where she looked for them, listened for the turning of the lock in the heavy door and the thudding of heavy boots invading her cell. She told herself she was a worthless thing, deserving only to be belted and used. She tried not to come, she really did, but there seemed to be so many of them and they were all so . . . so urgent and so vigorous.

Time ceased. She had no idea at all how long she was held in the prison. It all became a blur of white-walled cell, awful interrogation room, fire in her backside from heavy leather belts, screams as she pleaded that she was really Kano's woman, and grinning guards bearing down on her spread body.

They never removed her handcuffs except when they hung her up in the interrogation room, and she became almost accustomed to lapping up her daily porridge like a little dog. One of the worst things about the whole awful experience was that they never let her have a bath or a shower; the nearest she got to that was the two or three times they threw buckets of cold water over her, as much for their own amusement as to clean her up.

Then suddenly it changed.

The cell door burst open and S began to climb wearily to her feet, but instead of a bunch of guards just one man came in. He was in civilian clothes. She thought he looked familiar, but could not place him. He looked her over with an expression which changed rapidly from distaste to fierce anger, then he span round and began ranting furiously at the two guards standing outside the cell.

Things became suddenly dizzying. The guards grabbed her and rushed her out of the cell. Instead of taking her to the interrogation room they hurried her out of the building and across to another, one that looked like a house rather than a cell block. They practically dragged her through several rooms, shouting ahead as they went. Then they were in a large bathroom, and S was in a shower cubicle.

It had all happened so fast that she was still panting for breath when somebody turned on the shower. The water was beautifully hot, and S basked in it, lifting her face up to the jets and turning around and around so that every inch of her body could feel the benefit of the delicious warmth. The guards had not removed her handcuffs, which meant that she could not actually wash herself, but simply standing and turning under the hot, stinging jets felt like the most luxurious experience of her life.

After a few blissful minutes of this, the experience became even more luxurious. A young woman appeared and, removing the skirt and loose turban she wore, stepped into the cubicle with S and began to wash her. Turning the shower nozzle so that they were no longer in the spray, she shampooed S's hair gently and thoroughly then soaped her all over with soft hands. She moved the nozzle back to rinse S off, then repeated the whole process. After a second thorough rinsing, the woman turned the shower off and towelled S dry. The towels were rough and scratchy but felt wonderful on her skin, and soon S was glowing with contentment.

Next, the woman sat her down on the toilet seat – the first proper, European-style toilet she had seen since Master sent her to his estate, she realised – and began to brush her hair. Ever since she was a little girl S had loved having her hair brushed and now the sensation was so voluptuous and relaxing that she very nearly dozed off.

She was jerked back to alertness by the entrance of the man in civilian clothes. He still looked very familiar and, to judge by the way the woman brushing her hair leapt to attention, carried considerable authority, but S could still not remember where she knew him from. Then he spoke to her in English, and it came to her in a flash. It was Mr Patrice, the butler, Gladys's master.

'You look more presentable now,' he said, looking her over. 'You won't disgrace me on our way back to the palace.'

S's heart leapt with joy at his words. Back to the palace! Back to Kano! It did not matter in the slightest that her handcuffs were not taken off, nor that Mr Patrice clipped a leash to her pussy ring to lead her out of the house and through the streets, nor that the people they passed ogled and cat-called at the sight of a naked white woman being led along like an obedient little dog.

She was on her way back to her Master, and life could not be more wonderful.

Fifteen

Mr Patrice did not speak to her on the way to the palace, but S was so happy it did not matter. Nor did it matter that he led her through a postern gate to the rear of the grounds and took her straight to the kitchens. When did matter was the sight of Gladys scrubbing the floor.

Without thinking S began to rush towards her, only to be pulled up short by a painful tug on her leash. Looking stern, Mr Patrice pulled her towards him, the dragging of the leash on her pubis making her movements awkward. He unclipped the leash then turned to unlock the handcuffs.

'You will work with that woman,' he said coldly, pointing to where Gladys was busily scrubbing, her head down. 'You will not talk.'

Not being allowed to talk was the hardest thing. All S wanted to do was hug Gladys and pour out how happy she was to see her. Instead, she went to collect a bucket of water, soap and a brush, and knelt down by her and began to scrub the floor. But there are more ways than words for true friends to communicate, and their eyes met again and again and told each other volumes.

Why Mr Patrice had called Gladys 'that woman' rather than by her name was a worry, as was the fact that they were both kneeling naked and scrubbing the hard flagstones of the kitchen floor, being stepped over and cursed and even kicked by the other kitchen staff. But the delight of being back with Gladys and back in Master's palace could not be denied, and S scrubbed away with a will.

It began to become clearer at the end of the day when the two women were taken to their sleeping quarters, a cell like the one S had been kept in by the guards, but somewhat larger and containing double bunks with blankets and mattresses as well as a wash basin and a flush toilet. It felt like sheer luxury after the estate and the rebel camps and the prison. What felt even better was that S was at last able to throw her arms around Gladys no sooner had the heavy iron door clanged shut, and hug her so hard she laughed about her ribs cracking.

They kept their voices quiet for fear of alerting any guards who might be outside, but they talked and hugged like long-lost school friends. Gladys had been scared that S was lost for good. She herself had been brought to the palace the very first day they had arrived at the capital because, she explained, she was a local and could plead her case. What had happened to S had been a mystery until somebody had heard gossip from the guard station about a white rebel woman the troops were having fun with, and Mr Patrice had heard it and put two and two together. Hence her rescue.

It was not over yet, though. The reason Gladys had been demoted to scrubbing the kitchen floor, and now S too, was that they had consorted with the rebels and were under suspicion until Prince Adenkano their Master judged otherwise. They were to be put on trial in a few days, when he returned from his journey abroad. The rest was up to fate and how convincingly they could explain themselves.

* * *

S was excited almost beyond bearing when she was led off to what she had come to think of as 'the trial'. She had been bathed and brushed and made up by silent women. Mr Patrice, the butler, had replaced her three steel body rings with gold ones. Although nobody had said a word she knew, just knew, that Kano had returned and she would see him at last. She was happy as Mr Patrice fixed a heavy collar around her neck and bracelets around her wrists, then locked her hands to the collar behind her neck. She smiled with dignity when the butler clipped the leash to her pussy ring, and walked as proudly as she could as he led her through the palace. She was Kano's woman, his voluntary slave, and her heart thudded at the thought of seeing him again after so long.

She pulled her elbows back, presenting her be-ringed breasts as well as she could to please her Master, and straightened her spine even more as the door swung open and Mr Patrice led her into the room.

He was sitting on the high chair, the one S thought of as the throne. He was looking wonderful, his robes of white linen covered in swirls of red and gold and black. Gladys was already in the room, manacled as S was and kneeling before the throne, her head bowed.

The questioning was surprisingly gentle, as though Gladys had already told their story and been believed. Gladys did most of the answering and gave what facts and figures they had gained about the rebels, with S only required to confirm their veracity now and again.

The questioning was over quickly and the two relieved women were taken off separately, Gladys on a leash held by the butler, Mr Patrice, and S by a young man she did not know, who tugged unnecessarily hard at the chain clipped to her pussy ring.

He led her along a series of corridors and then into her old familiar cell, the one she had lived in when she was first brought here. Being back there gave her a feeling of deep contentment for this, really, was where it had all begun. When he unclipped the leash from her pussy ring the young man thrust several fingers into her. It hurt a little at first but she was too happy to care. She was back with her Master, and that was all that mattered.

She stood still as the young man toyed with her intimacies, and bent her knees to make things easier for him. He grinned when she began to move on his hand, unable to resist the sensations his fingers provoked in her. She gave a little mew of disappointment when his fingers left her, but immediately dropped to her knees when she felt the pressure of his hands on her shoulders.

He was circumcised and as rigid as a bone. He kept still as she licked the length of his dark shaft, breathing in the musky scent of his excitement. When her soft lips slid over the bulbous tip of his erection he gave a low moan, and his hips began to rock. She took him deeper, her tongue swirling on him, her nostrils flaring for breath as he filled her to her throat. She moved her head back, suckling gently, until she felt the ridge of his glans against her lips, then pushed forward again, slowly, breathing hard, setting up a steady, irresistible rhythm.

He was young and vibrant and could not hold out for long. He shouted and grabbed her head as he erupted into an orgasm so copious that her mouth could not contain it all, and droplets of milky fluid oozed out of the corners of her mouth and down onto her breasts. She kept on licking and sucking him until he began to soften and decline and finally pulled out. His eyes were shining with wonder as he raised her from her knees and led her over to her little bed.

He had not released her wrists from the lock on her

collar, but she reclined contentedly on the narrow bed after he left, gazing at the familiar ceiling and wondering when her Master would send for her. The thought of her Master added to the sensations of what she had just done set off a delicious heat in her belly and she drifted into a voluptuous dream.

Her Kano, Prince Adenkano N'Kwandwe, her adored Master, was touching her, rolling her breasts with strong hands, biting her neck with white teeth, spreading her. She was as high as the clouds and splayed as wide as the universe, and he came into her with a force that set her dreaming mind spiralling and sparkling with the size and power of him.

In her dream her hips undulated like waves on the sea and her vagina became a maw, sucking at him, writhing on his shafting hardness, dragging him in, fucking him even harder than he was fucking her.

When her orgasm hit her eyelids fluttered open for a moment. It was not Kano's face above her but the young man's, his features distorted by his efforts between her legs. It did not matter though. She was in the midst of an overwhelming come, and her eyes drifted shut as her body rode towards the crest of it and beyond, and the dream continued.

S scurried across the kitchen clutching the huge cauldron she had just finished scrubbing. She was back on kitchen duty, this time along with Gladys, and now both of them were at the beck and call of even the lowliest maid or assistant cook. She soon worked up a sweat from both the heat of the ranges and the rushing around she had to do. The noise was as incredible as it always is in a large, busy kitchen.

It was the change in the noise which alerted her. There was a crash, then a hush, then a voice shouting. S put the cauldron down where it was required and span round to see what was going on. A large woman, one of the few female cooks, was shouting with rage and waving her arms about. With her head bowed, Gladys was slowly walking towards her.

S did not understand the words that were shouted, but she knew her friend was in trouble from her very posture as she approached the angry cook. Silently, Gladys went to a rack, took out a large wooden spoon, and handed it to the woman before bending over a heavy wooden chopping table.

The buzz of voices grew at the sight of this magnificent woman humbly bending over, her legs taut and spread, her back arched and her buttocks high. S held her breath. Gladys was worth ten of any of these people, yet she was submitting without a moment's hesitation to what would be both pain and humiliation. It was a salutary lesson in what servitude really meant, and it went to S's heart like an arrow. Would she ever be able to show such grace, such courage?

The sound of the first smack rang out and made S wince even though she was on the far side of the kitchen. There was a visible flexing of Gladys's full buttocks at the blow, but she did not utter a sound even though the stroke had been very hard. The next smack was just as loud, this time on the other cheek, and still Gladys managed to hold her silence. It took another six strokes, delivered on alternate sides, before Gladys allowed a whimper to escape her lips and her knees to weaken.

It was S who was weeping in sympathy for her friend as the next three strokes fell, the last of the ten bringing a strangled wail from Gladys's throat.

As soon as it was over and Gladys straightened up stiffly the noise of the kitchen resumed as though nothing special had happened. S got little chance to speak to Gladys during the next hour, though she did manage to squeeze her arm and give her glances of sympathy as they hurried past one another carting pots of water or trays of vegetables.

It was a male cook who decided that S deserved a spanking. She did not know why. She could not think of anything she had done wrong, but when he gestured her to get over his knee she obeyed automatically. He used his hand, holding her down with his forearm in the small of her back and spanking each buttock in turn with his right hand. Somehow S understood, through the mist of pain, that she was not being spanked because she had done something wrong. The hardness pressing against her belly told her that he was doing it because he enjoyed it, enjoyed the feeling of having a naked woman across his lap while he beat her bottom.

She managed to stifle the screams that tore at her throat as he spanked her harder and harder for what felt like a million years but was actually only a few minutes. She even managed to avoid coming when he thrust several fingers into her and worked them in and out for several more minutes in demonstration of his power and her lowly status.

She felt quite proud when at last she was allowed to stand up and she caught a look of approval in Gladys's eye. It seemed an eternity since Gladys had been, officially at least, her watcher but S still looked to her for strength and guidance. That look of approval and friendship meant a great deal and made her feel warm inside as she turned to resume stripping the leaves from the pile of maize-heads that lay before her.

S stood at one end of the long table and Gladys at the other. Her hair had been washed and brushed until it shone, and hung down her back like a glossy shawl beneath a cap of diamonds and sapphires that covered her head and ears and reached almost to her eyebrows. Her wrists were locked to her elbows behind her back with diamond-studded cuffs so that her breasts were thrust forward.

From her nipple rings hung little trays of condiments while from her pubic ring hung a long linen towel scented with rosewater. She looked along the length of the table to where Gladys stood. She was similarly decorated, and S found herself wishing that she could look even half as beautiful and womanly. A dozen other girls stood by the walls waiting for the guests to arrive, their skirts and turbans brilliantly coloured, their pert breasts reflecting the light from the chandeliers, but none of them came near to Gladys in exotic beauty.

From the way the guests reacted, or rather did not react, one would have thought that the sight of a dozen bare-breasted girls and two stark-naked ones waiting to serve them was perfectly normal. They were all in the uniforms of senior military officers, their chests covered with medal-ribbons, and numbered about twenty. Prince Adenkano, in contrast, was wearing simple camouflage fatigues, albeit immaculately pressed, and yet he looked by far the most impressive of the men present.

Despite the presence of so much delicious femininity, conversation at the table was quiet and serious. Even though she understood little of what was said S guessed that these army men were more concerned with dealing with the rebel insurrection than with the banquet they were enjoying. Like Gladys, she hurried backwards and forwards in response to the click of fingers or a raised hand, and bent forward so that this guest or that could help himself to the salt, pepper and spices from the little trays that dangled from her breasts, or to wipe their hands on the towel that hung from her pubic ring. But not one of them touched her. Indeed, they seemed hardly to notice her as she hurried back and forth, her little trays swinging.

It was a strange and rather disorientating experience. The constant tugging at her nipples and pubis was physically arousing. The fact of having to bend over the table at the wave of a hand and offer her bare breasts to an indifferent stranger was even more so. S realised with a blush that she actually wanted them to touch her, wanted someone to squeeze her breast or sneak his hand further up when he used the towel hanging from her pubic ring.

Neither happened, and by the time the men left at the end of their meal S was almost panting with frustration. Even the removal of her trays and towel set off shocks in her body, as much because the person removing them was the young man who had taken advantage of her earlier as from the actual physical sensations. The expression in his eyes as he clipped the leash to her pubic ring was very different from the blank indifference of the men she had served at the dinner.

He pushed her up against the wall of the narrow corridor even before they reached her cell. His hands were hard and frantic and her shoulder-blades ground against the rough wall as he grasped her buttocks and lifted her off her feet. He thrust hard between her splayed thighs, but at first missed his target. He thrust again and this time impaled her so forcefully she cried out and bucked so hard that she banged the back of her head against the wall.

It was deliciously brutal. He showed no consideration or finesse but fucked her hard, his hips flexing and bucking as he shafted her. It was exactly what her body needed after the frustrations of the dinner party, and her legs locked around him as her pelvis writhed and ground against him and she sobbed into a violent orgasm long before he reached his own climax. When he did, flooding her with gouts of heat and crushing her against the wall, she gave a wail that turned into a gasping sigh and slithered down the wall like a rag doll when he pulled out of her and let her go.

S was awakened by what sounded like a distant thunderstorm. The young man had led her to her cell after he'd had his fun with her and now she lay manacled by her left wrist to the frame of her little bed. She sat up and listened hard. It was not thunder that had woken her, but the sounds of explosions and gunfire! The palace was under attack by the rebel forces, just as she and Gladys said it would be!

Then she realised that the noise was coming from quite a long way off. They were definitely the sounds of a battle going on, but they were too far away to be actually around the palace. She relaxed a little, then became alert again when the sounds got nearer. She became terrified when she began to hear shouts and the sound of rifles firing. She tore at the manacle holding her wrist to the bed but it would not budge.

She could hear shouts and boots thundering outside. She tried to drag the bed towards the cell door, desperate to find out what was happening. She had it halfway there when the door burst open and a group of wild-looking men burst in. For a moment they paid her no attention but crouched, pointing their weapons through the door and scouting the corridor with their eyes.

Most of them rushed out after little more than a

minute, firing their weapons and charging madly. Two remained, and they certainly did pay attention to her. They took a long look and said something to one another. Then one of them raised his rifle and aimed it towards her. S gave up her life as lost and collapsed into a ball on the floor. The crash of the rifle was unbelievably loud in the confined space of the cell. It took her a minute to realise that she was not dead, had not even been wounded. Then everything became a maelstrom as the rebel soldier who had shot away the chain that held her to the bed grabbed her by her hair and ran her out of the building.

The noise was appalling, shouts and screams and explosions and gunfire. S was dragged at a flat sprint across the palace grounds and thrown bodily into a clump of bushes, where a group of the rebels had set up a firing post. The fall knocked her dizzy and she was only vaguely aware that somebody tied ropes around her wrists and ankles and thrust a piece of rag into her mouth as a gag.

She came to her senses to discover herself bouncing on the hard metal floor of a truck as it raced across country. Whenever the truck hit a pothole she was tossed into the air, to bang painfully down again and crash dizzyingly from side to side. She lost track of everything except the mad careering of the truck, and thanked her lucky stars when it came to a halt. Then the canvas flap at the end of the truck was whipped aside and she knew she was in deep trouble.

In the dim light of early morning three men stared in at her as she pushed herself as deep into the far corner as she could. At first she cowered back, then, as one of the men climbed up into the truck and came for her, she resigned herself to what they obviously intended to do with her. She became limp as he took

217

hold of her arm and dragged her towards his two companions. He lifted her bodily and tossed her down to where the other two men waited, both grinning hugely at the prospect of their prize.

Sixteen

They carried her a little way off from the truck and dumped her on the grass near the foot of an acacia tree. The one who had hauled her from the truck knelt and untied her wrists, only to tie them again in front. He pulled her arms up above her head and tied them to the stake one of his companions was driving into the ground.

They were in no hurry. Two more stakes were driven in, each nearly level with her hips and about a foot away on either side. Then they untied her ankles and bound each of them to one of the stakes. She was now bound in the most vulnerable way possible, her knees forced high and pulled wide, her arms stretched above her head so that her breasts were thrust out prominently. There was absolutely nothing she could do to help herself as the three men got themselves ready, stripping off their uniforms and tossing them aside, revealing hard, eager bodies.

S was mentally preparing herself for what was about to happen when, instead of falling on her and having their way, the men began to shout at one another and then to scuffle. Fists flew. One of them made a dive for her, only to be dragged off by the other two, who then clashed in their turn.

From her bound and helpless position S watched with amazement as the three rebel soldiers fought over her. Each time one of them made a dash for her the other two would wrestle him aside. The sight of three naked men struggling over who was going to have her first was both comic and arousing. Comic in that it did not really matter who had her first; the way things were they were all going to have her anyway, so what did it matter? Arousing because in the growing morning light their sweating, struggling bodies took on a kind of primeval glamour. S found herself wondering which one would win, when the real business would start, and felt her breasts tighten at the thought.

The sudden crash of a gun close by froze the struggling men. Then, not even pausing to grab their clothes, they ran for the truck and, to the sound of more shots, gunned the engine and raced away. Bound as she was S could not at first see what had caused their sudden panic. She craned her head back as far as she could and saw a figure emerging from around the bole of the tree.

The figure was tall and broad, wielding a rifle as though it was a toy, and S's heart leapt as she recognised Nkwame. It was a different Nkwame from the immaculate sergeant-major she had known before. Now, he was wearing jeans and a torn shirt, and looked dishevelled. Even so he still exuded an air of command and strength which washed over S as a blessed feeling of relief as he cut her free of her bonds.

Nkwame had a Jeep two hundred yards away, concealed behind some bushes. Grabbing her small hand in his huge palm Nkwame ran S the distance to the vehicle and bundled her into the passenger seat before leaping in himself. He started the engine and roared away amidst clouds of dust, weaving across country, bouncing the Jeep so hard S had to cling on to the dash-handle with both hands for fear of being thrown out.

By the end of an hour's wild driving S was still breathless from the frantic speed of it all. Nkwame stopped at last in a small clearing among some trees, making sure the Jeep was well hidden. He had remained silent all the way, and still did so as he lifted several items of equipment from behind the front seats of the vehicle.

S climbed out of the Jeep and sat against the bole of a tree. She found herself watching with fascination as her huge rescuer worked with neat efficiency. He broke bunches of thin twigs from the shrubs all around them and stuffed them into a tin can that looked as though it had once contained several pints of stew. There were holes pierced around the bottom of the can, and Nkwame lit the twigs with a Zippo lighter, making sure they were burning well before cramming thicker twigs into the can until it was full. Then he took another can, slightly larger, and filling it with water from a canteen placed it on top of the first can.

It was a brilliantly efficient and effective bush stove, boiling the water quickly and giving off almost no smoke at all. When the water was boiling he tipped half into a billy can into which he had scooped a handful of tealeaves, then quickly opened a couple more tins from his pack and tipped them into the remainder of the boiling water. His movements were deft, almost casual, yet soon the aromas of freshly brewed tea and a meaty stew seduced S's nostrils more headily than the smells of the most expensive restaurant could ever have done.

He even had spoons; wooden ones to be sure, but spoons none the less. The tea had no milk or sugar but still tasted delicious. The stew was a mixture of corned beef and pulses and, once Nkwame had sprinkled a little salt into it, tasted wonderful. They

221

both ate ravenously, neither having eaten since yesterday. Only when they had finished and S leaned back against the treetrunk, thinking that this must surely be the most memorable breakfast she had ever eaten, did Nkwame begin to talk.

They had to lie low during daylight, he told her, because there were likely to be both rebel and government troops around. That suited S perfectly, for her hectic night had left her weary. The rest of his story came out slowly as she leaned her head against his shoulder and drifted in and out of awareness.

He had been a soldier since his teens, and had fought in Mozambique and Angola and now here. He believed in the honour of the military, and had believed in the propaganda of the rebels when he joined them as a mercenary. Then he discovered, first by accidentally overhearing a meeting of senior staff, then by actively searching, that the rebel leaders had no intention at all of 'freeing the people' as their slogans proclaimed. Their sole aim was in fact to take over the country's wealth and milk it away for their own benefit.

'Even your Prince Adenkano is better than that,' he said with a sigh. 'At least he gives his people houses and nobody starves.

'I saw them kidnapping you,' he continued. 'They were not concerned with the attack. They were only out for what they could get, like most of the others. They would have raped you and then sold you off to some brothel for profit. It decided me. I had already deserted, but I stole our Jeep here and followed. The stupid fellows were so busy crowing over their prize they never heard me coming.'

The thought of the fate he had rescued her from warmed S's heart. He had been her protector, and Gladys's too, while they were in the rebel camp. Now he had rescued her from the unthinkable. At the same time, however, weariness was dragging at her. She slid over and nestled her head against his chest.

'Thank you, Nkwame,' she murmured, stroking her forehead against the cotton of his shirt, then drifted into a welcome sleep.

She awoke feeling soft and relaxed. His arm was around her shoulder, cradling her as though she was a child. He was deep in sleep, snoring quietly, and the sunlight was catching his face, highlighting his nose and cheek-bones and shadowing his eyes. His face was hard and mature, but somehow gentle too, with a sort of peace to it. Snuggled against his hard body, still half in the realms of sleep, S felt suddenly more secure than she had for a long, long while, and she nestled closer.

Her mind drifted to how this big man had cared for herself and Gladys while they were in the rebel camp by rationing the opportunities his men had to fuck them, and then on to the few nights he had had her himself. That first night, the night he had begun cheating with the raffle, may have been shattering but the others had been gentler. Although he had been taking her because he had the right and the power to do so, it had been almost like love-making rather than mere fucking. The recollection of his body hard on hers, of his hands and mouth on her breasts, of his penis spearing her, set off that familiar heat in her insides, and she snuggled still closer.

When Nkwame suddenly stirred S became fully alert. She sat up, blushing as she realised that in her half-dream her hand had been stroking the groin of his jeans. She glanced at him over her shoulder, embarrassed at what she had been doing and the images that had been playing through her mind –

images of the penis she had been fondling through the denim, but naked and erect and bearing down upon her.

Nkwame's eyes told S that, if he did not know what she had been thinking, he certainly knew how she was feeling. He sat up straight, smiling gently. His arm went around her shoulders and S felt a hot shiver run from her spine to her breasts and down to her belly. With his free hand Nkwame turned her face towards him and strong fingers stroked her cheek with the delicacy of a butterfly's wing. Nothing was said as he lay down again, stretching his body on the grass. At least, nothing was said in words; it was all in the eyes, hers as well as his.

S moved to kneel beside his reclining body. She unbuttoned his shirt and pulled it aside, exposing the thick, glossy slabs of muscle on his chest and belly. She smoothed her hands over him, her fingers delighting in his warmth and the firmness of the curves of his body. She leaned down to kiss and breathe him, moving back into her waking dream. Still inhaling the maleness of his body, her fingers worked at the buckle of his belt and then his zipper. He raised his hips to help her as she pushed his jeans down over his hard thighs.

He was not wearing anything under his jeans, and reared up even before she touched him. The aroma of his maleness flooded her senses as she bent her head. As her fingers moved on the silk-on-steel hardness of his shaft and her tongue began to savour him, S knew deep down that what she was doing was for her own delight more than his. Her lips slid down over his thick glans, and she became greedy.

The muscles of his belly and thighs flexed as his loins began to move to the rhythm of her bobbing head and stroking hands. S went into that enhanced state of being where every nerve from her fingertips and her tongue to her breasts and vagina rioted in a single sensation of hot, spiralling tension. His hands stroked her breasts and set off tiny explosions. When a hand moved up between her spread thighs she grunted and almost swallowed him whole as ripples of excitation shot through her.

He had to use gentle force to lift her face from him she was so carried away with what she was doing, but then, when he lifted her and moved her, she clamped her knees astride him with a deep moan. She began coming even as she impaled herself on his dark shaft, cramming herself down on him until their pubic bones were crushed together, her vagina gulping at him, swallowing him deep until she had no capacity to breathe. She rocked on him, her hands pressed against his chest for support as her pelvis circled and ground against him in a frenzy.

Whether it was one long orgasm or a dozen was irrelevant as she rode him wildly. He gripped her breasts with iron fingers, and that only made it better. He pawed at her flexing buttocks as he erupted into his own orgasm, redoubling hers as his heat pumped into her depths. She swooned down onto his chest as his pulsings eased, nestling her face into his neck and pressing her aching breasts against his chest. He stayed in her after he had come, and even his slow shrinking felt wonderful to her, as though their bodies really were merging and becoming one single sexual entity.

S awoke with a shock to find that Nkwame was lifting her off his body. She had fallen into a luxurious dream still astride him, still relaxed against his chest, and he had let her sleep there. But now nightfall was approaching, and Nkwame wanted to move on. Rummaging in a kit-bag, he pulled out a shirt and tossed it to S.

They drove through the night, avoiding roads and villages and using only side-lights. The terrain became more and more hilly and then thickly wooded. As the first glimmers of dawn began to light the east Nkwame pulled the Jeep into a wide, grassy clearing and shut down the engine.

'I know this place well,' he said. 'It is not far from where I lived as a boy. We will stay here for a while, until the fighting is over.'

S looked at him nervously.

'Don't worry,' he said, smiling and patting her on the shoulder. 'I'll take you back to the palace. Maybe in a week.'

He smiled again at her look of obvious relief, and busied himself preparing a camp. From the back of the Jeep he took what seemed to S to be a very limited pile of equipment. There was his rifle, of course, which he leaned carefully against the side of the vehicle. Next came the cans he had used yesterday to prepare their meal, followed by a pair of water canteens, a rolled-up rubberised groundsheet, and finally a fierce-looking machete with a blade a yard long. He held the two canteens out to S.

'Through there,' he said, pointing to a small gap between the surrounding shrubs. 'and downhill a way is a stream. About three hundred yards. Go carefully, just in case there is anyone about.'

S sneaked from tree to tree, Nkwame's warning making her probably more cautious than she needed to be. The stream was just where Nkwame had said it would be, but his terse words had not prepared her for how beautiful it was. A little stream tinkled through a narrow defile overhung by trees. Lush, very green grass lined its banks. Uphill a little way was a small cascade, which was causing the lovely noise of running water, and further down lay a small pool reflecting the trees and dappled early morning sunlight. It was cool and quiet, and for several minutes S was lost in the peace and loveliness of it.

She pulled herself together with an effort and knelt to fill the canteens. They were surprisingly heavy when full and she had to lug them back up the hill, panting by the time she reached the clearing. The transformation Nkwame had wrought in the short time she had been gone was astonishing.

The groundsheet had become a tent, pegged down with sticks and supported by two sturdy poles and a ridge-pole cut from the branches of the trees. A fire was glowing in one can, and the second can was ready to receive water for boiling. Nkwame was busy on the far side of the clearing cutting the long grass with the machete. He carried a large pile of it over to the tent and tossed it onto an already thick layer of grass he had cut while she had been gone.

'For sleeping on,' he said, as he took the canteens from her. 'Easier on the bones.'

The procedure for the meal was the same as the day before. Once the water in the first can was boiling, half was poured into another can to make tea. Then a can of meat and another can of diced vegetables was tipped into the remainder, a little salt added, and a stew began to build. Long before it was ready S's stomach was rumbling at its wonderful aroma.

Sitting under a tree, they ate their stew and drank their tea in a companionable silence. Had it not been for the Jeep and the presence of Nkwame's rifle, which he kept always at hand, it might have been a picnic. Afterwards, Nkwame became all business again.

He insisted on showing S how to operate the rifle.

He taught her how to load and unload the curved magazine and to operate the safety catch. He showed her the metal slide which switched the weapon from single shot to automatic. He warned her about how much the weapon would kick if she ever needed to fire it. He made her practise a dozen times, switch to automatic, safety off, arms down and rigid to fight the kick while firing from the hip. She could not actually fire it in case anybody heard the noise, but he made sure she knew at least the basics.

Checking that the little fire in the can was safe, he astonished S by announcing that she was to keep guard while he took a bath.

'I'm sweaty and smelly,' he said with a grin. 'The pool down there is nice and cool. You can go second if you like. Come on.'

He moved down the hill to the pool with much less nervous caution than S had showed when she went to get the water, but nevertheless with a cat-like alertness. He positioned S upstream, near the little cascade, then went to the edge of the pool and stripped off his boots, shirt and jeans, taking a small object from a pocket as he dropped them to the grass.

His warning about keeping guard scared her, and S looked around wildly to see if enemies were coming, not paying him any attention. A loud splash drew her eyes back towards the pool. He was standing in the middle of the pool, which only came up to his knees, and splashing double handfuls of water over himself. The sight made S catch her breath.

He was nothing less than magnificent. Although she had had sex with him and throbbed in his embrace, she had never seen him utterly naked and the sight stunned her. She had seen photographs of body-builders back in her former life, and of athletes and models, but this man made them look inadequate. His body was hard muscle without being knotty and bulbous like theirs often were. He was huge, more than six and a half feet tall and proportionately broad across his shoulders. The water he doused himself with ran down his skin in sparkling rivulets and accentuated the curves of his taut muscles. It was as though he was a dancer, moving to music.

He shook his head vigorously then leaned to pick up something from the bank of the pool, and S held her breath at the perfection of his spine and buttocks. When he began to lather himself with the worn bar of soap he had taken from the pocket of his jeans she found herself wishing he was facing towards her rather than away.

Without her even knowing it, a hand slipped down to her crotch as S watched Nkwame bathing. The suds bubbling on his skin, only to be washed away with splashing water, made his mahogany skin shine in the sunlight. She had never felt like this before. Guard duty was out of the question as she watched this incredible male animal bathe himself, her fingers working voluptuously on her clitoris and labia as she tried to stifle the gasps of her orgasm.

Nkwame flopped back into the shallow pool and rolled and frolicked, rinsing himself and at the same time playing like a joyful child. But there was nothing childish about the figure which at last stood up and walked towards her, water streaming down his torso. The thick curls of his pubic hair glistened with silver water droplets and his penis, still thick and long despite being soft, swayed from side to side as he moved.

Only with an effort was S able to drag her eyes and mind away and pretend to be still on guard. Blushing to her ankles, she handed him the rifle without being able to look him in the eye, then scampered down to the pool for her chance to bathe, whipping off her shirt as she ran.

The pool was so cool it knocked the breath out of her, but somehow this contrast with her own internal heat only increased her arousal. She picked up the worn bar of soap from the bank and began to lather herself. She was acutely aware that just as she had been able to watch Nkwame he could watch her, and her bathing became a show, a conscious performance of bending and stretching and turning and running her soapy hands over her tingling skin. It was as much for her own pleasure as his – if he was watching.

With her head bowed as though she was concentrating on washing, she looked up under her eyelashes. He had put his jeans on, which S found disappointing, but he was very definitely watching her. Her skin tingled with a new thrill. She turned her back towards him and bent forward to scoop up handfuls of water to splash over her hair, knowing exactly the view she was giving him of her femininity. She straightened up and arched her back, raising each arm in turn to soap her shoulders and underarms and then her breasts.

She did not need to glance in his direction now because she knew he would be looking. What man could possibly look away from the display she was deliberately putting on. She sat down in the water at last, then lay back to rinse herself off, turning and rolling in the delicious water, revelling in the sensations of cool cleanness on her body and the knowledge that she had so rapt an audience.

She stood and waded out of the pool, picking up her shirt but leaving it dangling from her hand as she walked naked and Eve-like towards the big soldier.

Neither of them could wait to get back to the camp. S was breathless by the time she threw herself on to the piled grass in the makeshift tent, then much more breathless as Nkwame speared her with a cock that was now by no means soft.

He fucked her wildly, but such was her state that she fucked him even more wildly in return, locking her legs around his broad back, clawing at his chest and shoulders, ramming her cunt against him to the tune of animal grunts as the orgasm she had started earlier with her fingers now exploded on the glory of the thick cock piercing her to her depths.

It did not last long – they were both too worked up for that – but it was so intense that had a Centurion tank rolled into the clearing and fired at them, neither would have noticed.

Seventeen

The week she spent in the hidden camp with Nkwame
became like a pastoral idyll for S. He taught her the
right kinds of wood to use for the fire in his little
cooking can. He went away for short periods and
came back bearing edible leaves and roots and,
usually, a small animal he had caught. He never made
her watch the cleaning and skinning, so she ate the
resulting meals with relish. They bathed together
every morning, soaping one another and splashing
and giggling like children.

And they fucked, over and over and over again.
There was no hurry. They each rejoiced in the other's
body, taking their time, learning one another until no
words were ever necessary. He would look, and she
would roll back and open for him. If it was S who
looked and Nkwame was not ready, he would lie
back and offer himself for her mouth and she would
kiss and suck him to erection, then impale herself and
ride him long and voluptuously, so lost in her
on-going orgasms that sometimes, when she came
back to earth, he was begging her to stop.

The little clearing they inhabited would have felt
like an Eden had not Nkwame so often checked his
rifle and the surrounding countryside. In the end he
told her that it was time to take her back to the
palace, for surely the fighting was over by now. She

felt very mixed emotions. On the one hand she longed to get back to Kano, her wonderful Master, the man to whom she had offered herself as a voluntary slave. On the other hand there was Nkwame, once a rebel but now her rescuer.

He gave her no choice in the matter, simply loading his gear into the Jeep as evening began to fall and hustling her into the passenger seat. He drove faster than before and remained unusually silent, as though he was preoccupied with a difficult problem. He stopped the Jeep a little before dawn, parking it among some thorn bushes for concealment, and turned to S, his expression serious.

'I can't take you all the way to the palace,' he said. 'They will shoot me as a rebel if I do, so you will have to walk the rest of the way. It is only about four miles. But we have another problem.'

At S's look of puzzlement he explained. She had ostensibly spent more than a week as a captive of the rebels, but she looked remarkably fit and healthy. Looking the way she did, the palace guards might suspect that she had not been an unwilling captive, which might cause her serious trouble. If she was suspected of co-operating with the rebels they might shoot her as well.

There was a long silence as both of them pondered the problem. It was S herself who suggested a possible solution. At first Nkwame vehemently rejected her idea, but she insisted and at last he gave in.

She pulled off her shirt and handed it to him, then picked up the big machete and moved off among the bushes. Searching carefully, she found a number of the long, slender fronds she was looking for. She cut off half a dozen, all roughly three feet in length, and carried them back to Nkwame. He had finished ripping the shirt and was now trampling it in the dust beneath his big boots so that it became little more than a rag. As she handed him the bunch of slender switches she had gathered he still looked reluctant.

'Please,' she whispered, scared herself by what she had begged him to do. 'I can take it, honestly. I have to.'

S turned and draped herself across the radiator of the Jeep, spreading her legs and arching her back to raise her buttocks for him. Her fingers clawed at the sides of the vehicle as she readied herself. The first stroke swished down, landing full on her bottom and spreading fire.

'No,' she gasped. 'You must do it harder. You have to mark me! Harder! On my back and legs too.'

He thrashed her from her shoulder-blades to the backs of her knees. At first she had to keep begging him to go harder, but soon his instincts took over and all she could do was cling to the Jeep and writhe under the onslaught.

When he stopped she could do no more than lie there, the fire in her skin deepening and dulling to an all-encompassing glow as she fought to get her breath back. Nkwame stood still and silent as, with a groan, she straightened up and turned. She tried to drape herself backward over the Jeep's bonnet. It hurt, and at first she could not manage it. She forced herself at last, and looked to Nkwame. His head was down and he was looking away.

'Please, Nkwame,' she pleaded. 'Do it for me. They would have done it.'

As she stretched herself back and raised her arms along the bonnet S realised how outlandish it was that she should be practically begging a man to whip her breasts and belly, yet the dominant emotion she felt at that moment was a deep sense of arousal. She arched her back and parted her legs, unconsciously offering herself as erotically as possible.

235

'Not too hard, please,' she whispered throatily as Nkwame reluctantly readied himself.

He began on her breasts, hard enough to sting and make her gasp and wriggle, but not so hard that the switches cut her skin. Without knowing it, S stretched her arms higher and pushed her breasts up to meet the blows, for with each one a bolt of lightning shot through her body and added to the heat that was growing in her belly. By the time Nkwame moved down and began to beat the fronts of her splayed thighs S was moaning quietly and rocking her hips towards the whip, lost in the swelling of an incipient orgasm.

Nkwame, too, was beginning to get carried away by the wildly erotic process and began to beat her harder, which only seemed to intensify her wild reactions. Her eyes were clamped shut, her mouth was wide as she gasped and grunted, and her head was rolling from side to side as her body undulated towards the strokes of the switches. When he moved up and began to beat the very tops of her thighs and her belly, the first stroke was appalling but the second set her body bucking. When he landed a stroke exactly across the swell of her mons her orgasm exploded in her so violently that she toppled off the bonnet of the Jeep and lay sprawled on the earth, sobbing and clutching her crotch with both hands as the spasms surged through her.

She could not look Nkwame in the eye when at last she recovered herself and heaved herself to her feet. It was not so much that she was ashamed of the wanton display she had just put on as confused by it. She had asked Nkwame to beat her on her breasts and thighs as a sort of camouflage for when she got to the palace, but it had turned into a shockingly erotic experience.

Still looking away, and still throbbing from her wild reaction to the beating, S carried out the second part of her plan to convince the palace guards that she had escaped from the rebels. She had to be dirty, as though she had struggled cross-country much farther than four miles, which was all she really had to walk.

There was a patch of bare soil in the lee of a thick clump of shrubs. S lay down on it and began to squirm around, rubbing handfuls of dust on her skin despite its soreness and pouring more handfuls over her head to dirty her hair. Then she took one of the canteens of water and poured it over herself, matting her hair with mud and streaking her body as though runnels of sweat had run off her.

When she finished she looked at Nkwame, who nodded his approval at the results of her efforts. She felt another prickle of arousal as his dark eyes appraised her dusty, naked body, a prickle which increased as she bent to pick up the tattered shirt and pulled it on over her head, aware that as she did so she was concealing nothing from this huge and gentle man. She turned to face him again, caught up by an irresistible urge. For the second time in her life she said the words that would have been unimaginable to her six months ago.

'Would you fuck me please, Nkwame. I want you to fuck me.'

She could not believe she heard herself saying it, yet knew at the same time that she meant it with every atom of her being. She lay down upon the grass and raised the front of her torn shirt, raising her knees and spreading herself in wanton invitation as he unbuckled his belt and pulled down his zipper.

Even as his thick glans touched her pouting labia her arms and legs clamped around him as though she was a pulsating octopus, and she sucked him in with a wail of ecstasy. He tried to take it slowly, but her rampant body would have none of it. She clawed and thrashed and lunged against him, bruising herself in her frenzy to get him inside her as deep and hard as she possibly could. It was over quickly, too quickly for her greedy body, and her sheath writhed and sucked at him long after he had finished coming and was trying to pull out.

She mewled with disappointment as he slipped out of her, and her legs stayed clamped around his body as her hips continued to grind against him. At last her tumultuous orgasm spent itself and her limbs sagged, releasing him as she lay spread and gasping for air.

He offered her the machete when she had recovered enough to think about beginning her walk to the palace.

'You can say you stole it to help you escape,' he said. 'Also, looking like you do you might need to defend yourself if you come up against any men!'

S looked down at herself. Nkwame had made a thorough job of ripping and trampling her shirt and it hung on her in tatters, revealing an awful lot whenever she moved. Suddenly she realised that the walk back to the palace might hold more dangers than browsing wildlife, and accepted the machete gratefully.

She smiled up at the huge man who had started as her captor and protector but was now assuredly her friend and lover. On an impulse she flung her arms about his shoulders, hauled herself up to his level, and kissed him mouth to mouth, every atom of her love and gratitude pouring out with the passion of her lips and tongue.

She left him with a sense of regret, several times

feeling the urge to turn back. But something deeper made her go on, made her walk carefully towards the place she really belonged, four miles away with her Master, Kano.

The journey may have been only four miles but it took almost the rest of the day. Instinct told S that she needed to remain as inconspicuous as possible, so she avoided roads and trails, flitting from shrub to shrub and copse to copse. She met nobody until she got to the environs of the palace shortly before sunset. Then, inevitably, she came up against a group of soldiers guarding the perimeter of the palace grounds.

They were lounging and talking against a wooden roadblock, but became instantly silent and alert as, screwing up her courage, S stepped out from behind the shrubs she had been hiding in and walked towards them along the middle of the narrow, unmade road. Seeing a half-naked, dusty European woman walking towards them down the middle of the road threw the men into confusion. Some levelled their rifles at her while others shouted at each other and gesticulated wildly.

S stopped twenty yards from the barrier. Inevitably, none of the guards spoke English, so it was impossible for her to explain her situation. Taking a deep breath and almost shouting with frustration, she poked a finger at her chest.

'Prince Adenkano N'Kwandwe! Me, me belong Prince Adenkano! English! Me English! You fetch English!'

More rifles were pointing at her now and a couple of the guards took cover, as though they thought she might attack them. Realising that she was still clutching the machete, she tossed it to the ground and dropped her shoulders, bowing her head in a gesture of surrender. There were some more shouts, then one of the soldiers ran to a Jeep parked a short way down the road and roared off in a cloud of dust. The others kept their rifles trained on her.

They kept her standing there in the middle of the dusty track for ages, the evening sun descending towards the horizon but still giving off enough heat to make the sweat trickle down her body. After a while a couple of the guards became bolder and approached her, although they still had their rifles cocked and ready. S kept absolutely still as they drew near, moving on the balls of their feet and whispering as though they were stalking some dangerous prey.

They looked her over warily, moving round her at a couple of yards' distance then, when she did not move, crept closer. One of them touched her hair, lank and dusty as it was, and said something to his companion. The other man, bolder, pulled aside one of the rips in her shirt to reveal a bare, muddy breast. He shouted something to the guards who had remained behind the barrier, and in an instant S was surrounded by them.

Somehow she managed to keep still as hands plucked at the rents in her shirt to peep at the bits of her body which were thus revealed, and to pull at her hair, and then to flick up the tails of the shirt to expose her nether parts. The strange thing was that none of them touched any part of her except her hair, although they all took their time examining her breasts and thighs and backside. It was as though they thought that touching this strange creature might be dangerous in some way.

That this might have indeed been true was demonstrated by the way they leapt back from her as a Jeep and a Land Rover slewed to a halt behind the roadblock and a number of shouting men leapt out. One of them was white, and with a sob of relief S recognised him as baas, the estate manager. There was a hubbub of shouts and orders, and S found herself bundled into the back of the Land Rover. She almost wept with relief even though a pair of metal handcuffs was instantly clapped around her wrists and she was pushed roughly to the floor of the vehicle as it bounced rapidly down the road amidst a cloud of red dust.

When they first got to the palace S was locked into a tiny cell, still handcuffed, but after only an hour or so a guard and two women came and released her. The guard removed the handcuffs, avoiding her eyes as though he felt guilty about something, and the two women led her off clucking like mother hens about how dusty and dishevelled she was.

They gave her a long, luxurious bath in steaming, sudsy water that smelled of roses and cloves. They washed her hair several times, then brushed and combed it until it floated around her shoulders. They examined her all over and attended gently to several scratches and grazes she had picked up, actually without even noticing them. Her pubic hair had regrown and they shaved her carefully, dusting her with sweet-smelling talc. At last, when she felt as clean as she had ever been in her life and relaxed to the point of sleepiness, they took her to her old familiar cell. She rolled down on to the bed and was asleep even before one of the women finished tucking the blankets around her.

Eighteen

This time there was no 'trial' as before, kneeling before Prince Adenkano in his counsel chamber. Instead, S found herself back at her original duties as though nothing at all had happened.

The next morning she worked in the kitchens, fetching and carrying, scrubbing pans, carting out peelings and waste. The differences were – and they made her strangely uncomfortable – that there was no Gladys around to take comfort from, and that nobody touched her, nor even shouted at her much. Indeed, it was embarrassing when, having dropped a bucket of peelings, she instantly bent over the nearest table and presented herself for a spanking, and nothing happened.

She stood there, prostrated across the wooden table, her buttocks tensed for the impact of a belt or a wooden spoon, for several minutes. When it did not come she craned her head around. The kitchen was unusually quiet, and everybody she could see from her awkward position was looking sheepish, as though she had broken some unknown new rule.

In the middle of the day the two women who had looked after her last night came to the kitchen and hustled her away. They showered her, and made up her face and, as they began to decorate her with jewellery, her heart began to soar. She was going to see Kano! She knew it in the depths of her being, and even though they did not know each other's languages she urged the women to hurry up.

She did see Kano, and even caught his eye at one moment, but her role was once again to assist the girls who served at table. It did not matter; at least and at last she was back where she belonged, serving her Master. All would be well!

She was allowed to wield the big ostrich-feather fan when Prince Adenkano took his evening meal. It was unusual, and thrilling, in that this time he ate alone, served by two nubile girls in skirts and turbans while S stood, naked except for the jewels hanging from her body rings, behind his shoulder wafting the heavy fan.

Later, S stood obediently by the wall in his bedroom as the two girls who had served his dinner stripped off their garments and bathed him then accompanied him back to his bed. She watched enviously as the girls vied to pleasure him, their slender bodies wriggling like eels, their hands and lips and tongues working with eager expertise.

She automatically adopted the pose she had become familiar with before her Master had sent her off to his estate, hands clasped behind her back, feet apart and head high. Just as automatically, her mind slipped into the passive mode she had learned to adopt back then. She accepted that she would be no more than a witness to what was going on between the people on the bed, and that she was no more than a decoration to the scene.

Thus, she did not at first realise the significance of Kano's beckoning finger. When she did her heart leapt with a wild joy and she almost dived into the mêlée of bodies on the bed. Now it was the two local girls who became the witnesses as S paid homage to her Master's manhood, stroking and kissing him, then rolling onto her back and calling out her joy as he penetrated her with a single glorious thrust.

Her days took on a pattern which would have become comfortable but for two nagging thoughts. She worked in the kitchens every morning, skivvying and scurrying; then she was showered and decorated with make-up and jewels, and assisted at the serving of Kano's mid-day meal; she wafted his fan during the evening meal, and went to his bedroom each night. She was not always summoned into his bed, but when she was her skill and effort put the local girls in the shade and her orgasms were always genuine and volcanic.

Her two worries were persistent, though. The first, a constant concern, was the absence of Gladys. During the last few months S had come to rely on Gladys as a friend and supporter, and missed her sorely. The second worry, although it was perhaps less a worry than an occasional pang, was what had happened to Nkwame. Had he got away safely? Was he well? Had he made it back to his home?

Both worries disappeared in a hurricane of emotions when her Master, Prince Adenkano, announced that she was to be given as a reward to a man who had served him well. It was more than two months after her return to the palace and, although she constantly wished she could see more of her Master, could serve him more closely, S was getting almost used to this form of her voluntary servitude.

These days her Master was the only one who used her body for pleasure, though not nearly as often as she wanted and desired. Nobody spanked her except the Prince himself, when she had got a bad report from the head chef or Mr Patrice the butler – and even then it was with her laid out across his bed, and as a prelude to or intermission between glorious bouts of sex.

If anybody could be called truly content it was S in those weeks and months, and then came the bombshell. She screamed when she heard his quietly spoken words, and threw herself sobbing at his feet. It could not be!

'But you can't do this to me,' she sobbed as two attendant guards pulled her to her feet and held her facing the Prince, tears streaming. 'I love you!'

Kano's posture was stern and forbidding, but there was a strange softness in his eyes, that gentleness that had so warmed and encouraged her when she was being trained by Seigneur a lifetime ago in England. There was a long pause, during which S was able to gather some measure of self-control.

'Is it not the case that you gave yourself to me willingly so that I should be your Master?' His voice was soft and compelling.

'Yes, Master, but –'

'And is it not also the case that as your chosen Master I have the right to do with you as I wish?'

'Yes, Master, but –' Her protests were weaker now, for what he said was true.

'Then listen . . .' Kano's tone was patient, even kindly. 'There is a man who has done me magnificent service. Without him this foolish rebellion would have been much more difficult to crush. I have given him land, and given his tribe certain rights and privileges in perpetuity. But he is also in need of a wife. You are to be that wife. It is the highest honour I can pay him.'

'But I love you. You are my Master, and I love *you*!'

He smiled and patted her on the head as though

246

she was a little child who did not quite understand, his eyes as gentle as those of the Kano of old.

'And you will come to love your new Master just as much.'

Such an idea was inconceivable to S, and she began to weep.

'It is decided,' he said, more firmly now. 'Do not shame me by making an exhibition of yourself.'

When Mr Patrice came for her the next day S was like a zombie. She had cried herself out, confused between a sort of pride that she should be regarded as the finest gift Kano could give, and sorrow at being sent away from him, and could hardly register what the butler was telling her. She stood numbly as the young girl who accompanied the butler pulled at her arm, and followed like an automaton when she led her to the shower. Normally the stinging spray would have enlivened her, but not this time. The slow, intimate process of being depilated should have aroused her, but now it left her indifferent.

She registered that her hair was being brushed and her face made up, and that jewellery was being put on her – rings on her fingers, a circlet of diamonds about her forehead, more diamonds clipped to her nipple and pubic rings – and a fine silk-gauze veil draped over her.

She glimpsed herself in the mirror and was fascinated by the image she presented. The veil covered her head and shoulders and fell in soft folds to just below her breasts, and at first glance made her look almost bridal in appearance. The material was so fine and translucent that her face and breasts were clearly visible through it, and the fact that she was naked and bejewelled below it made the effect all the more erotic.

She contemplated herself in the mirror for a few

moments. She knew that very soon her Master was going to present her as a gift, a reward, to some unknown man and the idea made her feel strangely ambivalent. He had already given her away, in a sense, when he sent her off to his estate and she had spent months away from him, at the disposal of anybody who wanted to use her. He had made her a slave to his servants and workers, so lowly that she had been made to sleep in his kennels. Now, he was presenting her as a gift to somebody who was apparently a war hero and who deserved the finest reward he could give. From the lowest of the low to the richest prize was a dizzying transformation.

As she looked at herself in the mirror she wondered who he would be. She no longer resisted the idea of leaving Kano. After all, he had given Gladys away to Mr Patrice and she was content; he had even taken her into his bed again at least once. Maybe the same would be true with herself. She just hoped that whoever her new Master was he would be kind.

Her meditation was interrupted by the entrance of four girls. They were dressed identically, although you could not really call it being dressed. Each wore a cap of silver chains which completely covered her hair, and had a single large diamond suspended on her forehead. Looped between the silver nipple rings that decorated their small, pert breasts were ropes of pearls which glistened against the glossy chestnut hue of their skins and seemed to draw light from them. They wore tiny skirts made entirely of strings of diamonds, just like the one S had worn when she had first entered this exotic country, though against their dark skins the diamonds seemed to gleam more brilliantly. Around their wrists and ankles were dozens of silver and gold bangles, some with little bells that tinkled as they moved.

The girls fluttered around S cooing about her appearance and making sure that everything about her was perfect. Then they formed around her like a troop of bridesmaids and led her out of the cell. She wondered whether it would be for the last time.

The little procession made its way to the wide lobby outside the banqueting hall and waited in silence before the huge double doors. From inside, S could hear the muffled noise of many voices and felt a little shiver of nervousness. Mr Patrice appeared from somewhere and checked her appearance, adjusting the veil even though it was not really necessary. Impersonally, he rubbed a hand between her legs to see how smooth she was and then produced from his pocket a long, thin chain, which he clipped to her pussy ring. Then he too stood waiting.

Several more long minutes passed, then a gong sounded from inside the banqueting hall and the sound of voices died away. One of the heavy double doors swung open a little way and a figure squeezed out. To S's astonished joy, it was Gladys! Unable to contain herself, S threw her arms around her long-lost friend. They hugged for only a moment and then, smiling broadly, Gladys held S back a little way, her eyes shining.

'Oh, you look so beautiful!' she said, laughing and hugging S again. 'And you're so lucky! So lucky!'

Swept over with joy at seeing Gladys again, S did not react to that last statement, though a tiny part of her mind did doubt whether it was entirely true.

Then Gladys became suddenly business-like. Stepping back, she looked S over carefully. She adjusted the veil a little so that it hung further back on her head, the front hem now stopping just above her jewel-laden nipples, leaving them and the soft under-swells of her breasts entirely bare.

249

'Now, hold your hands behind your back,' she murmured. 'You won't be handcuffed, but you have to keep them there. It is a sign of submission. Shoulders back, there's a good girl. Hold your head up. You must be proud!'

Acting proudly when she was about to be given away to a stranger seemed wildly incongruous to S, but she held her head up because her beloved Gladys asked her to.

'I am to be what you English call your Matron of Honour,' Gladys said, more briskly now. 'You must do exactly as I tell you. It is an important ceremony and you must do well.' Her eyes softened and she gave S another hug. Once again she blurted, 'Oh, you're so lucky!'

She stepped back again and, taking a square of thick black silk from Mr Patrice's hand, draped it across S's head over her translucent white veil. The black square covered S to the tip of her nose, and though loose acted as a very effective blindfold. Keeping her head high as Gladys had told her to, she craned her eyes downwards. The glance confirmed what she already knew, that her breasts were full and hard and that her nipples were standing out like nuts. How could she possibly be aroused under these circumstances! Yet she was.

Gladys took the chain attached to her pussy ring from Mr Patrice and began to lead S forward into the banqueting hall. The hall was hushed, but S could tell that there were a great many people there. The thought of all those eyes on her as Gladys led her slowly across the hall made S even more aroused. She squared her shoulders, thrusting her bejewelled breasts further forward. Even though he was about to give her away, she wanted Kano to feel proud of her.

Gladys brought her to a halt and told her to kneel.

As she obeyed she glimpsed part of a gorgeous white, red and gold robe beneath the edge of her blindfold, and knew that she was kneeling in front of her Master, Kano. She straightened her back and moved her knees apart, feeling his eyes on her breasts and sex, hoping just a little that he might change his mind.

Her own mind flashed back to the moment all those months ago back in England when Seigneur had asked her to voluntarily give herself to an unknown Master. She found herself fighting the urge to giggle at the sudden wish that whoever her new Master was he would not beat her quite so hard as Kano had on that fantastic first night.

'Who are you?' The voice, Kano's voice, cut through her whimsy.

'I am S, Master.' She was surprised at how clear her voice was.

'And what are you?'

'I am your servant and slave, Master.'

A voice whispered in her ear, and S realised that Gladys was kneeling beside her. Obediently she leaned forward, taking her weight on her hands, her arms straight and her back arched. Gladys had whispered that she was to be ceremonially beaten as a public demonstration of her servitude to her Master. The very thought sent her blood racing.

Kano had beaten her lots of times before, and to S it had become virtually an act of love, but never so publicly. She remembered the ceremony at which she had given herself to him. Then there had been only a single, light stroke across her offered buttocks. Only later, when he had taken her to his bed, had he beaten her thoroughly – and afterwards he had fucked her so long and so beautifully she had wanted to die and stay in heaven. Perhaps this ceremony would be like that one, just a single stroke for demonstration purposes.

Then it landed and she screamed with shock and agony. It was nothing like a ceremonial blow! A line of searing pain striped across her buttocks and her instant reaction was to grab her bottom with both hands and howl. Gladys grabbed her at once and pulled her back down.

'Keep still and shut up,' she hissed. 'Don't make him lose face!'

S gritted her teeth and forced herself back onto all fours. She could, she *would* take it. The second stroke landed so quickly and so hard that she had to fight to stay down, but could not help giving an audible whimper. Determined not to let Kano down, she bit her lip and arched her back to present herself better. Tears were streaming by the time the next four strokes were over, but she had managed to keep still and silent and she felt a little surge of pride when Gladys patted her hand approvingly.

Through the veil and the black cloth that covered her head she heard a buzz of quiet conversation from whoever the audience was. The buzz was one of excitement, and through the conflagration in her backside S felt a renewed flush of arousal at the erotic spectacle she must be presenting.

Gladys whispered to her again and, stiffly, she knelt up, still resisting the temptation to rub her hands on the burning skin of her bottom. Within the very limited view her veils allowed her she saw a pair of shoes appear. They moved close. The front of her veils was lifted a little, still not allowing her to see much – not much, that is, except for the erect penis which appeared before her face.

It was not Kano's penis; she knew him too well, had seen him close up and sucked him too many times to be mistaken about that. And besides, this man was wearing trousers whereas Kano was surely

252

clad in robes. He was big and pushed forward, bumping against her lips. She knew he must be her new Master and that this was the act with which she was required to publicly demonstrate her submission to him.

For a moment she could not do it. It was so public, so final! Then Gladys hissed at her and the penis nudged at her face again, and she licked her lips and opened them wide. He felt and tasted vaguely familiar, but that thought disappeared as S became engrossed in the task she was performing. He smelled clean and intensely male. The feeling of his silky hardness sliding between her lips, filling her mouth as she moved on him, was heady. The presence of an audience became lost on her as she worked on him, the cumulative effects of all the erotic things that had happened in the last hour combining with this one to set off heat-bombs in her womb.

By the time he came she was already coming, her pelvis rolling in rhythm with the movements of her mouth on his shaft. She gulped his issue down greedily and kept sucking until he pulled out of her mouth with an audible plop, and so forcefully that she almost toppled forward. As he stepped back her veils fell forward again and she could see nothing save her breasts and her knees.

Nineteen

She expected that then the square of black silk would be pulled from her head and her new Master would be revealed to her. Instead Gladys instructed her to stand and, still tugging at the chain attached to her pubic ring, led her back out of the banqueting hall. S was mystified. She had been publicly spanked as a sign of her submission and then performed just as public fellatio on the man who must surely be her new Master, yet still she was not allowed to know who he was.

Gladys removed the silk blindfold once they were out of the hall and, smiling wildly, hugged her until her ribs cracked. But S was still lost. What was happening?

Gladys hustled S out of the rear entrance to the palace and into the back seat of a limousine. S winced as her sore bottom touched the leather upholstery, and asked if she could kneel on the floor instead. Only when she had settled stiffly into position did Gladys begin to explain.

Her new Master was now a major tribal chief and a very important man indeed. No, she would not tell S who he was but swore with wide-eyed sincerity that she would be happy when she saw him. The reason for the mystery was that S was to become a bride rather than merely a slave to be handed over. It was a great honour. She would be his first wife too! Such a privilege . . .

Gladys's enthusiasm was not at all infectious as S knelt awkwardly in the limousine as it bounced across potholed roads on a journey that lasted at least two hours. Her words, though, did sink in.

He, whoever he was – and despite her pleas Gladys would not tell her – had performed heroic service for Prince Adenkano and more or less single-handedly directed the battle which had put down the rebellion. He had been rewarded more highly than any other, and been granted a special request. And his request had been S. Not for his slave, which would have been easy, but for his wife.

She was to be married to him according to his full tribal ceremony, and Gladys was to be her guide and Maid of Honour. To Gladys it was wonderful, but to S it was still mystifying and rather frightening. Why was Gladys so happy? What was going on? She had gone through with it, had submitted to her Master's will, and was now headed towards a new Master, but was mystified and more than a little frightened by the prospect.

It was almost dark by the time their journey ended, so S could not see much of what looked like a large native village. Gladys helped her to climb stiffly out of the car and led her into a solidly built circular building with a thickly thatched, conical roof.

Inside, a dozen or more women were waiting, and they instantly gathered around S and began to fuss over her. S stood still as the women took off her veil and jewellery, feeling swamped by their ebullience and then embarrassed at the way they cooed over her hair and stroked her skin, and even tugged at her body rings. They, and Gladys as well, were acting as though this was the beginning of some kind of party, but their excitement still did not infect S, who stood and moved numbly to their gestures and Gladys's translation of their chatter.

The women examined every inch of her body and cried with obvious approval over the stripes decorating her bottom as she bent forward so that they could inspect her more easily. She tensed but managed to keep still when curious fingers began to explore the cleft between her striped buttocks, pulling them apart and tracing delicately across the pucker of her anus. When they began to explore the lips of her exposed sex keeping still became more difficult, but once again she managed it.

Once the women were satisfied with their examination they bathed her, making her stand in a large wooden tub and soaping her with their hands before pouring ewers of warm water over her. After they had rubbed her dry with scratchy cloths they sat her down and fed her. She was allowed to do nothing for herself. Food was placed into her mouth; a wooden cup was held to her lips so that she could drink; her mouth was gently wiped with a soft cloth. Then they led her to a narrow bed, lay her down, covered her with thick blankets and, picking up the oil-lamps which had illuminated the hut, departed, leaving her in confused solitude.

Her head buzzed with questions. Who was he? Why had she been left alone? If she had been given to him, what was the difference between being a wife and a slave? What had Gladys meant about being married according to tribal customs?

The questions swirled until the exhaustion of the day took her over, and she slept.

The ceremony began almost as soon as S was awakened next morning. She was made to sit on a low stool in the middle of the hut while several women wet her hair and carefully plaited it into scores of tight, thin braids which hung down all round her face. When they threaded many-coloured beads onto the braids, S felt that her hair had become a sort of beaded curtain through which she could only peep indistinctly.

Next, the women stood her up and massaged her skin with fragrant oils until she gleamed from her feet to her neck. The scent of the oil was a heady mixture of musks and fruits, and by the time the six hands had finished massaging every inch of her skin S was feeling breathless. The women, grinning to one another, paid special attention to her breasts and buttocks and her depilated vulva, as though they were deliberately teasing her into arousal. If they were, their efforts were all too effective!

By the time they led her out of the hut S was glad of the sheen of oil on her body, for she knew that her juices were flowing from her swollen labia and her breasts felt full and tight. The first person she saw when she emerged from the gloom of the hut was Gladys, a radiant smile on her face. She seized S by the hand, and clung to it all the while she explained the rituals that were to follow, though she would accompany her through them.

First, she had to go and stand in front of the portal of every single hut in the village, whereupon the whole family, men, wives and children rushed out. The first couple of times it happened S was embarrassed by the way every member of the family knelt and kissed both her hands and she was presented with a gift – a cooking pot, a knife, a necklace.

The next part of the ceremony was much more distracting. Once the gift had been given the head of the household stepped forward. He cupped his hands on the top of her head, then on her breasts. The first time it happened S flinched back and Gladys had to tell her sharply that this was part of local marriage custom; it was a ritual of welcome, and they would be offended if she did not return the welcome by accepting it.

But being touched on her head and breasts was not the only, or even the main, part of the ritual. Once the head of the household had given her the welcoming touches, each of his wives stepped forward in turn. Blushing, S obeyed Gladys's whispered instruction and parted her knees, keeping as still as she could as each of the wives, all of them smiling and the younger ones suppressing giggles, stroked their right hands over her vulva.

Gladys explained that this part of the ritual was meant as a sort of blessing on the organ with which she would please her husband. S could not be sure whether it was that thought or the touches themselves which caused the lurch of arousal that swelled in her.

There were thirty-seven huts in the substantial village. The progress from one to the next became dreamlike, a bewildering succession of smiles and gifts and increasingly lascivious strokings between her legs. When S rippled into a half-suppressed orgasm as yet another hand stroked her boiling sex a cheer went up, as though this was what everybody had been waiting for. The touches became just a little firmer after that, and a little more lingering, and more than once Gladys had to support S as her knees buckled with the power of the come that was sweeping over her.

She was weak and dewed with sweat by the time it was over and Gladys led her to a seat in the centre of a large, clear area between the surrounding huts.

Young women hurried back and forth, first washing her breasts and between her legs with cool damp cloths, then offering her food and drink. She had more or less recovered her composure when hordes of children ran up, each carrying a single long stick. They looked like birch-fronds, but S knew that birches did not grow in Africa. Or did they? She was confused.

The children dropped the long, whippy sticks into a pile at her feet, laughing and chattering before running off and joining the crowd, the whole tribe it seemed, which had formed a circle around her and was now watching avidly.

Gladys leaned forward and whispered in her ear. 'It is the custom here that the bride presents her husband with the means to discipline her if she is not good,' she said. 'You have to select two bundles of twelve sticks and bind them together as gifts for your husband. Choose well, for it is a sign of pride here.'

Dazed by the very concept, S knelt forward and began to examine the pile of sticks. Slowly, she picked out one after another, realising as she did so that she seemed to be picking out those that were the longest, thickest and whippiest. As soon as she finished selecting the first dozen rods an older woman took them from her and, while S selected the next twelve, skilfully bound their thicker ends together with a long leather thong, turning them into a fearsome-looking switch four feet in length.

The second bundle was dealt with in the same way and when it was finished the woman held both switches high and swished them through the air to show them to the circle of tribes people. At once, they started clapping and calling out.

'They are pleased,' Gladys said into S's ear. 'They say you have chosen well and will be a good wife, for your husband will beat you hard with such good whips!'

The thought sent a shiver through S. 'Please tell me who he is!' she pleaded, her eyes wide with apprehension, but Gladys was adamant in her refusal.

Moments later the women took her back into the hut she had slept in, and the wedding preparations continued. S was bathed and oiled again and her hair was redone, this time pulled back off her face. Thick, oily paints were smeared on her; white on her face and forehead, yellow on her breasts and her belly and vulva, bright red in the cleft of her backside and over her buttocks.

Then they placed a narrow but very effective blindfold over her eyes. Gladys was not there to explain, and S began to feel scared. Although she could not see a thing, however, she did not resist when her arms were gripped and she was led out of the hut. She knew by the hum of voices that the whole tribe was there, watching her being led across the clearing to her fate. A drum began a slow, almost hypnotic beat somewhere a little way off.

She knew from the change in the sounds that she had been taken into another hut. A shiver ran through her as she realised that this was it, this was the moment of truth. The hands of the women who had led her here left her, and for a moment she felt totally isolated and vulnerable. Then she felt a wave of warm relief as a familiar hand took hers, and a welcome voice whispered in her ear.

'He's coming!' Gladys squeezed S's hand as she spoke. 'I am to be witness. It is a great honour.'

'But what is happening?' S's voice was high-pitched and pleading, almost childlike in her nervousness.

'It's all right!' Gladys squeezed her hand again.

'You have to transfer the paint from your body to his to show that the wedding is complete, and that he has taken possession of you as his wife. Oh, you are so lucky!'

'But who is he? Please, please tell me!'

Gladys unexpectedly relented and whispered his name in S's ear. Behind the blindfold tears of relief and happiness welled.

Several hours later the sound of the single drum had been joined by the rhythm of several others in a throbbing syncopation. S had joyously and very actively transferred the wet paint from her brow and her belly and her bottom to her new husband. Behind her blindfold she was reliving the first night he had taken her though this night was even more intense.

She sucked him deep, pressing her forehead against his belly to transfer the white paint from her face. He did not come in her mouth, but held back to maintain his erection to transfer the yellow paint from her belly to his. S was incapable of holding back as his thick manhood thrust rhythmically in her. The transference of the red paint might have been uncomfortable had she not still been coming so much, for his cock was still very erect, and when at last he came she screamed out, clawing at Gladys's hand in her ecstasy.

Even though Gladys had told her who he was, S was swept with joy when her blindfold was removed after the consummation and the transference of her body paints. He was standing, huge and grinning happily, his loins smeared with copious quantities of white and yellow and red paint. S leapt up and threw her arms around his shoulders, weeping for joy.

'Nkwame! Nkwame! Nkwame!' She could say nothing else but his name in her joy that he, of all the people in the world, should be her new Master.

Still dizzy with joy and the afterglow of orgasm, S followed her new husband out of the hut in which their marriage had been consummated to face the tribe of his people waiting outside. Drums were still beating; the crowd was excited. Night had fallen and Nkwame's glistening body was lit by oil-lamps as he stepped naked from the hut. His people burst into cheers and ululations as they saw the paints on his loins, cheers which grew louder when S followed him out and they saw how smeared the paints on her own body were.

She blushed inwardly at the realisation that the whole tribe, a vast crowd of men and women and children, had been waiting, knowing precisely what she and Nkwame had been doing in the hut, and were now cheering the evidence of it. It felt almost as though the whole tribe, at least in spirit, had been party to the fucking she had just received, and the thought caused yet another pulse of heat between her legs.

Gladys and a small group of women in high spirits took S by the hands and hurried her off to the original hut again. There, they bathed her yet again and oiled her body, glancing at her large-eyed and whispering to one another. Gladys translated.

'They are calling you sister,' she said, smiling and stroking S's shoulder. 'They are saying you are a lucky woman to have such a manly mate, but that he is more lucky to have such a – what is the word? – such a sexy woman. They all heard the noises you made, but most of all they all saw how soft and drained his cock was when you finished with him.'

Then Gladys had told her about the one final part of the ritual which had to be gone through before the marriage ceremony was complete. When she first heard it S was terrified, but now that she knew who

263

her new Master was she felt better, though the prospect still daunted her.

When the women had finished petting and prettying her one of them – 'Your new Mother-in-Law,' whispered Gladys – handed her the objects with which her submission to Nkwame was to be publicly sealed and confirmed. Gripping one in each hand, S squared her shoulders and walked slowly through the door of the hut, her head high as, followed by the women from the hut, she made her way along the gangway of people which had assembled to witness this final ritual.

At the end of the gangway, a sturdy wooden frame had been placed in the clearing, its thick poles shiny from previous use. Next to it stood Nkwame. S caught her breath at how magnificent he looked, standing tall and imposing, the light of flickering fires gleaming from his mahogany skin, the pelt of a leopard draped around his big shoulders. He was keeping his face rigidly straight as she approached him, as befitted the dignity of a chief, though S was certain she could detect a proud smile in his eyes as she came nearer to him.

He was naked except for the leopard skin, so very different from the immaculately uniformed sergeant-major she had first encountered all those months ago. She felt a throb of heat in her breasts and belly as her eyes focused themselves at the join of his muscular thighs. She shook her head to fight off the distraction the sight caused, and concentrated on the next, the final, part of the ceremony.

Stopping in front of him she knelt, feeling small and vulnerable as he towered over her. She laid the two thick birches at his feet.

'Please, Master,' she said, her voice trembling with emotion. 'This woman begs you to accept her as your own.'

264

As he stooped to pick up the first of the whips, she turned and draped herself over the bars of the wooden frame, her hands gripping tensely, her legs wide and her buttocks offered high.

She clenched her teeth on the thick wad of leather Gladys had surreptitiously passed to her to help her avoid screaming as the strokes fell slowly and rhythmically, each one greeted by a cheer from the watching tribespeople.

When it was over and Gladys helped her up from the frame over which she had been ceremonially beaten, S glanced up to Nkwame's face. His smile and his eyes showed that he was proud. Proud of the gift he had been given, and proud of the stoicism with which she had borne the public beating. Her eyes dropped down and her vagina rippled with heat as she saw that it was not only his mind that was proud.

Without thought, and oblivious of the crowd watching, S dropped to her knees and kissed the thick glans which bobbed before her face. This promised to be a long and wonderful night!

NEXUS BACKLIST

All books are priced £4.99 unless another price is given. If a date is supplied, the book in question will not be available until that month in 1998.

CONTEMPORARY EROTICA

THE ACADEMY	Arabella Knight		
AGONY AUNT	G. C. Scott		
ALLISON'S AWAKENING	Lauren King		
AMAZON SLAVE	Lisette Ashton	£5.99	
THE BLACK GARTER	Lisette Ashton	£5.99	Sept
THE BLACK ROOM	Lisette Ashton		
BOUND TO OBEY	Amanda Ware	£5.99	Dec
BOUND TO SUBMIT	Amanda Ware		
CANDIDA IN PARIS	Virginia Lasalle		
CHAINS OF SHAME	Brigitte Markham	£5.99	July
A CHAMBER OF DELIGHTS	Katrina Young		
DARK DELIGHTS	Maria del Rey	£5.99	Aug
DARLINE DOMINANT	Tania d'Alanis	£5.99	Oct
A DEGREE OF DISCIPLINE	Zoe Templeton		
THE DISCIPLINE OF NURSE RIDING	Yolanda Celbridge	£5.99	Nov
THE DOMINO TATTOO	Cyrian Amberlake		
THE DOMINO QUEEN	Cyrian Amberlake		
EDEN UNVEILED	Maria del Rey		
EDUCATING ELLA	Stephen Ferris		
EMMA'S SECRET DOMINATION	Hilary James		
FAIRGROUND ATTRACTIONS	Lisette Ashton	£5.99	Dec
THE TRAINING OF FALLEN ANGELS	Kendal Grahame		
HEART OF DESIRE	Maria del Rey		

Please send me the books I have ticked above.

Name ....

Address ....

....

....

.... Post code........................

Send to: **Cash Sales, Nexus Books, Thames Wharf Studios, Rainville Road, London W6 9HT**

Please enclose a cheque or postal order, made payable to **Nexus Books**, to the value of the books you have ordered plus postage and packing costs as follows:

UK and BFPO – £1.00 for the first book, 50p for the second book and 30p for each subsequent book to a maximum of £3.00;

Overseas (including Republic of Ireland) – £2.00 for the first book, £1.00 for the second book and 50p for each subsequent book.

If you would prefer to pay by VISA or ACCESS/MASTER-CARD, please write your card number and expiry date here:

....

Please allow up to 28 days for delivery.

Signature ....